C000027282

# _Conquering the_
# _Bitch_

Self-published in 2021 by Yviebeth Bardug

Copyright © Yviebeth Bardug 2021

The right of Yviebeth Bardug to be identified as the author of this work has been asserted by her in accordance with the Copyright, Designs and Patents Act 1988.

All rights reserved. No part of this publication may be reproduced, stored in a retrieval system, or transmitted, in any form, or by any means (electronic, mechanical, photocopying, recording or otherwise) without the express prior written permission by the author.

This book is sold subject to the condition that it shall not, by way of trade or otherwise, be lent, hired out, or otherwise circulated without the author's prior consent in any form other than that in which it is published and without a similar condition including this condition being imposed on the subsequent purchaser.

# Acknowledgements

I would like to thank my husband for assisting me in ensuring the story continuity and for his encouragement to continue and finish this book.

# Table of contents

*The way how people view you, is a fraction of what you are, the reflection of what is seen in a mirror is just that, a reflection and not the whole. Do not let anyone add any weight to your life just because they valued and assessed a part and not the whole*

# Introduction

Waking up was a nightmare. Her head was hurting as if it was going to explode. She had tried sitting up several times now and her desire to vomit filled her senses, but she had to get a grip with things as she could not continue to live like this. She could hardly remember anything about the night before. She and a couple of friends had gone out drinking well into the night and had ended up drinking too much, as usual. It is strange but three months ago most of her friends would have said she was nearly teetotal since she hardly drank and if she did so it would usually be one glass maximum. This time she had gone over the top with several glasses of red wine, her favourite. She hated herself, she hated drinking, she hated not being in control of what she said, drink always made her feel paranoid the next day. In the morning she over-analysed every word she had said to people and misunderstood most of what people said to her. She knew she had to stop, she had had enough because thinking back she had talked too much last night, but she did not like people knowing too much about her emotions, her feelings and her thoughts or for that matter much about her life in general. She was what people called private and wanted to keep it that way. All she could remember of the night was her along with Richard, Damien and Tanya taking a taxi back home at midnight and that she had vomited. Tanya was absolutely livid with her having to pay an extra £50 to the taxi driver for the clean-up and this was on top of the fare of £35 ending up as a really expensive night out.

Liz had now been unemployed for exactly 63 days, her job as a Programme Manager dried up when the economic slowdown started hitting the IT industry across the UK but hit London particularly hard. Usually London, the hub of jobs, the employee was king, Liz found jumping ship was never an issue and it usually came with a pay rise. She had been riding on a high for the last five years, her latest job was a three-year contract at over a hundred thousand a year and was cut short by 3 months leaving her with no time to look around or plan ahead. It was not only annoying, but it was also a crisis and it was personal as well as country-wide with the recession hitting everyone. Even though she got paid for the remainder of the contract, a golden handshake she had negotiated mainly due to her reputation as well as the fact that she had worked previously with the director who employed her. The director knew she would deliver the work on time, but she knew it would be hard to get another job again easily. Those days were gone, there were too many people out there looking for the same thing.

At first, when they told her and a colleague (and flatmate) Tanya, that their contracts had been cut short, they both thought 'holiday', paid holiday more importantly! The thought of relaxing, enjoying their hard-earned cash, after such a long time working extremely long hours and under so much stress sounded fantastic.

People think that when you are unemployed with leisure time in your hands is good. It all sounds good and amazing but when you are forced to live a life of leisure and nothing else, boredom starts to seep through especially when all your friends are working. All the good things in life such as the facials, massages and swimming all lose their magic and become extremely boring if you have to constantly do them on your own. Lunches were no longer an attraction as she felt she had nothing to say to her friends and these became friends who never made an effort to call her or see her. She felt she was the one making the effort all the time in fact when she looked back she realised annoyingly that it was always her making the effort to meet people. The only time a friend made the effort was when he thought that there was the possibility of a job that might come through her and this was starting to not only being extremely annoying but depressing. For some reason everyone thought she had money to spare, they all expected she would travel further than she would have commuted by trekking for two hours all the way to the City just to meet them for a one-hour lunch then fight her way back home. Life started to become a dreadful drag and even though she knew a lot of people, she started to notice clearly and visibly who were her real friends those who genuinely cared for her and wanted the best for her. The painful reality of this was that there were not many real friends and to get a new one takes a long time of nurturing, growing and maturing. This was the awful fact that impacted her more than the lack of job. She felt horrendously depressed and let down.

To tops things up she had received news that her mum was dying of cancer which was diagnosed one week after losing her job. At first, she thought not having a job was a blessing in disguise as at least she would be able to go to Guilford, they had moved there after years in Edinburgh when they decided to move to have a change, and see her mum and stepdad more often maybe stay there for a month or so. Of course, all this was too good to be true, but everything was destroyed when her mum died two weeks after the diagnosis. After spending one week at her mother's side, she felt she had not been given enough time and she thought that it was not fair. It was lucky that their relationship had always been close. The cancer was all over her, in her kidneys, liver, and lungs. It had started in her pancreas, and it seemed to have spread fast. There had been no visible signs or warning, it just struck, pitiless of who and when it strikes, a hidden demon lurking in the dark waiting to strike. Saying that, her mum was the type that would never complain, not because she was worried of bothering me, but she was of the belief that nowadays everyone complained of everything. If something was bothering her, she must have assumed it was part of old age, an ache or pain that happens as you get older.

So many people do not get on with their mother, choosing not to speak to them for ages, hating them once they leave home but not for Liz as she adored her and wanted to be with her. She always enjoyed her company and they always laughed together. Everything with her mother was fun, she felt loved and safe and always wanted to reciprocate that feeling.

With all things in her life going seriously wrong she had decided to make some changes and the first one was that she would go and stay with her friend Charlie for a month or two. Charlie lived in

Edinburgh and had loads of friends and they would not ask her for much rent but would always make sure she was okay. All Liz wanted was to be as far away from her parents' house as she needed to think, relax and plan a way to rebuild her life. She guessed everyone has one or two friends who will help us so long as 'a favour for them is coming'.

She did not want to be surrounded by people who constantly asked her if she was ok as when it was obvious that she was not. Bereavement is not something that people understand unless they have gone through it themselves over someone remarkably close. In Liz's case, she hated anything to do with death not because of death itself but the finality it brought. At least when she stayed with Charlie, she knew Charlie would not ask anything as she was too selfish for that. It would suit her staying with Charlie, considering the mood she was in, not talking about her feelings or dissecting every day of her life since the diagnosis to the death of her mum was fine. She was going to mourn her in her own way without the help of nosy people. Yes, Charlie would never be bothered with anyone because she would just expect Liz to go to parties with her and if she didn't go Charlie would just go on her own.

Before she went to Edinburgh though she had to make sure that she found tenants and rented her house out as soon as possible since she did not want to sell it as a property in Turnham Green counted as quite an investment. She had bought the flat when she was twenty-six only four years after she got her first job with the help of some of the money her mum and dad had invested in a trust that matured on her 25th birthday.

Her flat was what she called her sanctuary and there she could hide from anyone and anything or at least she thought so until everything went wrong. This time everything had gone too wrong to just close the door for a couple of days. The flat was a maisonette style it had actually been a Victorian house which someone converted into two flats, the bottom flat was a very small one-bedroom flat where a single guy lived and whom she really never got to know but was always kind enough to put her mail through the letter box and keep the entrance tidy. His name was Robert Alloy who was an incredibly quiet guy of at least fifty who kept himself to himself.

The second-floor flat was hers. As you came into the front door there were two doors in the corridor and opening the one on the left took you up one flight of stairs and would face an oversized kitchen which measured twenty feet by ten feet and had been an addition done in the late seventies. For Liz, this was not only the first flat she bought, but it was also the first major risk she had taken, the flat had been empty for nearly two years it had to be gutted completely, due to a flooding the previous year whilst empty. A pipe in the kitchen breaking meant most of the units were stained or the wood had become warped with moisture and decay. All this could have been prevented but the then owner was not interested in preserving the building it seems that all he wanted to do was sell it. Apparently, the flat had been in the market for three years and it had been more of a hindrance than anything else for the seller. His son, the owner, had died in a freak accident in India and he died without a will hence the long time the place was in disrepair.

The second flight of stairs took you into the dining room (or what used to be the third bedroom) and the living room, which was gigantic and measured nineteen by fifteen feet and like the rest of the house apart from the kitchen had very high ceilings. This had been what had attracted Liz to buy the flat (apart from the price, which was low for London standards due to the building needing a great deal of urgent repair). The only sad thing about the flat was that whoever renovated it all those years ago and split the house into two flats did not have a care in the world for retaining those beautiful Victorian cornices, dado rails and ceiling roses that each room in the old days would have had. All these Victorian features had been crudely removed to be replaced with modern plain cornices, no dado rails or roses. Liz believed that those features themselves brought elegance to a property as well as making it interesting. She just could not understand anyone that would not respect the past and its beautiful architecture.

The living room didn't have a fireplace it had been covered by a layer of cement like the dining room however the advantage of the dining room was that it still had a hearth which meant it would be easier to try and restore the fireplace in that area. Unfortunately, Liz could not afford to do so the expenditure of that would have been too much then and she had already spent a small fortune on the flat restoring its old beauty.

On another flight of stairs, the toilet and the bathroom were found which she always thought was quite a selling point. There was no point in having just one toilet. A house should always have two or more depending on the number of residents. After all, what are you to do if you had been the willing victim of a very potent vindaloo? If the toilet was occupied, where would you run to? Unlike the old days the garden no longer existed so you were doomed to a very embarrassing outcome which would send any guest running in the opposite direction…literally with the friendship in tow.

Up another set of stairs were the two bedrooms. The master bedroom was the same size as the living room and the guest bedroom was the same size as the dining room, which was inhabited by none other than Tanya, Liz's best friend in London who had the benefit of paying a very small rent for the price of living in luxurious surroundings.

You may be at this point asking yourself if anyone can live in the lap of luxury in Turnham Green which although it is as good an area as it maybe it is not Knightsbridge or Kensington. Well, there is a simple explanation for this as the flat was luxurious, not only because of the materials used to refurbish it but also because it had been tastefully decorated to the highest standard. Added to that Liz made sure they had the latest mod cons including a wide screen LCD TV where they could see their favourite films, mega romances or sci-fi films, all with a happy ending. They were both romantics at heart and anything teary with a happy ending was for them, even though now and then they would choose a sad film which would make them cry all night.

The walls were a very pale cream, and the doors and skirting boards were white. Only the bedrooms and staircase were carpeted with a pale green colour pure wool carpet. The staircase was painted white and the main reason for this was that the previous owner had ruined it by staining it a dark brown colour which was impossible to remove so the only solution was to paint it. Maybe it was not considered a luxurious enough pad for a billionaire, but it certainly was for someone who only didn't earn much when she bought it and who in order to do everything to the highest standard had sacrificed two years of socialising so that she could afford the money for materials and workmanship.

The whole arrangement worked very well for Liz since Tanya was hardly there, she spent most of her time at her boyfriend Damien's house. The agreement was that they would always try and at least go out for a meal or spend the evening together once every two weeks, have a really nice 'girlie' session and a couple of glasses of wine and a gossip.

Liz knew that moving away meant that either Tanya would rent the whole place (she did not want to share a flat with a stranger) or she would have to move out so that Liz could rent the flat out to someone else and this would have meant problems for Liz as she was only going away for two months. Luckily, Damien and Tanya decided to move in together, a two-month trial (or so Damien called it). This meant that Liz did not have to worry about things and moved her stuff into the small room and Damien and Tanya moved to the large bedroom and Liz increased the rent.

Once she returned back in a couple of months, both Tanya and Damien could stay in the big room and Liz would reduce the rent to £1,000 since she was also to be in the flat. The plus was that Damien could rent his whole house to a corporate client and rake in more money! He was very lucky as he had a house right bang in the middle of Kew only having a short walk and then cross the road and he was in on the most amazing gardens in London if not the world. This alone will mean renting his property would give him plenty of money.

# Part 1

*To review the past and acknowledge it, is the
first stage of letting go of past hurts*

## Edinburgh March 2001

"Hullo luvvie!" Charlie's voice was as loud as ever. Liz was so embarrassed but glad that Waverly Station was so noisy that nobody would bother to check who was screeching so much. Her voice was one of those very posh but annoying types, the one that will put you off private schools for life, which was unfair as she knew a lot of private school students who were not only mega nice but down to earth. It annoyed her how people automatically thought of private school students as arseholes with a mum or dad being a paid-up member of the Conservative Party. This was the biggest misconception most people had but you only realise the truth if you are part of that 'circle'. In her mind it was the school that mattered not if it was private or state. There were some excellent private schools and some bad ones, the same can be argued for the state ones.

"Hi Charlie, thanks for having me stay." Liz was conscious that she had asked her 'friend' if she could stay for two months and she had to make sure Charlie knew that she appreciated this. She had not seen Charlie in two years the last time was when four of them, all girls, went on holiday together to Benidorm for two weeks. Charlie did not seem to have changed much, still as beautiful and as usual very false with a focused desire of being the centre of attention. Maybe she was a bit more flamboyant than before, maybe more deceitful. It would be interesting to find out what she had been up to lately.

"Oh! Don't worry, I am sure you would do the same, come on! I did not bring the car we can walk to where I live as it will take us only ten minutes." Muttered Charlie, walking fast ahead of her.

"But I have a suitcase surely we could take a taxi and I will pay for it?" Considering how wealthy Charlie's parents were and the size of her monthly allowance, yes Charlie was one of the few people she knew that received a monthly 'allowance', she was incredibly surprised. Even more surprised that she would not allow her to pay for the taxi she just wanted to make her walk!

"Don't be silly," mused Charlie "It's just a short walk plus your suitcase has wheels. "Anyway, how are you? I take it you are broke since you rented your house out?" Liz wondered where did this poison come from and more importantly why?

"I had no choice but to rent it out." Liz received a rental income of £1500 a month for it which paid the mortgage, she told people. She always made it clear to everyone that she had just about enough to pay loans, mortgages and general bills and food and extraordinarily little left for fun. Liz never discussed her private affairs with anyone, never mind money, she was very particular about it. She had been stung in the past and preferred never to let anyone know how financially fluid she was. She had saved a lot of money in the last four years, actually she had saved most of her money plus the money her dad had left her which after buying the house meant she did not have a mortgage or loans. This is something she had never told anyone; she had always made people believe that she had a mortgage just like everyone else. Now with what her mother had left her, she could afford not to work for the next ten years if she wished but that was not her style, she needed to be busy and use her mind.

"Oh! Not bad, if I could rent out my pokey little flat for that I would, mind you, I don't think I would have any friends that would allow me to stay with them for two months free of charge."

Liz was surprised at the retort - was it a purposeful dig? She had offered to pay Charlie £300 a month especially since her room was to be a large cupboard that had no ventilation and had just enough space for a bed. Charlie had then toned it down by stating "What are friends for!"

"Charlie, if you want me to pay £300 a month I can and will, but that is the maximum, unfortunately with all my outgoings I cannot afford anymore." The truth was that she was not willing to pay anymore, the outgoings statement was a lie as she did not have major ones and did not believe you should just buy things for the sake of it. Her money was generally spent on fun things, things that fed the soul. She did not think the room or the flat were worth it.

"No, that is fine, the only thing I ask from you is that you pay for your calls."

"Oh, that is OK, I have my mobile it's a 'pay as you go' one so I don't have to pay for any other charges."

They both walked from Waverley Station in silence, a heavy awkward silence, the fact that Liz had come asking, maybe more like begging a friend for not only charity but to help her pick herself up, noting that Charlie was probably the last person she should have come too but she really did not have anyone to ask to, not where she wanted to be anyway.

Down Hanover Street, cutting across Queen Street they turned right at the next junction into Abercrombie Place. Charlie lived on the 3rd floor of a Georgian building it was one of those converted buildings which must have been absolutely gorgeous in the old days. By the time they got up to the third floor, Liz was exhausted, the weight of the suitcase which at the start she thought was not too bad suddenly became a ton in weight, the only focus of her determination, pushing her not to give up or give in and complain. She was sweating and internally swearing, regretting coming to Edinburgh.

"Here we are." Charlie stated as she opened the front door one hand pointing towards the entrance as if she was going into a palace. A racing green door with peeling paint, its heyday long gone.

She was disappointed but what else could she expect. It was smelly and dirty; actually, it stank, a smell of unclean, stale and musty, fungi type which emanated through to the corridor where both had been standing, Liz felt as if she was going back in time to her university days. This was a typical late 80s student flat which someone of her age would have never expected to step into again not after all this time. Liz moved towards the living room and her disgust must have been visible. There was everything on the floor from dirty nickers to mouldy food and empty glasses of wine and cans of beer.

"Have you had a party recently?" Liz mentioned, knowing that no party had been held there for the last few weeks. It was definitely one of those places that had not been cleaned for at least a year if not more. This was a place where you cleaned your shoes on the mat as you left the apartment. Truly disgusting. Charlie, for being such a beauty and glamourous woman, she had no sense of pride when it came to her living quarters.

"Here is your room, a nice little cubby-hole. Sorry I had no time to clean it." Charlie was smiling but there was something strange, there was more of a smirk appearing on the side of her lips as if she were enjoying this. She knew her and Charlie were 'friends' and guessed that she thought Liz needed her and she always thought that if she was drowning Charlie would not help her but what surprised her was that her smile showed some hate and disdain. Maybe it was her imagination, maybe she was just tired and depressed and needed some well-deserved sleep, her mind was playing tricks for sure.

"Anyway, I guess you are really tired, so I will leave you to sort yourself and I will see you tomorrow morning. Peter is in the bedroom, so I'd better go and see him."

Liz could not believe it, this must have been her storeroom, the bed was buried under masses of clothes, books, old banana skins and everything else you could think of. She could not believe that this person whom Liz would call a 'friend' lived not only in this state but made absolutely no effort towards her, even an enemy would have shown more respect this was disgusting.

She wanted to scream, it was nearly past midnight, Liz had taken the 0600 train to Edinburgh and on top of that Charlie had made her walk to her flat which in all honesty had taken 20 minutes as her suitcase was always getting in the way. The fact that the room was not clean meant she would be cleaning it for at least an hour and to top things up Charlie's boyfriend was there waiting for her 'in bed'. Well, that was no surprise, it seems that maybe that was one of the few things that Charlie was exceptional at: men in beds.

On reflection, maybe she was being unfair and guessed that as it was a Friday night and it was one of the few days when Charlie could see Peter because he worked in Aberdeen during the week. She wondered if he was annoyed at her staying there for two months.

Whilst lying in bed, she had decided that she was obviously not welcome in Charlie's flat. It had taken her two hours to clean the room and at nearly three o'clock in the morning she was exhausted. She had moved most of the clothes, shoes and magazines into a very neat pile outside her bedroom. The rubbish had all been put in a bin bag and placed outside the front door and she would take it down later that morning after she had snatched whatever sleep was left in the night.

If Charlie had said 'no' to her, she would have understood. If she would have said to come for a maximum of two weeks and after that you pay me £300 per month but you can stay only for two months as a maximum, that would have been fine too, but no, Charlie with her usual big grin and constant happiness had told her it was okay especially since she had lost her mum and her job. Did she not realise that when you are grieving the last thing you need is land on a dump, she would have been more than happy to pay £300.

Never mind, she was going to get up in the morning, nice and early and be extremely nice to her and the new man in Charlie's life, Peter. She would offer to clean the flat as a one-off and maybe offer again to pay but this time upping her offer to £700 in total for the two months she was to stay there.

She woke up at 6.30 a.m. and for some reason for the last two months she had not been able to sleep for long. She was a bit surprised though that she was up so early especially when her windowless room was so dark and also since she had only been able to fall asleep around three in the morning after taking so long to clean and sort the place.

Having had a shower and dressed by 7.30 a.m., she decided she wanted to go and get some food from the corner shop. Charlie had a spare key in the kitchen and Liz was able to find it without too much fuss and made a quick list of what she was going to need for the next couple of weeks, mainly just the basics. She knew she was going to be out most days, or at least the evenings with her old university friends so she did not want to get too much food. She was just going to nip to the corner shop she saw further down Hanover Street and buy bread, cereal, milk, etc.

"Hi, how are you?" Liz jumped so high with fright she thought her head was going to touch the ceiling. She had not been expecting anyone to be up at 8 a.m. on a Saturday, especially in the kitchen. Standing in front of her was an absolutely gorgeous male specimen, far too good looking for this world.

"Hi, I am Liz, Liz Stanton, Charlie's friend and I am staying here for a couple of months in the small box room. You must be Peter."

"No, I am not Peter, I am Christopher Wandsworth. I am staying for the weekend, sleeping here in the kitchen." Christopher pointed at a sleeping bag behind the door. You nearly crushed me when you came into the kitchen looking for the spare key. He was smiling with a very honest and friendly smile "That was some awakening but worth it, I guess. Whilst you were in the shops I went for a shower." He was still smiling when he finished saying this and Liz knew he was not annoyed she had woken him up, he seemed very relieved for some reason but then again it was probably her imagination playing tricks.

Liz could not for some reason or another close her mouth and was shocked that this guy was sleeping on the kitchen floor which had not seen a hoover or brush for at least six years. Suddenly she realised maybe she was not as bad off as this guy, at least she had a mattress!

"I know what you are thinking and I agree that this place is filthy." Christopher's grin said it all, he did not care what she thought of him or his remark and if he did, he was obviously too polite to show it in more detail. Most people would have walked out, why hadn't he? He was obviously very wealthy or at least he looked it. Why did she not walk out? She could not even answer that about herself, she could have easily gone to a hotel but guessed she was too tired to argue and at this stage in her life and wanted a simple easy-going time. Falling out with someone at this critical time when one was grieving for their mum as well as feeling the insecurity of not having a job was not something people did. Under better circumstances, she would have stood her ground and asked for respect, no, demanded respect. Not now though, which she was sure would end up eating at her for years to come.

"I am a friend of Peter, Charlie's boyfriend. Peter asked me to meet him here for the weekend, I came last night from London."

"Did you take the train?"

"No, I flew, it is easier, plus I had some airmiles I wanted to use."

"Oh, I came by train, was in at 11.30 p.m., I don't know if I would do it again though, it was a good journey even though we had to stop in Newcastle and change trains as our was faulty. I was completely exhausted by the end of it."

"Yes, I heard you, you were cleaning your bedroom until 2.30 a.m." Christopher looking at Liz's face go red quickly added "not that it bothered me, I could not sleep either, too much on my mind."

It was true what he had said, he had too much on his mind, he had been asked by his friend Peter to spend the weekend with him mainly because he wanted to talk to him face to face as to how he should finish with Charlie. Apparently, Charlie had been a constant nightmare phoning Peter every hour of every day and pestering him to either come down or she would go up to Aberdeen. Peter liked Charlie, as a fun girl but nothing else; he was worried in case she wanted a serious relationship. He was not interested in a serious relationship and even if he was, it would certainly not be with Charlie.

Last night Chris had managed to go to sleep at 3:30 a.m., roughly the same time as Liz, he was angry he was sleeping on the floor, on a dirty floor. He was told there was a room for him but then Charlie had remembered only a couple of hours before going to pick up Liz at the station that she had promised the room to a friend. Not that it made a difference to him as he was glad, he had not spent 2 hours sorting out that box room and he was certainly not annoyed at Liz, who seemed to be a very nice girl. His anger was directed at Charlie because she had never forgotten Liz was coming; she was just playing games with the three of them. This girl was poison, someone to tread with carefully, after all sometimes when we know there are snakes in the grass, we walk carefully but never without shoes.

He looked at Liz very quickly and felt sad, sad because he had heard she was going through a tough time, sad because her friend did not care and sad because she looked lost and depressed. You could tell she was making a big effort to try and appear happy and relaxed which to most would be convincing but not to him. He had seen depression before and he knew from experience what losing a loved one meant.

"Can I offer you some breakfast? I've got some cereal from the corner shop and some milk." Liz was not sure if this offer was to be welcomed but she did not know what else to say, "I have just boiled the kettle if you would like some coffee."

"Coffee would be nice; I don't usually have anything to eat in the morning, but it smells too nice to say no." Christopher was sure Liz could tell he was lying but he did not care, he was actually starving and would have welcomed a fry up rather than cereal but did not want to offend her. Chris, unlike most of his wealthy friends, enjoyed a fry up and thought one every so often was good for the soul, a thought that Liz would certainly share with him.

"Morning, morning, morning, how is everyone?" Charlie had appeared at the kitchen door with what would have deemed to be nearly naked. She wore a little cropped top that just covered her boobs (very large boobs) and a 'G' string. Liz could not believe Charlie had appeared in the kitchen with just that.

Liz quickly looked at Christopher's face to see his reaction but there was nothing there, no sign of delight, curiosity or admiration, just a very nonconformist, nearly dismissive look as if he had not seen her at all. At least he did better than Liz did because for a start she could not keep her head straight and kept moving everywhere trying not to look at Charlie who was obviously trying to get as much attention as possible. Liz looked first at Chris quite intently and then to the dishes and this was well after she had put away her tongue which had been hanging out due to shock and the fact that Charlie's nipples were clearly visible under her top. She portrayed the kind of picture that will invite to say: 'Available' - obviously the truth was different as only certain men were able to get her and they had to be rich or with mega potential.

It was obvious that Charlie was an extremely beautiful woman and she knew it. Her skin was a lovely olive shade, she had very long and toned legs, her blonde hair was perfect and her eyes were big and blue which along with her beautiful blonde hair made the whole package desirable. But her most gifted attribute were her size 36E breasts, a thought that in Liz's mind would scare most women but certainly be a plus for a guy. The weight her back must be exposed to must be horrendous thought Liz with her 36D breasts. Though nature had been overly generous with her, a fact she was not very thankful for it and wished for a 'B' which would have been more than enough.

"I see the two of you had met." declared Charlie, pretending to yawn "Liz, I see you bought us breakfast. Good. I will take some cereal for me and Peter, is there enough hot water for a coffee for us? I take mine black and Peter takes white with one sugar."

Christopher's face showed surprise, total surprise, as if someone had slapped him the face and Charlie had noticed it as well. He was shocked and annoyed at the cheek this woman had towards her guests, she did not even try and be nice, she assumed everyone was here to serve her.

"Well, she is staying free of charge for two months, so I guess I can ask her to supply the food." Charlie was on the defensive, she realised that she had just taken, as usual without having at least the decency of asking. It was hard for someone that was so egocentric to suddenly change her ways and realised too late she had lost face again!

"Actually, I did offer paying £300 per month, I buy my own food, pay my own bills and I am definitely, from my last job description, not a servant. If you have, for any reason changed your mind about the agreement we have please be kind enough to tell me and I will move out." Liz's tone was tough with no emotion, she had only been here some hours and was already fed up having been insulted several times already.

Christopher said nothing, the atmosphere in the kitchen was heavy and uncomfortable and after a couple of minutes she thought he would have said something, but he didn't. Oblivious to any embarrassment anyone else might be going through, Charlie had to say something again.

"Come on Liz, what is wrong with you? I was just joking. Of course, I want you to stay, you are just being a bit touchy." Charlie gave one of those false smiles of hers, one of her favourites.

This comment did not go unnoticed. She was taking advantage of Liz's mother's death and Liz's state of mind to pin the fact that Liz was touchy. Of course, she was touchy, but this was definitely not one of the reasons. She was upset she had spent the night cleaning a room which obviously had not seen a hoover for a year, at least!

"Don't worry about it, there is plenty for everyone. Here, help yourself" Liz wanted to make sure that Charlie was aware that even if she did not have the choice of offering or not offering her food, she was not going to serve it to her either. She knew from university that once you gave in once to a polite 'let me serve you' Charlie would use you as if you were her servant for life.

"Morning everyone, what is up? Why the serious faces?" Peter had come into the room and he could sense some kind of embarrassment. The tension in the room spoke without words, the feeling was electric. He knew Christopher was not happy sleeping on the kitchen floor as he was used to better, no longer a student but a man of 37. He had only to look once at Charlie and he was filled with embarrassment "I see you have decided to be a bit overdressed this morning, Charlie?" sarcasm filled his words, which went along with a very dirty look, he did not care, that he was going out with a slut, there was no way around it, he knew what Chris thought of her, actually he knew what Chris felt for her as it was written all over his face, total and utter disgust and disdain.

He felt annoyed at Charlie for offering a bed to Chris and then telling him to sleep on the floor, it was so like her and showed that she did not care, she had no manners behaving as if she was the only one that existed, he wondered what man would be crazy to actually one day marry her? Definitely not him, he was here to have fun and then move on, but even that fun was beginning to be too pricey.

Chris wanted to go to a hotel after that, he knew that at a short walking distance he would be at the North Bridge where there were some of the nicest hotels in Edinburgh, also the most expensive ones but who cared he was an incredibly wealthy man. Peter knew that if it was not for him calming him down and asking him to stay, he would have walked out on him and his filthy, brass but beautiful girlfriend.

"Morning, Peter." Christopher sounded pissed off.

"Hi, I am Liz, Charlie's friend" Shyness overtook Liz. Peter was not at all what she had expected, he looked too decent, clean cut for Charlie. Confidence was oozing from him; he knew he was good looking and charming and of course being wealthy counted a lot towards that confidence. However, he struck her as a fair and honest man, his eyes looked just like those of a man who understood, or was this part of his charm? Liz guessed that in a way you don't get to be as wealthy as him unless you are ruthless and there again, you could be ruthless and fair…maybe, but she doubted it or maybe she was just too much of a cynic.

"Hi, I am Peter, Peter Wardlock, Charlie's *friend*." He emphasised on the friend, he wanted Charlie to know that was it, just a friendship. After all, he could never introduce her to his parents or the rest of his family. She was just too crazy for his family as beauty was the norm there so they would not be impressed by that since his two sisters were models and his brother Aaron had married a model as well.

Peter was surprised seeing Liz. She was very quiet, the shy type but confident and she obviously was the type of person who liked being on her own turf but there again, we always prefer that but some of us thrive with a challenge and change of scenery.

Liz struck him as someone that would face her responsibilities well and will appear to be sociable, but he got the feeling she wanted the quiet life, not too much fuss. She did not match Charlie's personality which was out to be loud, embarrass the more insecure and humiliate them to the point of them wanting to disappear. It was probably the fact that Liz was beautiful that attracted Charlie to become friends with her. He wondered how close friends they were. Charlie acted with everyone as if they were her best friends, but from meeting her group in Edinburgh this was not the case. He knew she hardly knew anyone to call her best friend, she acted aloof most of the time and her repartee consisted of laughing at everyone and everything. Definitely not someone you kept as a friend.

"Did you sleep well, Liz?" Peter asked the question knowing the answer, like Christopher he was embarrassed that Charlie had not bothered to clean the room.

"Yes, thank you. I hope I did not wake any of you up this morning. I just tend to wake up so early lately because I find that it is very difficult to sleep in. I tend to get a headache if I force my body to go back to sleep." She knew she was ranting but couldn't't stop herself. "I decided to go to the corner shop first thing and get some milk and coffee, sorry if I woke any of you up."

"Oh, you didn't!" Christopher and Peter both retorted in unison much to Charlie's amazement and surprise. She knew she had been rude to Liz by not being a good host, but she could not be bothered with her. She would not be bothered anymore however she had to change her attitude as she had noticed that both Christopher and Peter were both eyeing Liz up. As usual, men would look at her for fun and Liz as a partner, it was all very annoying.

At the start she thought it might be fun having her here at the flat for a couple of months but then she remembered how quiet and proper or at least more behaved than her Liz was. Liz was thoughtful and always looked after everyone, she always thought Liz was a snob. The thought of Liz being better than her annoyed her and for some reason she decided she would make her pay by making her uncomfortable.

She remembered Liz always making friends very easily, but thanks to her, most of them did not trust her. She had made sure of that. Liz never knew why people always looked at her with suspicion at university as if she was about to snatch their boyfriend. Unknown to her, Charlie had been spreading rumours, all untrue, of course, and most people did not fully believe them, but the seed of suspicion was already there. That was one of the reasons Liz knew she could not ask that many people to help her this time, her memories of university were still clear even though it was now more than eight years ago.

Charlie realised too late that everyone was looking at her as if she was some sort of a freak. Peter had sussed out by the way she was looking at Liz that she had been jealous of her. She was probably happy that her friend was going through a tough time.

"Liz, let me help you with the coffee and we can take it to the lounge, it is sunnier there and we can open the windows. Come on guys, move, Liz and I will take the coffee and cereal through." Charlie had a Cheshire cat smile, she knew she had thrown everyone in turmoil, everyone hated her two seconds ago and now they were wondering if they had imagined her previous nastiness. She had decided she would be more careful with how she treated Liz in public, as usual people liked her a lot, even without problems people always warmed up to her. But for some reason people were different with Charlie and she hated that, she wanted to be liked and admired by everyone.

"I am off for a shower and then I will join you" Peter stated with a dismissive attitude, as if he wanted no part in girlie fall outs. Chris went out of the kitchen in silence; he had to prepare himself for a pretty shitty weekend. Create mental reinforcements for whatever this weekend threw out to him.

Whilst Charlie and Liz were silently making coffee and serving the cereal, Liz's mind went into overdrive, depression was slowly taking over the lovely morning and she wished that she had gone to stay with Charlotte in Glasgow but knew it would have not been fair. The twins were just three months old and with their two -year-old daughter Beth being at the demanding and terrible two's age, she decided it was not a good idea. Their house was not that big and considering she had a live-in-nanny staying with them it would have just made it very crowded and she did not want to be in a crowded place for 2 months. On top of this, every weekend Charlotte told her how both sets of grandparents were arguing as to who should stay with them. It would have been too much and selfish on her part.

She had to just accept the situation, maybe she would only stay two weeks instead of two months and see what came up, she knew lots of people from university but none well enough to ask to stay with them for two months and she felt she needed that time to relax and rethink her life. She needed to refocus and felt that it would be impossible to do that here.

She did not want to go as far as Aberdeen to stay with her friend Kieran, even though he would have loved that. He was still single and still wild and she was sure he still lived surrounded by a mess, he would have loved someone like her to pamper him for two months and make him a delicious meal or two.

No, she decided it was best to stay in Edinburgh where she could meet lots of people, go out, see museums, parks and she could see Charlotte in Glasgow for one weekend. Liz was sure Charlotte could find an excuse for her to spend a day with Liz, Jonathan, her husband could take care of the children for one day. She would also visit Kieran for the weekend or a maximum of four days but that would it. Aberdeen felt too far and isolated and during a time when she needed to be surrounded by people and needed easy access to things she liked, she rather not dared to spend too long there plus Kieran had work to do which meant her staying in an empty house in a city where she did not know anyone and she felt she was not yet prepared for that.

Regardless, she had to decide today or tomorrow what she was to do and how long she was going to stay with Charlie, she wanted to get better not worse and she knew exactly that she could only trust Charlie so much, if at all.

After they all had some breakfast and cereal, they all decided to go to Princess Street Gardens to just lie down and read books; it was around 11 a.m. so they would probably be at the gardens around 12 noon once they got everything sorted out.

When they went out of the flat, the sun was shining, and it was actually quite warm and definitely warmer than yesterday evening but not the kind of warmth you would get in London where temperatures could go up to 28 degrees in the summer. No, for Scots, warm was maybe 12 to 15 degrees but for a Londoner, the weather would have been considered a little bit cold, especially if you account for the breeze which seemed to be always present in Edinburgh. For the Scots who went out en masse to sunbathe the moment the sun started peeking out, this was considered quite warm.

Regardless of it, Liz had a nice simple light blue fitted cardigan on top of a white cardigan, just in case, if there was anything she hated was being cold, she could not stand it and it would destroy her day of she felt a slight chill. She could always take her cardigan off if for some miracle or other the weather turned reasonably warm. Her mum always said layers were best solution for any type of British weather!

The gardens were beautiful and very well kept with lots of colourful roses and many other types of flowers. It was one of the nicest parks Liz had ever seen in Britain and it still remained one of her favourites. She remembered when her mum came to visit her whilst at university and she was mesmerised by the gardens. Usually, gardens this well-kept would form part of a private house or a trust not taken care of by the council. The only thing her mum thought was missing were gladioli because she loved gladioli and thought every garden must have them, all different colours if possible and if not, at least pink and white. Liz for a start preferred a garden with lilies, especially of the Japanese variety, she also like trumpet lilies and arum lilies but all these were not seen often in gardens, mostly they were sold as a bunch of flowers, which she absolutely adored. The Scottish weather did not lend itself for lilies!

Liz's love for flowers and nature overall, it was something she had inherited from her mum; she had always, even as a student, bought a bunch of flowers to brighten up the bedroom or the living room where she lived.

After lying there for nearly two hours and listening to her stomach grumble, Liz decided to put her book aside. She was reading a historical romance, the ones we hide when someone else tries to read the title and then looks at our faces, feeling sorry, thinking we are desperate spinsters looking for true love or are nursing a broken heart, looking for some kind of escapism. She could agree a little bit with the second reason, we all needed some escapism, otherwise life was too much and yes, she was reading one of those. Christopher was lying to her left, he was reading the Times, quite embarrassing actually to be near someone like her, but he did not seem to mind. On her right, Peter and Charlie had been snogging for the best of two hours, their mouths must be ready to drop, they certainly looked as they over did it, and both their lips looked like car tires.

"Guys, I am starving, shall we go off for something to eat?" She tried desperately not to look at their rubber lips, Charlie looked as if she just had a silicon implant.

"Good idea!" Christopher echoed her sentiments, he was also, she believed, thinking the same as her either silicon or tyres.

"Okay," Charlie sounded as if someone was trying to muffle her "but after it I want to spend time alone with Peter, maybe you two can go off somewhere?"

Christopher stared at her and Peter sharply, one thing is to think like that, another one to voice it so rudely. Liz understood his annoyance especially when he had been invited by Peter to spend the weekend here. Her position was different, but Chris was only here at the request of Peter. What a bitch!

"Don't be so rude Charlie" Peter sounded so surprised he could not believe how rude Charlie was. He definitely had to finish with her this weekend. He could not drag it on, if he continued this then he would end up losing his best friend and his family would certainly not talk to him. He would of course miss their lovemaking, after all she was a very sexual person and very beautiful, but he could no longer put up with this, it had to end, but how?

"I was not being rude, I just feel I haven't seen you for a while and I wanted us to go shopping, I have seen some very interesting jewellery shops" Charlie looked at all of us with an innocent face, yeah right, jewellery shops. She was after Peter to get engaged to her, she had only been dating him for four months and wanted the big stone.

Liz could not believe it, she had not changed at all, maybe if she could not be so blatant and loud a guy would stay with her for a long time, but at his rate and by the way that Peter looked disapprovingly to Charlie, she could only guess it would not last for long. It was written in Peter's face. It always happened, she pushed too far, too soon and was too rude. Liz knew that she would soon come to her crying because she had been dumped and she did not understand why. "It is funny", Liz thought, "me being the person she comes crying to, especially after what she did to me at university." Revenge is so sweet, especially when everyone was not aware, she knew, a secret she still carried, heavily but she carried it nonetheless.

"I know a really nice pub down Constitution Street, just off Leith Walk, I can't remember its name, but it has really nice food and a jazz band that plays there all the time. We could take the number 10 bus down to the bottom of Leith Walk and then walk for a couple of blocks, what do you think?"

"Oh, was that the pub that on our last day of our course you were sick in?" Charlie smiled at Liz knowing that being reminded of that time would embarrass her.

"Yes, the same one, can you remember its name?" Liz was not deterred and pretended not to be affected by the comment.

"No, but food is good there, I have been there several times." Charlie realised that she had to be careful, Liz had only been in Edinburgh for one day, and you could tell she was ready to pounce on her.

"Ok let's go and get something nice to eat" Christopher muttered as he got up and dusted himself. He could not wait to get rid of Charlie for the day.

The pub they went to was halfway down Constitution Street, which was a strange looking street as it had some old buildings and some very nice restaurants hidden away and some very old houses that were in desperate need of repair, covered in moss, where chunks of rendering was falling off. The pub itself was amazing, no, it was gorgeous it is very old looking and just the type of place you could sit in on a Sunday morning reading your newspaper waiting for the fried breakfast to arrive. The bottomless coffee was great and the atmosphere was very good. There were four brown leather chairs near the fireplace and the moment they walked in they all practically dived towards them as if they were the last seats left in the world.

One of the features that Liz liked about the pub was that you had a sense of space as well as a cosiness which was very hard to find, a real fire was roaring in the fireplace, even though it was not too cold and it gave a sense of belonging, of feeling secure, like the sense you get when you go home to your parents after a very hard and stressful week, a feeling of welcoming and of peace.

Leith was such a lovely area, it had changed a lot since she had been a student, for a start. When she lived in Edinburgh, Leith was considered one of the roughest areas of Edinburgh it was a red-light district but not quite as bad as it sounded. Now, Leith was considered to be one of the exclusive areas to live, where trendy people from London or rich students lived. It had the latest in restaurants, pubs, cute little shops, barbers and hairdressers, the only thing that was really missing were the nice flower shops, so far she had only seen one.

Lunch went without much ado most present eating in silence, obvious the desire of wanting to leave and be somewhere else. Peter looked rather glum, as if he was getting ready for the slaughter, praying. Christopher made polite conversation with Liz and Charlie, but it was mainly directed at Liz, he looked as if he did not want to speak to Charlie but felt he had to. It was such a shame as the food and the pub's atmosphere was amazing. Definitely a place to be on a Saturday or a Sunday, just to chill.

"How about you and I going ice skating after lunch, Chris?" Liz had taken advantage of everyone calling Christopher 'Chris' and decided she would do the same, he seemed to like it as he never said anything, he actually smiled.

"Maybe that was not such a good idea, but I just love skating."

"Are you joking?" Disbelief crossed Chris's face.

"No, what is wrong with that?" Liz, in her short existence of 32 years she had gotten used to being looked at oddly when she made suggestions like this. She learnt to shrug them, as if they were of no importance. "I have not ice skated since the age of 24, that was actually my last time, I thought it would be funny and fun! Do you know what age I am Liz? A man of my age frolicking about in ice skates would look quite embarrassing."

"It is okay, I can pretend to be your daughter demanding you entertain me" A flicker of mischief passed through Liz's face, she was teasing him, pretending he must be around 50 and she was not far off it!

"I am not that old thank you very much, I am actually just 37. However, in view that you seem determined to make a fool not only of myself but yourself, I have decided to brave it." Liz took that small piece of information and stored it. Interesting that he was 37 and single, unless he had been married and divorced but she doubted it, men like this, once nabbed don't regain their freedom that easily!

Both Charlie and Peter looked at each other in disbelief. Peter because he thought it was the greatest idea he had heard in a very long time. He had not been skating since he left university which was nearly 17 years ago. He was surprised that Chris had accepted, since he had never seen him do that before, he was too careful with himself, would rather play rugby than be found skating with a girl. Peter now wished he was going, annoyance filled him and made him depressed, he wanted to have fun and he was stuck with Charlie.

"Well, it seems to me that both of you want to play at being children, that is fine, Peter and I will go shopping" again her cutting remark came as a surprise, her tone of voice had no trace of humour, she sounded so jealous. Liz knew that Charlie had always been jealous of her, but she never thought it was this deep-rooted resentment, she thought there was still a friendship but the more she spent time with her the more the realisation that she had been fooling herself for years transpired. Charlie should be at least trying to be her best friend, especially after what happened, it was her fault and she had forgiven her, well, sort off.

After they paid the bill, Chris and Liz decided that in order to take advantage of the time, since it was already 2.30 p.m., they would take a taxi. They left Peter and Charlie outside the pub and rushed at the first taxi that appeared down Constitution Street.

The journey to the Murrayfield ice rink was good, the chit chat was the usual, what do you do, what do you like, etc. Information that normally would have been asked within the first couple of hours of meeting, however because it was such a weird day and situation, they never had the opportunity.

Liz actually found out that, both Peter and Chris had gone to Cambridge university. Peter got a job in Aberdeen at a firm of actuaries and Chris had gone into banking based in London. They had been friends for nearly eighteen years and had always visited each other at least five times a year. In the last three years they had gone on holiday twice, once skiing for three weeks over Christmas to Chamonix and the other time, Chris was sent to the Caribbean regarding some business venture and Peter joined him for a week.

It seemed that they were the best of friends, Peter had been married once and Chris helped him get over his divorce, which she had heard it was pretty crazy, very much a messed-up affair and one of the reason Peter kept most women at a distance, something you should admire and if possible use, but certainly not make a commitment and definitely not a permanent one for that matter.

Chris had dated women for years but the moment they started pressurising him to get married he would dump them like hot potatoes. It is funny, she could not believe he was actually confiding this to her. She felt he was trying to get her interested soon to be added to his hot potato list of unwanted femmes. Hmmm regardless, she felt special and honoured!

Liz could not believe her luck and when they walked into the skating rink not only where they were playing 80's disco music, but Chris and her were the only ones over 12, she just could not stop herself laughing. Apparently in the evening older people came for the disco but nobody as old as the pair of them.

They felt that the looks they received from people were hilarious. They even heard a couple of girls commenting that geriatrics should not be allowed in. Of course, Chris and her, behaving in a very mature and adult way, told them to piss off.

Yes, they probably were the ones that sent those two girls to therapy. They were probably shocked when Chris, as he fell, took two fingers to the air in defiance, especially since he saw a very nasty smile slowly draw on those two girls' faces as they saw him crash against the wall and hit his head.

"See what happens to old people like you when you do young people's sports" It was not a question; it was a statement by the girl with the red hair, seeing him flat on his bum deciding she could not miss this opportunity to be cheeky.

"Shut up carrot head" With this comment even Chris was surprised, especially when the girl rushed to her friends crying. He could not believe he had behaved like an utter pratt. Boys calling someone names were one thing, but adults were another.

"I can't believe I did that, what is wrong with me?"

"Don't worry about it, she did look like a carrot anyway, a nasty one" She winked at Chris "We have been here for an hour, I think we have done enough, this fall will probably set you back years, you will fear ice rinks and your children would have to be deprived of skating because of it." She could not stop laughing, in fact, Liz laughed so much that even Chris started seeing the funny side, he was in agony, but he could not stop himself laughing.

As he started getting up, his legs were all over the place and that is when they just heard this ripping noise, the material at Chris' crotch had decided it had enough of being pulled left right and centre and it just ripped through, Liz's eyes were by then streaming with tears and Chris looked as red as a beet root. Just as well he was wearing blue boxers that matched the colour of his jeans or it would have been a funnier sight than it already was. By then most people by now were pointing at Chris, who was failing desperately to stand up.

"Come on Liz, help me" it was a funny sound that came out of Chris when he said it, almost a gargle, he was obviously trying not to laugh or not to cry and scream at the same time.

"I am sorry, come on, give me your hand" She was struggling trying to hold his hand; she was hardly balancing herself as she could not stop laughing. Her ribs were starting to be sore; it was just too funny and sad she guessed.

"Oh, thank you, now, let's go and have a pint of something, I need something strong" Chris was trying to get up but kept sliding, it was just too funny, he actually looked scared which made him look pathetic, a very good looking but pathetic guy.

Liz decided that she was having a very good day, Chris made her laugh and in the last three hours she had not thought of her problems and disasters surrounding her life. She felt like a teenager, she felt that Chris and she had known each other for a long time, they relaxed in each other's company, and there was no lying, just two good honest friends, new friends but still friends.

Before they had noticed it, they had ended up having three drinks in a pub near the ice rink. Their conversation had been so animated that the time had slipped by. time was irrelevant as they both found themselves comfortable in each other's company, at ease sharing experiences, non-judgmental, just enjoying themselves.

"I am a little bit hungry, fancy going for a light meal? Maybe Thai or if you fancy something different, we can get a kebab as a takeaway?" "I fancy something spicy with a bit of a kick" Chris was looking at her, it was a very long look, it held her gaze for a while and it said: "I am very comfortable with you, I like you, let's not destroy it by going back to the flat yet." He had not voiced his thoughts, but his gaze said it all and the fact that he was suggesting going out for a meal also meant he enjoyed her company.

"Actually, do you fancy Indian food? I know a restaurant by the Leith docks, the food is fantastic, in fact, one of the best Indians I've had and the service is equally impressive."

It did not take much to convince Chris, he seemed relaxed and eager to please, and maybe he did not want to go back to the flat too early and was looking for an excuse.

It had only been seven thirty by the time they had arrived at the restaurant, they did not have to queue, and they were given a table facing the waters of Leith. If it was not for the fact that both of them knew this was not a date, it could have been seen to any passer-by as a very romantic meal out. Maybe it was the scenery of Leith or the conversation they were having, one could not tell, but they both enjoyed themselves thoroughly.

"Here, have my business card. When you get back to London maybe we can get together again and reminisce on this wonderful weekend" Liz did not know if he was being sarcastic or not, the fact that he winked at her was a giveaway, but she was sure he did enjoy himself tonight. Chris seemed honest when he said to meet up, it would be nice to keep in touch with him, he was a lovely guy.

"Thanks, I will" Liz put the card on her bag and noticed he had written his home telephone and mobile on the back of the card, she smiled "if you have another card, I can write my mobile number as well if you want. My plan is maybe to stay in Edinburgh just for one month or so, I might go to Glasgow or Aberdeen for a week after that or in between that."

"Thanks, I would like that" his smile was so broad, but his eyes were focused and intense, Liz knew then that he really wanted to see her again, it was obvious and he wanted her to know "if I am up here visiting friends or clients or even on my way to Aberdeen to see Peter, I will call you."

The rest of the evening went flying, two souls that connected at some level. Was it fate or was it just chance? Their common interest was that both were stuck in an unwanted situation, but they discovered they have so much in common.

By the time they got to the flat it was 10.30 p.m. at night, Charlie was annoyed she was in a foul mood and close to being upset, she was not even behaving like an adult and she was completely nasty.

"So, what happened to you? Did you get lost or maybe did you just decide you did not want to be with us?" Her comments were being directed at Liz. Her guess was that Charlie liked making the decisions here and she did not like that Chris and Liz had decided to just stay out for the day, after all, she was not exactly welcoming their presence at lunchtime.

"Now come on Charlie, this is not fair" Chris was sounding incredibly angry. You could tell by his jaw that he was trying very hard not to lose his temper or raise his voice. "If I recall well this afternoon, you did not want to spend time with us this afternoon, you were not exactly welcoming us with open arms. Also, we did not arrange anything for the evening; actually, Liz and I left two messages on your mobile, Charlie."

"Charlie, just leave it please." Peter sounded stressed; he must have had this all evening "do not ruin the day anymore than you have already. Have you checked your mobile? Maybe, after all they did try and get hold of us."

"I left a message on your mobile as well as Peters." Chris stated, he knew he did not have to explain, and he knew that Peter was not bothered "I guess you did not take it with you."

"I forgot to take it with me, don't worry, Chris. We only came back at 7.30 p.m. so there is no problem at all, plus you can do what you want - I am not your guardian." Peter smiled at Chris whilst he said this. He looked tired and exhausted, totally drained.

"I think if nobody minds, I am going to the pub for a drink before it closes for the night, I had a really good day and I don't want it destroyed, maybe when tempers have gone down a little bit, you can all join me, I will be in the pub at the corner."

"Do you mind if I join you now, Chris?" Liz was a bit apprehensive as she did not know if he just wanted to be alone, she certainly did not want to be left alone with them.

"Not at all Liz, you are welcome!"

"I will join you in half an hour with Charlie." Peter, without even asking Charlie had decided they will be friendly, he was fed up with her trying to rule everything, she had been stuck with her all evening with her moaning and demanding attitude. If she did not want to go to the pub, then she could stay here on her own, which Liz doubted she would do. She would not apologise; he would act the martyr and sulk for hours.

"Ok, see you later." Chris closed the door with purpose, he had slammed it and it showed how annoyed he had become, his weekend was ruined, he could have been in London at Janine's dinner party, his current flame, but Peter had begged him to come up to Edinburgh. He would never do this again, not if this spoilt brat was involved in it.

Chris left the next day; he left incredibly early in the morning and very quietly. He had said his goodbyes after the pub that evening and they had exchanged numbers, which Liz thought was really nice. He was obviously still annoyed at Charlie and Peter as well for putting him in this kind of situation, it was not fair. He had ruined his whole weekend and being such a busy man, his weekends were a valuable asset. The only plus he thought was meeting Liz, a lovely charming and very lost girl, she was obviously suffering a lot from the death of her mother.

# New Beginnings - 1991 Looking at The Past

Charlie had always been the party animal, always laughing, planning fun parties, the joy of the party. Liz remembered everyone wanting to be with her or near her when we went to the pub or had a party or went to a party, you were guaranteed that something fun or unusual will happen. She was the girl to be with if you wanted to be noticed and popular.

looking back when Liz had started university, she had been so stressed thinking nobody would like her, worried in case everyone thought she was prim and proper, but she should not have worried as her class, which had around 65 people had all sorts of types, punks, posh, scruffs, sporty people, everyone. Nobody cared or at least seemed not to care and most importantly everyone seemed equally nervous, having probably the same questions and doubts as Liz. Nobody knows what goes on in people's minds and everyone assumes the worse, either someone is having a bad time or is having too much of a good time. At the end of the day, Liz realised she needed to think that everyone was the same with feelings, nervousness and anxiety.

She remembered walking into class on the first day and after looking at everyone, decided to sit beside this girl that was dressed like Cindy Lauper. Liz thought, "well at least she looks like fun." Her name was Charlie Summers and that was it, they became friends, or at least Liz thought they did. They went everywhere together, did everything together but luckily, never fancied the same people which was great and Liz always thought her taste was a little bit wild but then again, thinking back she now realised that she chose the mild ones that dressed as they were wild but weren't. From experience, it was the posh ones that were the wild ones, they seemed so prim and proper but behind the scenes nothing stopped them, that and the added arrogance made them a dangerous breed. Sadly, it was exactly what Liz liked about them.

Liz very soon realised Charlie was jealous of her, Charlie always thought Liz looked and acted above her station. She was what most people would have called an inverted snob or at least a pretended inverted snob. It is funny as she went to private school and was very posh but for some reason felt she was not, as if she wanted to forget her privileged background. She always acted as if she needed to prove something to everyone.

Liz also went to private school but for some reason everyone assumed the opposite which proved her theory that nobody really knows what they are talking about. Most of the time comments about schools are due to jealousy because they really do not like themselves or the individual in question and cannot admit it. Liz was more than sure that Charlie would have had the biggest chip on her shoulder if she had been born poor of low middle class. It was all pretense for her.

Liz started remembering, drifting slowly into the past as she now and then did but more often than not lately, like looking to understand her mistakes and learn, which she found hard. Sometimes the last thing she wanted to do was remember. She had started dating this guy called Timothy, he was 'nothing much to look at', semi attractive, more 'nice' than a unforgettable kind of guy but kind and generous and he encouraged her in everything and always pushed her to do better, to strive high; to be honest, they should have really have been just friends but one night one thing led to another and they ended sleeping together, not that she had considered myself an easy target as she made him wait for three months before it happened. Still, looking back, they should have just been friends, passion and deep attraction does not mean 'forever love'.

It had been the first time Liz had slept with someone, but not for Tim, as she called him. He went out with quite a few people before her even though he was not your classical good looking guy, he had a 'charm', everyone trusted him, he could basically have anyone he wanted, whenever he wanted them. He was good and reliable; someone you could count on and would not let you down without a solid reason. Liz was very flattered he wanted her, out of a crowd, he wanted her which was amazing.

Liz had not fancied him at first, but he grew on her, slowly and strongly, someone she could rely on, confide, depend on and more importantly, trust him with her secrets and dreams. Young love, seeing everything for the first time, fresh without any doubts, prejudices or scars from past hurts or prejudices, but it seems we were not meant to be. Fate had plans for them and she should have seen it coming but maybe she did not want to hear it and this was the only way she would have taken note.

Charlie had phoned Liz one night really distressed, Richard her boyfriend at the time had finished with her. This in itself was quite a shock and never in the three years that Liz had known and been Charlie's friend heard, of anyone finishing with her. An act for sure, but Liz was naïve in the way of conniving behaviour and had believed everything. A final act that had made Liz grow and realise that nobody really cared, everyone wanted something, had a reason for everything, being it for self-gratification, spite, jealousy or just for financial gain or a one up on someone. Faith in humanity gone without Liz realising it, deep on her neurological mind, her cells learned and judged.

Everyone in the year had successfully graduated from university and were at a loose end trying to find jobs, which for some reason or another were not being very successful. Most in her year were signing on at the dole office, which to be perfectly honest most would not recommend to anyone. Signing on is the most humiliating and degrading experiences ever, the embarrassment as a graduate not to have found something after graduation, not only that, having to get up early to go on the queue to make sure your signature was done so you can obtain he much coveted price of hardly any funds to survive.

Charlie just wanted to have fun and saw being on the dole as something she could do for the next six months or so to see what happened. She had been dating Richard for a year and now that she had graduated and Richard had got a job in a Swiss bank, she had expected him to propose; after all he had been working for a year. Why she thought this is unclear, how long you had a job generally did not rule if you wanted to propose to someone or not, it was more the fact that someone love you but to her his was irrelevant, her assumption was that everyone wanted her and adored her and there was not question Richard wanted to marry her.

Richard struck everyone as a very ambitious, hardworking but fun guy. Most importantly a bachelor through and through for at least the next ten years or so. He did not seem like a man who would fall in love and marry, no, he was the type who would play the field for years, then marry and cheat on his wife and maybe later on divorce or be divorced and be shocked about it. Certainly, a man that thought he was untouchable, guilt free and in his mind, totally honest. He would not rob anyone but cheating to him did not fall in the category of guilty or a bad guy.

Nobody had ever told Charlie what everyone thought, but Liz always felt she had been wasting her time. Anyway, as Liz was on her way to meet Charlie, minding her on business, she got a call from Tim saying he will meet me at his flat later on that evening. Liz had told him that she had to see a lecturer at the pub as it was his leaving party and most of the class were to be there to say goodbye to him, she asked him to meet her there, but he declined.

Tim had told her that he did not want to go out; he had had a bad day and just wanted to relax in front of the TV and not think about anything, mindlessly playing with the remote control to anything that may take his fancy. Probably rugby or football, she had thought!!

"Can you come round to my flat later on?" Tim sounded tired; Liz did not want to push him to come out.

"OK, I will be there around midnight, I got your spare key, so if you are asleep, I will just sneak in" Liz's singing voice came through the receiver, happy and carefree, knowing she was loved and secure in his affections.

Tim had been already working as a junior actuary for 1 year, he was older than Liz by two years. At the young age of twenty-two he was considered one of the rising stars at university, with the expectation to have great achievements by the age of thirty. He had graduated a year early with a distinction in Applied Mathematics from Edinburgh university. He was ambitious but not too ambitious, he knew what he wanted and balance was one of the things he craved for, he did not want to go abroad to New York, where he was originally offered a one year posting by his company with an extremely attractive salary. He wanted a reasonably easy life, hassle free, near his friends and family and no early burn out which was what he foresaw would happen to him by accepting a job in New York. He truly believed that pure greedy choices early on in life only sent you to an early grave and most definitely and unhappy life.

Richard and Tim had both graduated from Edinburgh university at the same time, both having done Mathematics and by way of a weird coincidence, they both worked for the same company. Their attitudes and work ethic were very different, Tim was more laid back, whilst Richard only thought of success and money, at any cost, his arrogance at least two steps ahead of him. It was Richard who had introduced Liz to Tim. On the surface there was no sign of competition but deep down you could see there was, Richard wanted to be the winner, the top dog, he saw himself as the one with the prized wife and family, the nice car, house and job. Not something you saw straight away but you were given glimpses now and then, by the throw away comments, that you would only notice if you were really people watching. Most people were superficial, nobody connected to their inner voice anymore to ask if someone was indeed good, not that wanting the best was bad, so long as it was not done wrongly.

"Hi Charlie, it's me Liz'," Liz had been, unsuccessfully trying to get hold of Charlie for close to an hour now and her mobile had been busy, when at last she answered, she didn't sound as upset as she had expected.

"Hi Liz, when are you going to be here?" Charlie sounded anxious.

"Well, I was going to go there now but just for half an hour and then I will have to go. I promised John Lehrer that I will be there for his drinks party, after that I was planning on going to Tim's flat, he is not coming out, he had a really bad day and wanted to relax!"

"Why do you bother with John, Liz, who cares?" Charlie's disdain of the non-rich, which in her mind was anyone that earned less than £150,000.

"I promised and he has always been good to me, I like him Charlie" This was one of Liz's failures, why explain why she wanted to go out and meet this guy? She owed Charlie nothing "plus most of the class will be there and it would be nice to see everyone together one last time." John had been a good English literature lecturer, he liked him, he was down to earth and wanted to help students. She felt duty bound to go to his leaving do.

"I don't know why you are so anti him Charlie" As usual she was successfully getting under Liz's skin, irritating her no end. She was horrible to this guy for no reason, if anything, Liz would have thought she would have been the first to be there since she did not like being excluded in a day out or a pub crawl.

"I am not anti him, he is just an arrogant asshole, that is all, he really thinks he is above the rest of us because he is a lecturer when in fact, he is only three years older than us!!" Charlie sounded even more on the defensive, desperate to clear the reason as to why she did not like him, but not sound like the bitch that she very clearly was.

"I don't think you are being fair; I say this because you liked him until he started dating Jenny Coggin. Is it because you can't stand her?"

"Never mind Liz, I am not getting into this discussion, I am not in the mood. I tell you what, don't come round, I am going to watch some television and then go to bed, you just go to the pub and I will speak to you tomorrow" with that Charlie was gone, no goodbyes, nothing, she just hung up on her.

Liz had not been this angry in a long time, she swore she would not go and see Charlie the next day unless she apologised first, she was tired of her selfishness and tantrums. She had to make a stand and she would go to John Lehrer's pub crawl and have a great time.

What Charlie never told Liz was that she had a six-month fling with John; this was whilst he was seeing Lara Taylor. Her hatred towards him started when he finished with her and Lara to go out with Jenny, not only that, but he had also proposed to Jenny six months later and now, a year after their engagement, he was leaving Edinburgh university to go to Dublin and live near her until their wedding.

Nobody in her class knew of their affair, which in all honesty, in Charlie's mind had been a disastrous and humiliating experience. She had been obsessed with him, only to realise too late that he used her for sex. He had never taken her out for a drink or a meal or even given her a present or a surprise, their affair never moved from the four walls of his bedroom. In the end, it was not the fact that he left her for someone else that hurt; it was the realisation that she never meant anything to him.

Liz was meeting everyone in a pub in the Grassmarket, she was already late by thirty minutes and was worried in case they had already moved to another pub, she tried the Beehive and they were not there, so decided on the Last Post, which was lucky, she had only been one hour late but most people looked as if they had been drinking for three hours at least.

Liz had been there for only two hours when she started feeling extremely low, she wanted to be away from everyone, she did not know if it was because she had an argument with Charlie or because she had drunk three glasses of wine or because it meant that John's departure meant that the university life which she had led for four years was over. She probably would not see most of these people for a long time if at all. She decided, there and then, to go home to Tim. She wanted a hug, to feel she belonged.

She wished John all the best and that she will see him and Jenny at their wedding in Ireland. She was, along with another guy and two girls, the only ones to be invited to the wedding. It was weird because Jenny had been in their class, but she never really mixed with them, more like an outsider looking in. The four invitees were John's guests and not Jennies. Liz felt a sense of peace, was nice that she will see him again; he had been a good friend and a lecturer.

Tim lived in the South side of Edinburgh, a beautiful part of Edinburgh called Morningside, since she was going from the Grassmarket, she decided that it would be quicker to go through The Meadows, a very large park in Edinburgh at the back of the university. She crossed the park and went down Marchmont Road and then turned right to Warrender Park Road then Bruntsfield Place and then followed the road down to Morningside. After 40 minutes of walking, she was at Tim's, finally. Relief washed over her, she was 'home', she felt a welcome feeling over her body.

Tim's light was off, but she saw a glimmer of light coming through when she looked up to the window, possibly from the bathroom, she guessed, or he must have left the corridor light on for her and he must have gone to bed early. The door on the street to the tenement block wasn't very secure as it could be opened by just pushing at a certain angle. When she went in there was a dimly lit large stone staircase with three flats on each floor. She ran up the three floors to Tim's flat.

She used Tim's spare keys to his flat and sneaked in without making too much noise, not wanting to wake him up as she knew he had a bad day. She thought she would just sneak into bed and give him a big hug. She will not wake him up, she will tell him tomorrow about her argument with Charlie and me feeling low at Johns night out. No point disturbing the guy now.

The bedroom door was ajar, she heard muffling noises, panting with some kind of groaning, not one but of two people. Suddenly, she felt her heart racing at 100 miles per second, she knew, she felt it deep in her core, a coldness came over her. She had a feeling she was not going to like this, she wanted to run. Liz had not put the corridor light on, but Tim must have left the living room lamp on, which gave the whole flat a shadowy, eerie look but gave Liz enough light to see where she was walking. She felt as if she was part of a film, she was waiting for someone to jump on her and knife her.

Still tip-toing, thoughts pushing through the back of her mind, she started worrying about a possible break in, unheard of but still possible. Edinburgh was well known as a peaceful city. She did not want to call the police and look like a fool if nothing was wrong.

She pushed open the door, very slowly so that nobody was disturbed, her heart stopped, she was just looking, staring in disbelief, they were oblivious to her presence, her eyes with tears swimming on them, her throat was sore and dry, her sight adjusting to the darkness, her tears not enough to free flow down her face. She knew she had to be in control, survival mode had kicked in, fight or flee reflexes full on. She knew that she could not show her anger and despair. Guessing being only 10 p.m. Tim must have thought he had enough time. She wondered how long they have been seeing each other, how they must have laughed at her, how could he have had a lover, her of all people. She could not make a sound, her mouth and lips were dry, so dry as if she had been exposed to the desert sun for hours, parched to best describe them, her lips moved but no sound came out, they were trembling, all she remembered was her mouth being covered by her hand in order to muffle the sound of disgust and shock that came out of her throat.

All these thoughts were going through her in what felt like a lifetime, but it was in actual fact only two or three seconds. She started backing off, she could not witness it anymore, she had to get out of there without them realising that she had witnessed them making love, her boyfriend, her lover and companion her Tim, and someone whom she considered her best friend, Charlie.

She got as far as the door, the tears started falling to the floor, her hands were shaking but she had managed to open the door and close it without making too much noise. She was hoping that the noise from their lovemaking will be enough to muffle the noise made from opening and closing the door, they were being so loud; he was like a wild animal, something he had never experienced with her, he obviously found Charlie amazing, more than that, he must desire her passionately to act like that. Liz was conscious of trying to be quiet, it had taken her less than 5 minutes to run up the stairs, it was now taking me more than five to go down the stairs; she was conscious that she did not want to be discovered. Fear of discovery and being publicly humiliated gripped her, the only thing that made her achieve her silent goal. Her pride kicked in.

"Please God, don't let them hear me, I don't want to be discovered" Liz muttered to herself. "I can't take a face-to-face humiliation."

Liz got to the front door on the ground floor, knew that if they looked out of the window, they could easily see her, it was not dark enough to disguise herself in the shadows, the streetlamps were too bright, but she had no choice. She decided to put her jacket over her head and walked hugging the wall until she was far enough away from Tim's flat. If people thought she was stupid, so be it, she thought. Finally, far enough she could breathe, her heart pounding, body shaking and tears on free flow.

To go home, which was near the Commonwealth Swimming Pool, on St Leonard's Lane, off St Leonard's Street, it had taken her nearly three hours normally it would take only twenty minutes, Liz had been walking very slowly, crying her eyes out, stopping several times, as if not believing what had happened, as if everything had been a dream.

When she arrived at her flat, she was the only one there as her two flatmates Lorraine and Kieran were still out, probably somewhere in Leith where the pubs remained open until six a.m. The phone had been ringing when she walked through the door, it was probably Tim pretending he had been waiting for her, after all, it was now nearly 1 a.m. in the morning.

"I wonder how they are now, pretending she went to visit him because she was lonely and upset, both waiting for her" Liz without realising that she had said it aloud, she had to find a way of not seeing him, finishing with Tim, pretending it was for another reason, it will be the only way. She will keep on Charlie's friendship but never trust her again; she will never trust anyone again. She wanted out of it with her pride intact. Her head keep repeating the words like a mantra: "keep you pride, keep your pride."

"I hope that 'what goes round comes round' for Charlie and Tim and I hope you pay for the hurt and upset you have caused" she whispered to herself. Liz never even listened to the messages on the machine, she knew who they were from, she just went to bed and cried herself to sleep. She had never even bothered to change into her t-shirt; all she wanted was the duvet on top of her to shut herself away from the world.

Early in the morning, Liz got up, groggy from crying and lack of sleep, her mind foggy, wondering if it had all been a dream. Her stomach feeling as if a revolt was going on in it, her head hurt, pounding and throbbing; her eyes were swollen and sleepy eye sticking to the lashes. She felt empty, did not want to get up, did not want to face the world. What was she do to? How can she maintain her pride? She felt and was humiliated. Sickness mentally and physically was starting to engulf her, she started vomiting but nothing was coming about, she was in shock, her worst fear had materialised. She had slumped herself in the corner of the kitchen, staring for what seemed an eternity, her mind racing with thoughts, their time together, their lovemaking, their laughs and friends. Why was life so cruel, why? What had she doen to deserve this?

She had stayed in Edinburgh after graduation because of Tim, was trying to get a job here so that both could be together and now, there was no reason for her to stay here, she had to go, but where?

The phone was ringing again, that is what had woken her up, in her confusion and stress, she had fallen asleep in the kitchen floor, she had not realised it and must have just dosed off. Where were Lorraine and Kieran anyway? What time was it?

"Hello? She sounded as if she had been asleep for one hundred years, but she could not, however, hard she tried, sound okay.

"Hi sweetie, it's me, Tim. Where have you been, I was worried all last night when you did not come round?" Was it guilt she was hearing? Was his voice okay, did he feel bad, did he feel pain for what he had done?

"Hello? Liz? Is everything okay? Tim sounded genuinely worried, her guess was because guilt was eating him. She wondered why did he do it? Why did people cheat? Was it because he could not miss an opportunity, challenge, was bedding Charlie a challenge?

"Hi, I am here. Sorry I am just very tired; I came in very late so I decided not to disturb you" Liz guessed if anything Tim might think she had a hangover.

"I spoke to Jenny today and she said you left at nine p.m. last night. Where did you go?"

This was typical, she was not going to be allowed to come out of this with at least some pride. Why is it that she could never just hide and escape without people noticing? She wanted to cry, scream and run. She wanted to ask him "why did he do it?." Why did he not just finish with her and then go out with Charlie?

"I went to meet Kieran and Lorraine in Leith and then we just stayed out, they are still not back, I came back here around three a.m." She hoped that he would not have the chance to speak to Kieran or Lorraine until she did first, this will also buy her some time to think of what to do with her life.

"Do you want to meet up for lunch? It is nearly 12 noon; I could meet you in Bruntsfield if you want or that nice restaurant we like in Lothian Road?" He sounded guiltier "I missed you last night" He was definitely feeling guilty, she wondered at what time Charlie left? They probably could not make love again after mid night just in case she went round; she wondered where Charlie had slept? Did she go

49

home, or did they just stay on the settee? Going to the bedroom together after midnight would have been too dangerous.

"I really don't feel like going out Tim. I am actually thinking about going to Glasgow to see Charlotte" she muttered. "She invited me a couple of weeks ago but could not go, so this is a good opportunity." She tried to sound as if it was the norm for her to just go off to a different city at a minute's notice.

"Liz, are you OK? You don't sound OK. Can I see you before you go to Glasgow? Maybe I can meet you at the station?".

"No, I am OK", she whispered, trying her very best not to cry. "I just need to get some things cleared in my mind" She lied. She hated lying but she was not going to give him the pleasure of finding out she knew, she wanted to make sure he was left guessing, he had to pay one way or another.

"Like what? What is bothering you?" He was not aggressive with his questioning, but you could tell something was bothering him. "Did she know?" He thought to himself, panic rising, his heartbeat speeding up, he felt faint and sick at the same time, unaware that she already knew.

"Just stuff. Please, don't push me. I need some time; I need to think." She had to try and cut him off nicely or she would get upset and tell him that she knew.

"I love you. You know that don't you?" he started sounding desperate, as if he knew that she knew. "I wish I had been with you last night; I am sorry I was so tired" He lied. He felt she knew, she was lying, he had been found out.

That did it for Liz, she snapped. How dared he said he was tired after he must have spent hours and hours making love to her. How dare he!!

"I told you I am fine, please leave me alone. I will call you on Sunday night when I am back" with this she hung up on him, tears were falling down her face, she knew what she had to do, she will call Charlotte and ask her if she could go and see her.

The phone range several times but she didn't answer it, she knew it was Tim and she also knew that he would come and see her as he did not believe she was to go to Glasgow. She did not have time to chance it. She got showered and dressed in a record 15 minutes, put two changes of clothes in a rack sack and went out of the house. She made a mental notice of phoning Kieran in his mobile so that she could ask him to cover up.

Within 20 minutes, after spending ten minutes trying to hail a taxi, she was at Haymarket Station, the train to Glasgow was due in 10 minutes, so she was OK. She rushed to buy her ticket and went down the stairs to the platform. She could now start relaxing, she could feel the tension leaving her body, the sadness of it all was still engulfing her.

She had decided to go to Haymarket rather than Waverly because knowing Tim, he would have gone to Waverly station. He was a desperate guy trying to save his relationship and he would do anything.

The good thing is that he did not know where Charlotte lived or her phone number, so she was safe, at least until Sunday night. She managed to leave a message on Charlotte's mobile saying that she was in Glasgow and if she could stay in her flat; she explained she needed a friend, the rest she would explain when she saw her.

Charlotte must have realised something was wrong, Liz's voice was teary in the message, she knew Liz never showed emotions unless something devastating happened, with that in mind, she had quickly phoned Liz back telling her she will meet her at Queen Street Station and they could both have a coffee and then go to her flat.

The journey to Glasgow took forty-five minutes by train, she found a quiet seat where people would not stare and ogled at her. Her tear-streaked face and red eyes could not be hidden. She felt as if people knew what had happened and they were feeling sorry for her. She could not stand it. Her mind was in turmoil, she felt worse than yesterday, devastated, lonely, that was the worse, she had a sense of loneliness about her that was ripping her apart. She wanted to call her mum but did not want to bother her with things like that; her mum always worried about her and it would not have been fair.

She had managed to quickly talk to Kieran on her mobile phone on her way to the station and without explaining much. He seemed to have understood, at least she thought he did.

"Liz, is there anything wrong? You don't sound OK? Kieran's voice showed concern you have not done anything, wrong have you? So typical of Kieran to assume she had done something wrong. She was such a good girl that the moment something happened they assumed she suddenly went wild or lost the plot.

"No, I have done nothing wrong, don't worry. Something happened that I will never be able to talk to you about, something personal. Please don't ask what, I will be OK. Just make sure that everyone, including Tim and Charlie think that I have spent all Friday in a pub with you guys in Leith". A small favour to ask and she knew Kieran would not push her, even though he was probably itching to know.

"OK, we were only in Robbie's until 11.30 p.m. and then we went to Christopher's Fellini's flat. Every one of the usual groups was there apart from Louise, she went to see Phil probably for a shag." The smart comment coming from Kieran could not be missed, he had fancied Louise for 2 years and she kept turning him down only to end up going out with guys who used her for a one-nightstand or for a 2-month fling, nothing was ever serious and it upset Kieran that she did not respect herself enough to say 'no' to other guys.

"Liz, when you are back on Sunday we can talk and if you don't want to talk, I just want you to know that Lorraine and I are here for you."

"Thanks Kieran, you are really sweet. I will be back very late on Sunday, but I will definitely have a chat with you on Monday." Kieran and Lorraine had both been really good friends since her first year of Uni. She did not manage to get into the university halls of residence but was lucky enough to find a flat where they needed someone to live in the box room, at £90 a month. She was so desperate; she couldn't say no to it even if it was an illegal little room with no ventilation.

This was in her first year. She got on so well with both Kieran and Lorraine that she decided to stay for as long as she could, which now amounted to nearly four lovely years. Both Lorraine and Kieran were doing medicine, and this was their final year. Most of the time they were studying but when they went out, they did it with style either by getting completely drunk or they would try and score. Regardless of it when they went out you were guaranteed of not seeing them until the next day by noon at least.

Lorraine had always been the super confident, 'fight for your rights' kind of girl, the girl power of that time. Liz had always thought she looked like a lesbian, very camp and pushy. Even Kieran though she was gay, until six months ago she introduced us to her boyfriend of one month called Guy, an unusually looking guy with very attractive piercing eyes, plus he had a very prominent scar starting at the bottom of his earlobe all the way down to his chin. He displayed it like a proud peacock and to be honest, when you first met him it made you think twice if you were safe; it gave him a rough kind of look. A look that said don't mess with me. The funny thing is that he was so gentle and proper, but that scar just made you feel you could not push him too much or the gentleness would go.

Liz had always wanted to ask him where he got it but never had the courage, too personal, she guessed it happened whilst he was working, he was a bouncer in a disco somewhere in Lothian Road, don't know which one, she have never been a disco goer but when she did go it was around Edinburgh university and not Lothian Road.

Lorraine got on really well with her and she liked her, but she definitely could not confide in her. She would tell her to start a revolution or something like that and to be honest she was not in the mood to fight, she just wanted to hide and curl away, bury her head in shame, even though she was the innocent party. Liz really missed her mum, gosh, if she could just be here, but she did not want to bother her, she would worry too much, it was not fair.

On the other hand, there was Kieran, gentle and caring, he always fought for the underling and very confident and calm. He was extremely good looking, from a very wealthy family from Aberdeen. She thought his family had been in the whisky business for over three hundred years from his mother's side. From his dad's side, apart from him owning a large consultancy firm, she did not know more than that. Kieran exuded wealth and confidence in equal measures. Even though he was from Aberdeen, he hardly had a Scottish accent, maybe a very faint trace. She though the main reason for that could be that he had been sent to a boarding school since the age of eight years old. Most of his friends were either English or foreigners, very few were Scottish. This, he always believed was a real shame but then again, he also believed that he was not as 'lucky' as people thought he was. To him boarding school was the worst thing that could happen to anyone, even though his parents loved him, and he knew he was loved, he they never understood why they sent him to boarding school. He felt abandoned and sometimes angry that he missed his formative years away from his parents.

Kieran and Lorraine could not have been the most unlikely people to share a flat; they were like chalk and cheese, totally different in even their outlooks and ambitions. Kieran wanted to be a consultant specialising in neurology, whilst Lorraine wanted to go to Africa and be a doctor for a charity, she wanted to single handedly save the world. Boy, was she going to be disappointed! The world does not want to be saved, all it wants is to take and take until there is nothing left.

Kieran was messy to the point of driving anyone nuts; he never washed the dishes or cleaned the flat unless you forced him, saying that, if you told him to do something, he would do it. Lorraine on the other hand was an extreme, worse than me, every time she cleaned the flat it smelled like a hospital. She was not OCD, more like someone that like a job extremely well done and expected everyone to be of the same standard.

Regardless of how different everyone was and with all their quirkiness, the flat and friendship worked well and everyone was good and understanding. Everyone respected and helped each other, at the end of the day, one can do whatever they want and believe in whatever they wanted, as long as they respected someone else's opinion and made sure that it was not an obstacle to the friendship. After all, we are all different and have different tastes and aspirations and had and will have different journeys.

Money never was an issue, just because someone was wealthy did not mean they were better and vice versa. Just because you were poor also did not mean you could bully someone out of a group or insult them because they went to a good school or had a nice car. It was not fair after all, if they were in the other's shoes, they would not exactly throw their fortunes to the wind and become paupers. Nobody had a chip on their shoulder because of their background or life experiences or journeys. We were all good people, fair people and most importantly, understanding people.

# A Cold Heart - No Turning Back

*'No man ever steps in the same river twice, for*
*it's not the same river and he's not the same man'*
*Heraclitus.*

The train was starting to approach Queen Street station, since she was the fourth carriage near the start of the of the track, she looked out to see if she could see Charlotte, worried in case she was let me down like Charlie and then she saw her, she had a pair of orange corduroy trousers on, a red shirt and a bright green and purple scarf. This was definitely 'her', flamboyant down to a 't'; her clothes were loud and bubbly like her personality. It is funny, it did not matter how Charlotte dressed, she was still beautiful, it suited her, she was one of those women that you could dress on a sack of potatoes and she would still look very attractive. Liz thought she must have added the scarf just for show; then again, it was not as warm as one would expect it to be in mid-August and Liz guessed the wind meant that you had to have a scarf to protect yourself.

To her surprise, Glasgow was colder and windier than Edinburgh, it was usually the other way round, with Edinburgh freezing you to the bone, not because it was colder but because of the wind penetrating whatever number of layers you had decided to use to protect yourself from the wind.

"Hi Lizzie" Charlotte gave her a big bear hug and that did it, tears were streaming down her face as if a lake had overflowed, Liz could not even say hi back, she just cried her eyes out for what seemed 10 minutes. Passengers and passers-by were staring at them as they passed by us, obviously wondering what was wrong, if we had not seen each other since childhood, if Liz was delivering bad news or had received bad news or if she was emotional because she was a long, lost lover. You could tell people were quizzical, wondering but in a rush to get to wherever they were aiming for, shops, a connection, home, but were still curious. Liz did not care, she worried constantly about what people thought of her, this time she did not care, she had not seen Charlotte in four months and it felt as if she had not seen her in years.

Throughout university Liz used to see Charlotte once a month, at least, but these last four months have been weird, with no money and being on the dole, she just slipped into denial, not seeing friends or family, just going about within the circle that was left in Edinburgh.

"Sorry Charlotte, I am sorry."

"Don't be silly, that's what friends are for you dumb girl. Now, don't say anything, just take a couple of deep breaths and relax.." Her arms circled her in a tight embrace, a feeling that felt so good, she felt safe as if all my worries would go and she would find out it had all been a dream. Whatever has happened we will, between us, resolve it, like the old days, she sounded more confident than she looked; she knew something horrible must have happened. Liz realised then how much she had missed her, Charlotte was such a good friend, very protective and never condescending, just wanted to be there for her.

Charlotte had never seen Liz like this before, well, maybe once, when her dad died six years ago, she looked as if her world had fallen to pieces, her whole family was falling to pieces around her and she kept her strength until the funeral and then, just after that, everything went, she completely cracked, she had called Charlotte at eleven p.m. for a chat and when she had arrived at her house, she had cried nonstop, she was desolate and broken, a shadow of her old self.

Liz had told Charlotte she wanted to appear strong for her mum but that she could no longer cope with things. Her mum had sunk into a depression and her little brother Luke who was ten did not understand fully what had happened. The idea of 'death' is always slow to sink in and the fact that you will never see that person again really hits you, not at the start but later when you have something to say, to share or laugh together about and you realise they are not there anymore. When you find that you can barely remember their accent, their favourite word, their laughter, their hugs. All that remains is a hazy image and a feeling of loss, you know you miss them and loved them dearly, but you cannot picture them anymore. Guilt comes and hits you really hard if you find yourself laughing or forgetting more of what they looked like. You cry not only because they died, but because you lost them, a feeling of selfishness rises up like bile on your stomach, yes, you need them, why have they gone? You know everyone goes at one point, but it does not matter when they depart, it is always too early. Why? We have years to get used to this happening. Questions like this come up and guilt engulfs you, and unless you have someone to talk to, you can spiral down into depression.

Liz was her mum's sounding board, she had been fourteen, confused and with a mother than needed her to act much older than her years. A little brother that needed love, as much as her mum and just as often. She cried very little when comforting her mum, she just held her tight, telling her beautiful things that her dad had said about her, telling her how much he had loved her, making her appreciate the time she had spent with him was worth at least something even though he was now gone.

It is funny how death affects people a different way, Liz's mother had always been a tower of strength for the family, nothing deterred her, she was beautiful a softer Maggie Smith with sad questioning eyes made of steel but deep down there was softness, a love so deep. Beth had always been a survivor but sometimes we find that what kept us going is gone and the walls start cracking. Her father was her mother's wall, her strength, she never realised that until now, she really missed him, she was probably thinking how she would cope with of the next 20, 30 or more years alone without him, just thoughts and memories. Dad had adored her, silently taking care of her, loving her and admiring her. In all their time together they had seldom fought, enjoying spending as much time together as possible.

Their little family unit had been perfect, strong and most of all stable. But you don't realise how easily things crack when some tragedy strikes. Sometimes, without one realising it, when the strong person, matriarch or patriarch holding the family together dies or leaves, the whole family crumbles.

Things just got to Liz when she found her mum had obsessively started talking about herself and her loss, not caring about anyone else. She never grasped that Liz and Luke were also hurting and also needed to talk, vent out their feelings of loss and their fears. This is when Charlotte came as a blessing, it allowed Liz to be able to support Beth emotionally and help her with Luke and the beauty of it was that within 8 months, Beth was fine, sad and hurt and lonely and sometimes angry that she had been left behind, but the fighting power came back to her and realised that she had two loving children to take care off and nurture.

Happiness came back to the house after this, slowly but it did come back, everyone had recovered, got themselves back on their feet eventually, they knew it was that or give up and get destroyed. We all got up. With stronger foundations, each willing to find to bring back the happiness once lost, if not for their sake it was out of respect to Sebastian, her father.

Charlotte and Liz had both attended the same school since the age of nine, Charlotte started a year before Liz and from the moment they met they became best friends, only going their separate ways when Charlotte was accepted at Glasgow university to study medicine and Liz got accepted at Edinburgh to read English. They promised each other that even though they would be apart, they had to see each other once a month and always call each other, something that they have tried really hard to maintain. Charlotte was only 9 months older than her, but it felt as if she was the same age, she was so calm and supportive and there was no selfishness on her.

Charlotte's parents moved after a few years of her being in Glasgow to the west, they guessed correctly, she was not going back to Edinburgh so there was not point them leaving there. Their other daughter was in her last year at Glasgow when they moved to be closer to them.

They walked in silence to Charlotte's car, one that one must point out was a battered bright yellow Beetle with a bright pink flower on the bonnet, really old, at least by nine years, she had bought it from another student three years ago and as far as Charlotte was concerned, 'it' was her second-best friend. She was so proud of the car that she would show him off everywhere she went and did the customary horn salute when she met with another Beetle.

"I see you still have Lulu" said Liz pointing at the car, a smile plastered on her face. Charlotte was very fuzzy that her car had a name, why she chose Lulu, nobody knows, but it was a name she loved and nobody questioned it or asked her, it was one of those things one just accepts and knows that it made Charlotte happy. Sometimes we will do things for no specific clear reason at all and this, was one of those.

"Yes, she is not doing very well lately, problems with the exhaust and I had to change all the tires for new ones. I took it for an MOT and they don't understand how I have managed to pass the last MOT test, they reckon the tires have not been changed since the car was bough, can you believe it". Once Charlotte started you couldn't't stop her, she talked and talked for ever, which was generally quite nice as she made you laugh as well, it also meant she did not have to make an effort with conversation, she could just sit there and enjoy listening to her.

"Charlotte, in all honesty, have you changed the tyres in the last three years?" Liz looked at Charlotte with a reprimanded and suspicious stare.

"Well, not exactly, I assumed that they guy that sold it to me must have done it" guilt was slowly starting to etch itself on Charlotte's innocent looking face or no so innocent for that matter. Charlotte was too clever, and Liz knew so much about her it was quite impressive. Very few people got to know someone well but for Liz, Charlotte was an open book and vice versa, like identical twins. Most people at university buy a battered old car because they cannot afford a new one and if it died on them, they would just accept it and have it written off. But not Charlotte, she learned how to make the most out of 'Lulu' and it worked, and it kept going.

"Are you saying that a very clever, brainy student of medicine believed that the previous owner of this wreck would have done anything to make it road worthy?" Liz pretended to tell her off, but it was to no avail, she started laughing, this was so typical of Charlotte, living on the edge, trying to push things to the limit. She knew she was driving or had been driving a dangerous car and did not care until she was forced to repair it, she had fixed what she had to and taken care of it for it not to get any rustier than it already was.

"Ok, ok, I had no money, it is very hard being a student and don't want to ask for money. Plus, I needed some beer money. What is a woman to do if she cannot afford to go out? How am I to ever meet the man that is meant to be my husband?" Mischief etched on her face. She always had a smart comment at the end of her tongue.

It was funny, this is exactly the kind of conversation Liz had missed so much, it was always silly, light-hearted and funny easy banter but it sometimes carried what deep down we all dreamed about, we both wanted to be married to lovely guys one day. I guess that is what most women want and if not, it was what these two women wanted. Charlotte and Liz went further, they dreamt about living near each other, their husbands going to play rugby at the weekend, their children becoming as good as friends as they were, having wonderful Halloween parties, attending each other's Christmas parties, sharing laughs and cries alike.

They got into the car, which Charlotte was trying to convince Liz had central locking and that by magic she had pressed a button and both doors' locks had been released. In actual fact, the doors could not be locked, which meant that if a thief ever tried they would find themselves being able to easily steal this car. Of course, it is doubted anyone in the right mind would do it as it was too much of a liability, unless of course they were crazy about Beetles as Charlotte was.

"I hope when you are rich doctor the first thing you will do is buy a decent car."

"Of course, I will Liz, actually what I am planning to do is the moment I get a rich husband I will get a nice car, which I am sure it is going to happen well before the time I am a rich doctor." They both laughed nonstop, like old times, oblivious of the real-life hardships and challenges, a refuge for the bad times that Liz was currently experiencing and a welcome break.

Laughter was echoing though Lulu, the little fun car and you could hear it above the excessive noise that the engine was making. There was a feeling of home, of being welcomed, it felt so good. Liz's problems did not seem that bad now, it is funny, when a good friend is at hand, nothing seems as bad. That is what love does, being surrounded by 'family'.

"OK, being serious now, we will go home, dump your stuff in my room and then we will go to a nice little café that is just round the corner. We can have a coffee and a slice of nice strawberry cheesecake; it will be my treat and we can have a chat. I just want to hear what happened, let's not worry about what we should do." Her look of concern was genuine, she really wanted to help her friend "I want you to talk and get it out of your chest, all the hurt and anguish, then we can plan."

"Oh, also if you don't mind, we will just share my bed rather than you sleep on the floor, it is a double bed and it has plenty of space. I was hoping at least one of my flatmates would have gone away to visit their parents so that you can use their room, but they never bothered. I hope you don't mind." Charlotte gave her a quick glace as she drove, for her sharing a bed was not a problem.

"No, that is fine, as long as you don't sleep naked, I will not be able to stand that." Liz remembered that in the summer Charlotte tended to sleep with nothing on. "I guess I can understand it since it is fresher, but I cannot stand it if I am sharing a bed. The idea of a naked person lying near me or nearly touching me always made me cringe." Liz was not that way inclined and to be honest she could not do that with anyone she did not fancy either!

"OK, I promise I will put my pyjamas on." Charlotte put a hand on her chest looking solemn and then bursting out laughing.

"Good! Remember when we went to Rome and you came out with the blisters?" Liz's face was full of laughter, seeing Charlotte always reminded her of the good times. Well, she says good times, but Charlotte did suffer during that trip. "I had never seen blisters that size and you had it with fever and nausea!"

"Yes, I do, only too vividly thanks to your reaction to the sun." even Charlotte started laughing.

Charlotte and Liz decided to go to Italy on the summer of my second year at university, they had travelled all over Italy, from Florence to Milan, to Pisa, Venice and finally Rome. The heat must have been unbearable for Charlotte's very pale skin complexion and then she started getting some kind of heat allergy resulting with her skin coming out with giant blisters, it was horrible. She was in agony.

After spending nearly part of the day looking for a B&B to stay in they had at last managed to get into a 'Pensione'. they could not afford much, so they had decided to share the room and the bed. It was their last stop before going back to Scotland, so they were scraping the barrel.

An hour after they had arrived to the 'pensione', Charlotte apologised to Liz and told her she had to take all her clothes off, including nickers, the blisters and the heat were too much for her. Neither of them had realised how hot Europe gets in June and how the sun is so much more intensive than the UK.

Liz did not mind Charlotte being starker's, in fact she had told her to lie on the bed whilst she went to find a shop that sold cold drinks, something that seemed for some reason to be absent in Rome in the area where they were. She also checked that the tickets were okay for the trip home. Liz left Charlotte for exactly an hour. When she came back Charlotte was not in the bedroom and she became really worried. She decided to look for her in the toilets which had been just outside our hosts room, she shouted and heard nothing however, the owner of the pensione heard her and told her that there was another toilet in the floor above.

Liz had rushed there and shouted Charlotte's name, no response came, however the door opened slightly and she could just see and hear Charlotte whispering.

"Liz, thank God, where had you been, I had an accident" Charlotte looked as if she was going to cry. "Why did you take so long?"

"I told you I went looking for drinks and also to the train station. What is wrong?"

"I had a bout of diarrhea and just had to run to the loo, sorry I was not here in time" Poor charlotte, she started crying. Her face looking extremely distressed.

"What? What happened?" She could not believe her ears, but she knew what she was trying to tell her.

"I just managed to put my clothes on and get a towel and rush here but, I only managed to close the door, and everything went crazy. I am completely naked, I had to flush my nickers down the loo and my skirt and blouse are in a state. My money belt is also covered with it and I think my passport is stained."

Liz did not know if to laugh or not, she just could not believe it. She was so concerned in case anyone else heard them that she also started whispering.

"When did it happen?" I don't know why I asked, who cared, but she did not know what else to say and it was buying her time to think. Most people have good friends, but you very seldom get to share an experience like this with anyone. Poor Charlotte, she must be dying of embarrassment.

"Just minutes after you left, I have been in the loo for an hour now."

"OK, I tell you what, let me get new clothes for you, can you clean as much as the toilet as you can, I will just go to the corner shop to get disinfectant and toilet stuff."

"We have a sink in our room, you can wash your clothes and passport in there rather than here" Liz could not help but smile when she said wash your passport. She just had this vision of everyone that had to look at her passport would not have a clue that it had been covered on diarrhea, it was just too funny. "Hopefully, it would not smell for long!"

"Don't laugh Liz, I am really in pain and I am stressed. I think I've got a temperature."

"OK, I will also get some aspirin for your fever. I will be back in ten minutes" Liz rushed outside to their room and got clean clothes and underwear, gave it to Charlotte and then rushed to the nearest shop. She got the aspirin; she had to get Charlotte out of that toilet and in bed before she became any worse.

By the time Charlotte's ordeal had finished, Charlotte was fast asleep on the bed, she had two aspirins, drank half a bottle of the litre of water they had in the room and had cried herself to sleep and was totally naked. Since they had both been up at 5 a.m. that day, she had decided that she was tired as well, it was only 7 p.m. but she could hardly keep her eyes open, so she pushed Charlotte to the side and went into bed, with a T-shirt on and was fast asleep. Out for the count.

Hitting the floor half asleep had not been Liz's idea of having a good night's sleep, but she hated anyone naked unless they were her boyfriend. She hated it more when Charlotte was obviously missing and dreaming of her then boyfriend Toby and decided to cuddle her. The shock made her jump and since she was already at the edge, she just fell and hit her head which woke her up! Charlotte was not happy at her reaction, she said her reaction made her feel like a pervert, instead of taking it as a mistake; after all she had been asleep when she had attempted to cuddle her.

Anyway, back to the present, they had been driving through Glasgow, which to Liz's belief and everyone's surprise, she felt has a secret beauty. All the buildings were either Georgian or Victorian and most of them had been preserved really well, which cannot be said for most areas in London, with the war damage flattening most areas that used to be affluent in the eighteenth and early nineteenth century and which had been left as a legacy, an array of beautiful buildings and extraordinary architecture. Buildings, which no longer existed and, in their place, had rows of endless tower blocks.

Yes, Liz liked Glasgow or at least parts of Glasgow. The City Centre was changing all the time; work had started on the bus station and around both universities. She remembered the number of times they went to either Glasgow or Strathclyde university students Union for a dance on a Saturday night. The drinks were reasonably cheap, and their bars were always full of very friendly students that would just talk to you for the sake of talking or chat you up. This was different from Edinburgh, there could be a lot of snobbishness depending to which university you went to or if you went to a college or polytechnic, saying that not everyone was like that, there were still a lot of very friendly souls in Edinburgh.

"I will go through the side streets rather than on the main road as it is chock-a-block at this time of day" Charlotte was not specifically talking to Liz, it was more as if she was really talking to herself, approving what she was doing, patting her back for her quick decision making.

They ended up going down Union Street, Jamaica Street, over the Glasgow Bridge and then turning left at Norfolk Street and then right at Norfolk Court. With all the traffic going around them, which was quite a lot, it took them forty-five minutes to get to their destination, but they did get there.

The block of flats where Charlotte lived were not exactly the most beautiful buildings ever, it certainly did not have the grace that flats in Edinburgh flats had but they were practical and really big. Charlotte lived in a second-floor flat which had three bedrooms. The front door into her flat was painted what one could only describe it as a disgusting, actually, no, revolting is the right word, colour purple. To top it all, the handles were a very silvery shinny colour; it was a very gothic door. Every time Liz used to come to Glasgow to visit Charlotte or every time she thought of Charlotte she thought of 'the door'. It made you think as if you were going into an illicit den as if behind it, sordid happenings were about to occur.

"Here we are at last. What a trek, and to think we don't really live that far from the centre" Charlotte gave a sigh of relief, "Let's just dump all this stuff and go out, this weekend we will just pamper ourselves and make sure that you are in such good form that you will be able to face anything in the world by tomorrow, this includes meeting my boyfriend."

"Oh cool, you've got a boyfriend, who is he?" Liz was amazed at this, usually she knew everything that happened in Charlotte's life, so was a bit taken aback when the mention of a boyfriend came up "You did not tell me anything about a new man in your life?" There was no annoyance on Liz's voice, more a curiosity detected only by the tone in her voice and the raised eyebrow.

"Oh, it is nothing serious really, we met last Friday, and we have seen each other four times already" Charlotte dismissed it as a normal occurrence, as if it happened all the time, which they both knew was not true. Extremely were attractive but when guys saw them, they saw people that you knew were looking out for their 'partner for life'. Guys knew that a fling would not wash with them, they were serious girls who did not have flings, they fell in love, so most of them, apart from the very brave, approached them.

"I met him at the Glasgow university Union, he is the cutest guy I have ever met. Saying that, he is not what we would call, my 'type', but you can give me your opinion tomorrow, I need to know what you think. Oh, by the way, his name is Rupert."

"That is not fair Charlotte. As long as you like the guy, I will like him as well, as long as he makes you happy that is good enough. Don't expect me to turn round tomorrow and tell you I don't like him, of course unless I found out he was a psychopath waiting for the right moment to kill you!!" Both Charlotte and Liz smiled at this, they both knew and understood each other, were there for each other but firmly believed in live and let live. So many times, you have friends or family that try and influence your decision in your life, your boyfriend, sometimes because they don't like him, sometimes because they themselves fancy him and sometimes because they just don't want to see you happy and are jealous. This was not the case with both of them, they would certainly tell each other if they believed there was something seriously wrong with their partner but that is as far as they would go. Just because one or the other did not like the others partner was not a reason to try and destroy their happiness.

"Does he know I am here by the way?" Liz was conscious that she might be in the way to her friend's new budding romance.

"Yes, I told him I wanted to spend today with you, he was fine with that. He is going out with some of his friends and then he will come here tomorrow morning around 10.30 a.m. so we will be able to have some time to sleep."

"What does he do?"

"He is a medical student, on his final year. He is really brainy but just to warn you, he is not the stereo typical medical student, but he is an absolutely darling."

"Do you have a photo of him?" Curiosity was getting the best of Liz; she wondered what this guy looked like. Charlotte usually went for the very clean-cut type, boyish and with an innocent look, the type that you feel safe with and then find out that they have two or three girlfriends they had been stringing you along.

"Of course, not silly, I have not dated him long enough for that.." Charlotte's cheeky grin was pasted on her face "I am not about to waste film and developing charges on something that might not last."

"Well, it sounds to me as if you are in love, I have never heard you speak like this about someone before, it seems that you are desperate to get approval and you keep saying he is cute."

"Well, I suppose I do fancy him a lot, maybe not physically, his brain is yummy! He is so clever. Actually, yes, I think even physically but for some reason I am attracted to something else."

"He makes me laugh a lot, he is hilarious but not in a laugh your socks off kind of way, even though he can do that as well. He is more of the type that leaves you with a constant grin on your face."

"Anyway, let's stop talking and get a move. I thought we could walk towards town and find a pub somewhere. I know it is not the best area but like the last time you were here, we found quite a nice pub, rough but nice where we could have a chat without being bothered."

"That sounds fine. I am actually desperate for a coffee, and then I will probably have a pint of cider" added Liz, thinking it had been a day since she has not had a drink!

"Good. There is nothing like cider to cure the soul" Charlotte winked at her and opened the front door for them to exit.

Both went out facing the bright sunshine but very chilly afternoon. Charlotte did not change from her very bright attire, as far as she was concerned, she believed that her clothes made her feel happy and give her the warmth that was missing from the hard, Scottish weather.

Liz had her black jeans with a sleeveless black top made of pure cotton and a black suede jacket, its length reaching not past her waist. She also had an amber necklace; it was quite a chunky one, half the size of her palm and embedded into a metal plate hanging from a very chunky plain metal chain. This was what Liz called her favourite necklace, and it went very well with the black ensemble. You could say it was the epitome of 'safe', she very seldom ventured out using bold colours and she should really as her olive complexion would suit deep red and green.

"I dislike days when you feel as if it is really warm outside, the sun is shining and the moment you go out of the house you feel as if you are going to freeze your socks off." Liz stated absent minded. A trick by the British weather and it never fails to fool even locals!

They walked quietly down the main street looking for this dodgy pub that they have been to the last time Liz was in Glasgow. They had been trying to cure themselves of a horrendous hangover, she remembered they were still drunk walking to this pub at 1 p.m. The whole situation was hilarious, the barman looked at them oddly, especially since they managed to walk in a zig zag line to the bar thinking we were doing a convincing effort of walking straight.

Liz remembered the night before they had gone to one of the unions and danced until 2 a.m. and then went with four other guys from Charlotte's class looking for pubs that were still opened. They only found one that was opened until 6. a.m., it was probably the dodgiest pub Liz have ever been too, Liz was sure there were alcoholics and druggies in there, but it did for them, the six of them just drank until six and then after that Charlotte, Tina, a flat mate and classmate of Charlotte, and Liz walked back to the flat, they have managed to arrive there at 8 a.m. and went straight to bed.

"Oh, here we go, I think this was the one. It looks the same anyway, let's see inside."

"To be honest Charlotte, I don't think I could remember how the inside would look, I was too drunk."

"Never mind, I think this is the one, it does not matter if it isn't, it looks dodgy decent" Charlotte threw her head back laughing, knowing both words together did not make sense, after all, most pubs round here would never be decent unless some decided to give the place a complete face lift and change the clientele. Saying that, sometimes the oddest of people turn out to be the most interesting and 'safe' characters.

"Two pints of cider and one white coffee" Charlotte ordered everything to the quizzical looking barman. Turning round to Liz she said: "I thought we might as well order the alcohol at the same time as your coffee, otherwise I am sure we will be waiting for ever."

"Yes, that is fine. Shall we sit in that corner?" Liz pointed out at a corner that barely had any light, but it was in fact the lightest area in the whole pub. There was a smoky atmosphere covering the whole pub, but because the sun was beaming through the window above where Liz was pointing it looked as if fog was coming through into the pub, giving an eerie look.

Everyone in the pub were looking at us, probably wondering why such nice-looking lassies were drinking in an old man's pub. To be honest it was a lovely place, it had the original décor and there was no noise, you could drink and chat to your hearts content and there was no music blaring out that forced you to either shut up or shout.

It was now six p.m. Charlotte and Liz had spent three hours and drank four pints each in this pub, talking about everything that had happened with Tim to bits in Charlotte's life like her new boyfriend.

Liz felt as if a giant load had been lifted from her shoulders, it was so good to talk to someone about everything that had happened. She very seldom talked to people about her feelings, not because she did not have anyone to talk to, but because she was too proud, she could not bear people thinking she was weak, that she could not cope. She also did not want people to get and store ammunition against her, a fact she had learned very quickly. People store information for the future, and she did not like that.

In fact, people knew that Liz had a strength of character that very few could match, she was always determined to survive, to make the best and only now and then defeat stared at her in the face smiling, it was usually when the war had been too long, more than one battle was being fought. In this case, Liz, without realising it was worried about the future, her work, her student life had finished, and she had tried getting a job but could not because of the recession. On top of that Tim decided to cheat on her with Charlie, not that Charlie made the difference, it was the fact that he had cheated on her.

"OK, so, are you sure that is what you want to do?" Charlotte wanted to make sure that Liz did not make any rush decisions that she might regret at a later stage, she wanted to make sure that her friend was aware of the big change she was going to do with her life in a space of a week. "I want you to know that you are welcome to stay here, I am sure Tania and Louise will not mind you staying here for a month if things don't work out."

"Thanks Charlotte, I think I will be fine, saying that I will definitely come back to visit you, maybe not once a month as we have planned before as I need to sort myself out financially and get myself a job, but maybe one weekend every two or three months I will come back here to visit, or you can visit me."

"Yes, that is a point" Charlotte looked pensive "I think I only visited you four times in the last three years, you have always visited me. Why is that?"

"I guess I always made the point that I wanted to come to see you." You know I don't like staying in the same place all the time, so you offered me the opportunity of getting away from things very often, plus the nightlife in Glasgow has always been good. On top of that, don't forget that we always saw each other at Christmas down south in Surrey."

"True, however, I promised I will make more of an effort" Liz knew Charlotte could not be bothered with the travel, she had always been like that and Liz did not mind.

Charlotte always made an effort when she was in Glasgow, always had plans of what they would do, would cook beautiful lunches or dinners with her meagre grant money, would not allow her to pay for things and in the evening, they would always go out dancing to the unions or very cheap clubs.

As they were walking home, they both decided that they would go to Strathclyde university Union for a boogie, Liz had not had a good dance in ages and was really looking forward to it, plus, it meant that she did not have to dress up. She could go dressed the way she was but maybe without the jacket as they would take a taxi there and back so she should be okay. She hated taking jackets to the Union, they were such a hassle. Twice she had lost jackets because people either took them by mistake or stole them. Just as well she never kept money or keys in them.

Both had dinner with Charlotte's flatmates, Tania and Louise, both medical students, Tania was the same year as Charlotte and Louise was the year below, a sister of the last flatmate they had. Both Tania and Louise were coming out with them, which was good as they could split the taxi fare. The university union was really busy with people, all in good moods, ready to either have a good night, looking either for a nightstand, just some fun dancing or the partner of their dreams. The four of them hit the dance floor straight away, within seconds they were all dancing with guys, laughing and cheekily smiling at each other, as if they had finally caught their prey in their webs.

Tania was the first to disappear; she said she was going home early. We all knew what she meant, Charlotte once told Liz that Tania always stayed for around two hours and then went home with a guy, a bit of a loose girl but with a heart of gold. That is what Charlotte had said and who was Liz to judge. Tania was beautiful and brainy, guys fell at her feet by the clicking of her heels, she did not want a serious relationship, she just wanted to have fun and be adored by guys. She did not want to hurt anyone, but I don't think she was aware that most of those innocent men that went home with her were eventually hurt by her. She would date a guy for a maximum of a month, after that she would consider it too serious and dangerous. Let's just hope she was very careful and took precautions, now a days, you either got pregnant, got HIV or some venereal disease, nobody cared, and it annoyed Liz, Britain was turning into a careless society.

One day Tania will meet her match and he will either woo her and marry her or dump her as unceremoniously as she had dumped all the guys before him. Life can be cruel but sometimes you tempt fate by laughing at it and thinking you will always be in control and be lucky. Karma can indeed be a bitch!

Liz's theory is never play lady luck as she will twist the card against you as soon as she is bored and when you least expect it! Her rule was having fun, play for gold and to win but don't hurt anyone, always play fair.

At 1a.m. Louise decided to go home, alone, the guy she had been kissing had asked her for a date on Monday evening, wanted to take her out for a meal. Very unusual but it happened, Liz considered it unusual because most university students were broke, if anything, they will take you for a pint and expect you to pay the second round.

Charlotte and Liz decided to stay. Charlotte had dismissed the guy she was dancing with and went to a corner to finish her pint. Liz on the other hand had been kissing this guy for what seemed an eternity. He was a medical student on his final year called Jonathan, obviously looking for romance, that's what you usually found when you met a guy in his final year, they were slowing down, wanted a steady relationship to help them face the world as a professional adult. Giving hem some kind of stability in a world that seems exciting and scary at the same time.

Just when Liz was going to suggest they joined Charlotte, the DJ started playing 'What kinda boy you are looking for (girl)' by Hot Chocolate. Liz could not resist this, they both started slow dancing to this, if you could slow dance to it. It was lovely. Liz did not fancy Jonathan, she did not even know why she was kissing him, all she knew is that it made the pain Tim had caused eased a little bit, she knew it was not fair, but she needed this, wanted to feel desired, needed reassurance that there were men out there that liked her. She did not want to do anything on the rebound, she had to be careful and just could not hurt someone as nice as this guy, it was not her.

Charlotte was watching Liz, she knew, understood why she had been leading this guy. She knew Liz will not let it go further than that, Liz would not hurt anyone purposefully. Jonathan was really good looking, but did not feel too sorry for him, this is probably the first time in his whole life that he probably fancied anyone genuinely, he had a reputation at the university of being a heartbreaker, actually, that was putting it mildly, a cad was a better description. He was extremely good looking, a lady killer in fact and came from a very wealthy family. Some people said his grandfather had left him £3 million pounds when he was fifteen years old. His parents had put it on a trust until the age of thirty. Poor guy, he had at least another five years to go to fully enjoy it, but in the meantime, he would just have to enjoy himself with mum and dad's money who were not short of a bob or two!!

Must say though, for a man ready to inherit that amount, he was a hard-working guy, he was top of his class and never failed attending a class unless he was extremely ill or had been called for an emergency which was to be honest unlikely. He was a good guy, he valued money. Shame he did not value women the same way! Or at least not valued them until now.

It was now twelve thirty a.m. closing time really, Jonathan and Liz had danced and kissed for nearly an hour after Louise had left. She had dragged Jonathan to sit with Charlotte and they were very animatedly talking to all three of them when it was time to leave. Jonathan had asked Liz for her phone number in Edinburgh, but it did not matter really as things were going to change soon.

She had told him that she had gone through a very rough patch with her boyfriend and that they had finished and now she required some space, which Jonathan took very well and said he would like to get to know her and take things slowly. What Liz knew is that he would probably not want to take it as slowly as she planned. Never mind, she also gave him Charlotte's phone number, just to be nice and to prove to him that she was not going to try and run away.

Charlotte and Liz took the taxi back home after Jonathan and Liz spent nearly ten minutes kissing outside the university union.

Jonathan was a good kisser, excellent kisser actually and shame she was never going to see him again.

"He seemed nice." Liz mentioned as if she had talked to the man for ten minutes and not spent the last three hours snogging him.

"He is nice but be careful, he is known as a womaniser. Actually, this is the first time I have seen him smitten." Charlotte was carefully watching Liz for her reaction "He really likes you. Just be careful or he will break your heart" Charlotte's concern was genuine, she was worried in case her friend was jumping from one relationship onto another or worse, in case she was on the rebound.

"Don't worry, I will never see him again, he is not really my type, even though he is good company, certainly intelligent and most of all a good kisser" Charlotte looked at Liz in astonishment, not quite believing what she was hearing. Liz had never kissed a guy or dreamt of kissing a guy unless she fancied him rotten.

"Don't look at me like that Charlotte, I liked him but not enough and I can't get Tim of my mind. I know what I need to do but don't worry it will take a while for me to get over Tim, I really loved him or think I did and he hurt me. Not only that he had decided to hurt me with a friend of mine which is unforgivable.

Charlotte did not say anything as they arrived to the flat in silence. She understood her friend needed someone to show her affection and she got it tonight, at least she did not take it far enough to hurt this guy if that could be possible even though god only knows how much he deserved it. One of her friends had fallen for him in first year and she was so hurt that she quit university. Bastard!

They all woke up at exactly ten thirty with the doorbell ringing, Charlotte jumped over me, rushing towards the door and Liz was woken up with a leg going into her chest.

"Oh, no, Sorry Liz, that is Rupert at the door, I slept in!" Everything seemed to have happened at the same time, the leg on the chest and Charlotte talking. Liz opened her eyes in time for seeing

Charlotte leaping from the side of the bed facing the wall to the side where Liz was.

"God, you are going to break your neck doing this. He is not going to run away just because you did not answer the door within ten seconds." Charlotte must be absolutely crazy about this guy to be running around all over the place, she had never witnessed her like this before.

Liz could hear in the distance Charlotte speaking to Rupert taking him to the kitchen and offering him a cup of tea. She had decided that since he turned up at ten thirty a.m. sharp, the least she could do was get up, shower and get ready, at least this way she will be able to leave Charlotte with him alone for thirty to forty-five minutes. As Liz was on her way to the shower, she heard Charlotte shouting at her.

"Liz, come and meet Rupert" you could hear the excitement and maybe a little apprehension in Charlotte's voice. Liz peaked her head through the door which was ajar.

"I am not really decent for anyone to see me" she called, her hair was all over the place and looked as she had been put through a hedge backwards.

"Hi Rupert," Liz smiled shyly "Sorry but I cannot come in any further as I am not looking decent or at my very best."

"Hi Liz, how are you? Did you have a good night last night?" Rupert had very friendly tone and charming demeanor as if they already had met was welcoming.

"Yes, thank you it was lovely." Liz was surprised at the very laid back and friendly attitude he had, he was obviously very comfortable with Charlotte and in her flat but he seemed so at ease meeting Liz especially that early on the relationship. Meeting your girlfriends' best friend sometimes is regarded the same as meeting one's mother-in-law!

"Good night?" Shouted Charlotte all excited, her eyes wide pretending as if she was in shock and questioning such a stupid question, which was no "Liz spent practically three hours snogging Jonathan. Of course, she now says she does not fancy him, what do you think?" Charlotte had a twinkle in her eye. Rupert knew Jonathan, everyone knew of Jonathan and his reputation.

"Jonathan, as in Jonathan the medic?" Rupert seemed surprised, if not shocked.

"Yes, the one and only Jonathan" added Charlotte as if a prize had been won.

"Can you all speak as if I am here please?" Liz was not annoyed, more amused about the display of interest and surprise in Rupert's face, she raised an eyebrow as if to challenge them "Why are you so surprised Rupert?"

"I am not surprised, I am just incredulous that you only snogged, usually within 10 minutes he is trying to take someone to bed. He must really have liked you a lot not to have pushed, I am impressed."

"Meaning what Rupert" Her eyebrow still raised "are you saying I did not have the courage to spurn his advances?" she smiled "Maybe he did try hard and I just did not fall for them." Everyone laughed, it was good that Liz liked Rupert. Charlotte thought, she knew she liked him because if she did not, she would usually go quiet and try and avoid speaking to him.

"Rupert has suggested that we all go for a walk either in Glasgow Green or Pollock grounds and if we feel up to it, we could go and visit the Burrell Collection or Pollock House. What do you think?" Charlotte looked so excited; she was like a little girl of ten being offered her favourite ice cream.

"Sounds like a good idea, I actually have never been to Glasgow Green, so that would be different. Maybe we can, after that go to a nice place for lunch", "my treat" Liz could not stop looking at Rupert, not only he was extremely good looking, but he was a mixture between a goth and a punk with an extremely posh accent. He was dressed from top to toe in black and had pointy boots and a very long leather jacket which was probably no more than one inch above from the floor.

"That sounds like an excellent idea apart from you treating us to lunch, it should be the other way round, but we can discuss it on the way there." His voice was very firm but friendly, Liz knew she would have to battle with him in order for her to treat them for lunch, but she was not worried, she knew she would win.

"OK, but I will just keep insisting. Now, I will go and shower and get ready and leave the two of you in peace."

Whilst Liz was having a shower, the feeling of a hot shower of water on her back was just what she needed. It was as if she started relaxing at last, after all her mind was still in turmoil, she still kept thinking about Tim and Charlie, about their arduous lovemaking. It was not fair, she thought they were doing very well in that department, he never complained or asked for anything, maybe she should have asked. She started feeling like most people do in that situation, putting the blame on herself when it sat squarely on Tim's shoulders.

She felt much better after the shower, warm and relaxed as if someone had put a warn furry blanket over her and cuddled her. She guessed like what one would feel in the womb, safe and warm. She felt so good that she decided she would be less restrictive in her wardrobe and decided to go for her purple suede trousers and a black knitted polo neck to go and her Doc Martins as she knew the park might be a bit wet.

The park was beautiful and quite big, there were lots of people out an about, some playing football other just walking, admiring the view and taking in the beautiful day. It had actually turned out to be a very nice day with the sun out really strong, and it was getting very warm. Liz did not know if it was because she was feeling happy and relieved that she had made a decision, but she actually felt good, full of energy, unlike yesterday when she felt as if everything was falling to pieces.

Rupert turned out to be not only a lovely guy but an incredibly brainy guy, he was so interesting and very charming, when one talked to him, he would listen to you as if you were the only one there and by the way he talked to Charlotte, he was obviously smitten, the feeling it seemed was mutually!

Lunch came and went without much ado. Liz ended up paying for lunch after reminding Charlotte at least ten times the number of times she had paid for things, plus she helped her a lot yesterday. Saying that, lunch was quite expensive and it cost her including wine £56 but she guessed it was worth it plus they all had starters and desserts. A therapy session would cost more, which she could not really afford, you would have to book several sessions. This was cheaper and Liz felt the benefits practically instantly.

Time kept nearing for Liz to leave, go back to Edinburgh and enact her plan. After lunch they went back to the park and just lay on the grass for two hours, just talking about everything and everyone. Rupert had realised by the end how good a friends Charlotte and Liz were and even when we were having a girlie chat, they would include him and you could tell he was enjoying himself. He was actually quite good at offering his opinion from a male perspective. They also told him of Liz's decision regarding everything. He avoided giving a personal opinion, however, he wished Liz all the best and understood how she was feeling.

"Oh, look, a fairground," Charlotte noticed it far in the distance, at the opposite end of the park "come on, let's go!" They all rushed to it, running across the park, Charlotte and Liz were so fast and poor Rupert, obviously not keen on sport or proposedly taking his time, was lagging behind.

Liz had not had this much fun in such a long time, there were dodgems, octopus, big wheels, twist, cups and saucers, these later ones were for kids, but it did not stop them getting into them.

Liz was not usually very good at fairgrounds simply because she got dizzy and sick very quickly but this time she was fine. She didn't know if it was because she was desperate to forget Tim, whatever it was, it worked and as far as she can recall, she has never been sick again on a fairground.

Of course, one of the things one must do when at a fairground is visit the clairvoyant or psychic reader. Charlotte decided to go first, she was the brave one and deep down, she desperately wanted to know about her life, especially if she was going to marry Rupert.

"Hi, my name is Lavender" a beaming welcoming face peered at them through thin looking glasses. "Please place a donation of £10 at the edge of the table" The clairvoyant said in a very quiet voice to Charlotte. She looked around 60 years old, very friendly but incredibly fat; obviously she must have received lots of ten-pound notes and spent them on food!

"I will spend thirty minutes talking to you about what has been, your past, your hurts, familiar event. Proof of life really and then go through what will likely be happening in your future. You will then you will have five minutes when you may ask me questions." She did not spend any time asking Charlotte if she understood or not, she just dived into her work, looking at her crystal ball and spreading her tarot cards.

"The tarot helps me with some tricky information, I use them as a guide but most of the information it is either psychically or mediumistic."

She started talking nonstop, lips moving and her eyes not looking at the cards but at the top of Charlotte's shoulder, her eyes fixed on something or someone, very eerie but impressive, she was concentrating as if someone was physically there and talking to her. It also helped the fact that one of her eyes was not quite focused, and you were not quite sure where to look, her glasses masked a lot of her cross eye but if you stared directly at her you could see it.

"I see a young man, he works in a charitable profession, very handsome and charming. Yes, he is extremely charming and very popular with the girls. He has a quiet confidence that is mixed with sheer determination to achieve every goal in life, he is very hard working…. his initials are RJ, and you have known him for a very long time." Lavender peered at Charlotte as if Charlotte should have known who this was "He comes from a very wealthy background and from what I see, he will be well known in his field throughout the world. Yes, I see a lot of money, I see him broken hearted but eventually a happy man. I think he is a doctor or in a similar field."

"You will marry in five years' time to this wonderful man, you will have four children, two boys and two girls…. I see your career…"

Lavender talked nonstop for the duration of the sitting, pausing only a couple of times to look at Charlotte maybe to check that she was taking everything in. She talked about her love life, career, money, family and friends, was very detailed but not detailed enough for her to be able to say 'yes', she is talking about this guy. She did know somehow that Rupert was not the RJ she was talking about, would not be 'the chosen one'. It was a feeling, just the way she had described him and she was sad, very sad but she would not tell him as she wanted to convince herself that it will last between her and him and that he loved her and would marry her one day. That all this psychic mumbo jumbo was just that mumbo jumbo.

She knew she was being silly because she hardly knew him but for some reason felt a connection with him, something special that she had not felt in a long time but at the same time she felt it was doomed from the start, as if it was ending before it had begun.

"You will suffer a loss; your heart will feel it but will not admit to it. You will accept it as fate. You will move on, it is written." This left Charlotte with a feeling of apprehension and loneliness, who or what was this loss, when will it happen. She was worried about it being her mum or Dad or indeed any member of her family. Was it Lizzy, was it Rupert? She hated this. She tried asking for more details, but she never got any, sometimes they do that, they say, so that the reading will not rule your life, you will just let fate work its magic.

When Liz's turn came, the apprehension took over her. Liz had never been to a clairvoyant before and felt terrified. Rupert on the other hand refused to go, not because he did not believe on it but because he felt it was not a manly thing to do and he felt deep down we should mess with our future. Why not wait to be surprised.

"Now, you seem to be an interesting case, full of sadness and achievement and finally success and happiness. I have never seen so much of everything in one's short life" Lavender looked at Liz with not so much pity but a degree of sadness that such young life was marred with so much pain at such an early age. "You must not forget that we are here to learn, it is a journey ad nothing more, how well or bad we do it is irrelevant, it is what we learn in our journey.

Lavender went through talking about her mum and dad, her brother and apparently a little sister, which she told her was wrong, she did not have any sisters. The woman was adamant that she speaks to her mother. She talked about her love life and saw lots of initials, heartache and love. The initials JF kept coming up, apparently this man would love her, but she would not. He would go on to marry someone else. He would always love her but in the end will accept her as a sister since his love would not be returned, unrequited she called it. She saw the letter T, a very sad encounter, a tragedy, yes, even I knew she was speaking of Tim. Tim the bastard, the Tim the sex fiend, Tim the nymphomaniac, God how Liz hated him. She then went on to talk about the C's in her life, watch the C's they could be dangerous to her happiness, and they could be a blessing. She had so many C's in her life that she could not exactly stop talking about all of them, but it was weird that so many of her friends had names or surnames starting with C. Maybe it stood just for 'crap', I will have a crap life.

She talked about her career, success, etc. Liz eagerly wrote everything down so that she could check it in 10 years or whenever she was meant to marry or have that fantastic career. She would rewrite it when she went back to Edinburgh. It was all very interesting but doubted it would happen in real life.

"He loves you!" Lavender said as Liz was walking out, taking Liz by surprise "Tim loves you; he was just a fool. In any case, it was never meant to be, dear. Things will get better" Lavender smiled, and Liz smiled back, the first genuine smile in the whole weekend, and understanding passed between them and one that showed she felt for at least some of her clients.

It is very hard to feel pity for everyone, as some people only deserved what they got and others were just asking silly stuff, but Lavender felt sorry for Liz. She was a good girl, a nice girl and did not deserve this heartache. Most people did not believe in karma, but it does exist. The time most people believe on it is when they are much older, in their 50s and they see luck dished up in odd ways. For Lavender, karma was the great equalizer, an amazing universal force that brought everyone to their knees at one point or another in their life. Some people realise it in time and start overloading goodness to balance things early and avoid the big equalizer, others laughed at it only to be overwhelmed when it come knocking at your door, others fight against and blame everyone but them, those she felt sorry for, they will never shake the karma off as it will come around and around, negativity will be swirling in their life constantly because all they will see if anger and envy and they will never take accountability for it. Those were the worst kind, the ones that believed they only ha back luck not realising it was them that brought everything to their door.

At six thirty p.m. they all decided to go for a very light meal due to the substantial lunch and this time they had split the bill and had just one glass of wine each with Rupert opting for a dark beer. Rupert and Liz ordered a Caesar salad, which was a bit of a surprise for Liz until she found out he was a vegetarian. Charlotte ordered a steak and kidney pudding with chips. It would be interesting to see Rupert's reaction when French kissing Charlotte if the taste and smell of steak and kidney would be revolting to the palate of a vegetarian.

Dinner was fun and after it Liz was taken to Queen Street Station and took the last train back to Edinburgh. Her heart heavy from the goodbyes but she will certainly look at this weekend with appreciation. Charlotte was her best friend as she had cheered her up immensely, the power of friendship all over and it was good to meet Rupert as well, he seemed like a very nice guy, well balanced but more importantly a good guy.

Liz was dreading going back but knew she had to, not only that, but she also had to face Tim. She just hoped at the end of the day she was brave enough and can accept things more easily. It would be hard, no question about it, but it must be done.

# Tim

*'Never allow someone to be your priority while allowing yourself to be their option' Mark Twain.*

He had a horrible Saturday and rushed to Liz's flat as soon as he put the phone down, and only to find out that there was nobody in. He decided to rush to Waverly Station, taking the first taxi that appeared in front of him.

He arrived at Waverly but the train to Glasgow had left just ten minutes before. He did not know what else to do, depression started taking over him, he knew Liz knew, didn't know how, but knew. He did not think Charlie would have told her; regardless how heartless she was. She would not do that; she was too clever to shoot herself in the foot like that. One thing that Charlie would not do is ensure everyone hated her and knew this kind of news would put her in everyone's black book.

He could not understand what took over him last night, he had been depressed and annoyed that Liz wanted to go out to her lecturers last night out. He did not want to say, 'stay with me tonight', no, he wanted her to say she would stay with him, but she didn't. He was feeling low and sorry for himself when at 8 o'clock the doorbell had rung, it had been Charlie, crying her eyes out, she looked so lost and fragile, she was so beautiful. He had been an absolute idiot, a weak idiot.

He had never cheated on Liz; sure he had been tempted but always backed off never even daring to kiss a girl. He was always conscious that Liz would finish with him without any qualms. He loved Liz and he just did not understand what had happened that night, weirdly enough it felt as it had happened months ago. The whole event seemed surreal, long, long ago and worse still, it was as if he had an out of body experience, that it was not him but a double of him.

He started walking out of Waverley station, up the stairs that led to Princess Street. He was really down and needed to think. He needed to be alone and think alone. Starting to walk towards the North Bridge, he realised he was walking aimlessly, bumbling even, not knowing what to do. Feeling an incredible sense of loss., he wanted a drink. Still walking aimlessly, he found himself on the Royal Mile where he looked for a pub, there were lots of them, the Ensign Ewart was a good pub, it was usually quiet at this time of day, he would go there.

As he started approaching it his phone started ringing, yes, he had a mobile, one of the few students that had the luxury of a mobile then. He had asked his dad for money to buy one, he thought it would look good, after all, not many students had mobiles. In his class there was only one other that had one and he was also from a very wealthy family. He recognised the number flashing on the screen, it was Charlie, but he decided not to answer as he needed to think everything through. Knowing Charlie, she would either tell him she told Liz or start blackmailing him.

Why did he do it? Charlie was beautiful but he had nothing that attracted him to her, she was like a bitch on heat, a nasty, manipulative bitch that for years had only wanted to see Liz hurt and down on her knees. Liz was the only one that did not see that side of Charlie, always seeing the best in people and only too late realising the danger, usually when it was just seconds away of being hurt or humiliated.

After a couple of minutes, a message sign was flashing on his phone, he decided he will listen to it in a couple of hours; he could not face things as they were.

"A pint of eighty please." The barman knew Tim, this was one of his favourite pubs, he always brought Liz here now and then for a quiet drink in the afternoon, especially if they had just been for a walk or been shopping, well, more window shopping than anything else neither of them were 'shoppers' really.

"Hi Tim, how are you? You don't look good? What's up man?"
Johnny the barman was not concerned, he liked Tim, but he always
thought he had it too good for himself. He was always surrounded by
either wealthy or very beautiful people. Saying that, he really liked
his girlfriend Liz as she was a really nice girl and down to earth with
time for everyone, always having a good word to say about
someone. He knew Tim worked hard but he did not seem to
appreciate what God had given him, he acted as if it was his God
given right.

"I am OK Johnny, had a bit of a bad night last night." Tim did not
really want to talk, he wanted to avoid revealing to anyone what had
happened.

"You want to talk about it?" Curiosity led Johnny to ask, nothing
else, he did not care, well, not care enough.

"No, thanks, I will just go and sit in a corner. I just want a quiet
time. Speak to you later Johnny" Tim was not fooled, the barman
liked him because he was a fun guy but he did not regard him as a
friend, even though several times they had been clubbing together
after closing time. It was just one of those things where they got to
know each other, he got on very well with his group, mingled well
and above all he was fun which was what everyone wanted.

Sitting drinking his pint, Tim started thinking about this whole
year, how much he had grown to like and love Liz, the funny times
they had together, her giggle type laugh, her nervousness if she had
to go to a ball, her insecurities, and her smile. He felt as if
everything had been lost; he did not know what do to. He had been
thinking of asking Liz to marry him even though both of them were
far too young. He knew now that she would say no. How did she
find out? Maybe he was just being paranoid; maybe she got really
bad news this morning and rushed to her friend Charlotte. No, she
would have told him, she told him everything and she would have
phoned.

As he drank his pint he started going back, memories flooding his
mind, he remembered the day he met Liz. Richard had been dating

Charlie for two weeks and it was August, he remembered it clearly because everyone was talking about the company's late summer party. The main talk was about what to wear, most women opting for summer flowery ball gowns, men, black tie which meant a kilt for the Scots.

He had only been working for two months at the company, the same as Richard. Talk was that there was going to be a bouncy castle, free drinks and a sumo wrestling competition. He remembered he was really looking forward to it, just because he liked fun parties, anything that gave you an excuse to behave like a teenager or a child! He felt life was making him grow too fast and this was his outlet, a chance to relax.

Richard had told him that he was talking Charlie and if he would mind taking Liz, Charlie's friend.

"Don't worry Tim, strictly friends, plus, she is quite a looker, so it is not as if you will be stuck with an ugly duckling."

"OK, I will do it but just this once," Tim agreed, he was being hesitant, he did not want to spend the evening with someone he did not know, what if they did not like each other "as long as I don't have to spend the whole night with her."

"No, don't worry, it is really just a way of getting into the party, you know, partners only, I could not quite get away with taking two girls. Plus, for some reason Charlie is really annoyed that I have offered to take Liz as well. I just thought the bigger group the better, more fun."

Tim remembered the time he saw Liz, they all met at Richards flat, she was wearing a three-quarter length flowery silk ball gown. It really showed her figure, it was hugging her figure at the top, the bottom half being quite a loose flowing skirt her hair was swept up in a chignon which in a way made her look much older than her 20 years, but what she remembered is how beautiful and elegant she looked and she kept smiling all the time, a shy smile but a dazzling one.

He remembered the first time they made love; it was scary. He knew Liz was a virgin and did his best to not only be gentle but also the best lover ever, which wasn't quite hard as she would not be able to judge it. All he wanted was for her not to be disappointed and he wanted to make sure she enjoyed herself as much as him, that she would remember it as her amazing 'first time'. In the end, they had both been so nervous that it was a total disaster. Tim could not even cum and kept being extremely clumsy. It was actually quite funny looking back, both acted as if they were teenagers and naïve, which neither of them was, just because she had been a virgin did not mean naïve. On the contrary, Liz had messed about with other people but never gone the full way. She knew what pleased her but for some reason, maybe knowing this was going to be going the whole way just made her too nervous as well and she failed to even show a little bit of her knowledge and dexterity in the art of love making.

The second time they tried it was fantastic, it had only been a couple of hours later and it was unreal and surreal, as if they had both gotten years of experienced packed in a couple of hours. They did it twice after that, yes, when you are young you can really get going and never get too tired.

Liz's breasts were a perfect medium size, a man's handful they were, really firm and creamy looking, her waist was perfect and very slim and she had a lovely pear shaped bottom, her figure was like an hourglass, her hair dark and her eyes big, he remembered seeing a flicker of nervousness the first time, a look that said she was worried in case she did not end up being all he had imagined. He had never told her she was more than what he had dreamed of. Liz was not tall, she was very petite but a very beautiful one with a perfect figure, a figure she did not have to slave over too much to keep trim.

Their lovemaking was gentle but clumsy the first time, over in minutes, the second time it was hot, they had been nearly brutal to each other, his tongue probing forcefully into her mouth and then urgently going to the tip of her breasts, sucking and pulling and licking. He noticed Liz liked her breast kissed and stroked and when she was nearly peaking, she liked them bit slightly, pulled slightly as if to give her the last push. They spent the whole night just touching each other, making love and talking, probing different areas of each other bodies to find out what they each liked and how to please one another. Liz looked so happy, so relaxed…they both felt as if they had known each other forever.

He remembered laughing a lot and talking, he was like a teenager and felt so happy, so fulfilled. It wasn't just sex; it was more, he could not put his finger on it. It was not a sense of possession or ownership, it was feeling of sharing and understanding, bearing one's soulmate. Sexually both of them had been good to each other, they complemented each and had always been very active, making love practically every time they saw each other which was nearly daily, after such a long time in a relationship, they never seemed to have enough, always wanting more, demanding more. Was this the demise? Maybe they just did it out of habit? No, it could not have been, he always had a feeling of anticipation when he knew Liz was near him, a tingle, like an electric current running over the small hairs at the back of his next and a desire so strong that it could not have been a habit.

He hated himself, no, he loathed himself. The satisfaction Liz gave him could not be compared to the cheap, temporary satisfaction Charlie had given him, he felt cheap and at a loss, he now understood that pure sex did not compensate for making love. Making love gave you a feeling of fulfilment that just sex could not; he had lost everything only to find out the meaning of it too late. If only he knew Charlottes number, he hated himself. He started thinking again of last night, after getting over the shock of seeing Charlie cry and having given her a glass of red wine, they sat on the settee, she was talking about how she felt for Richard, how hurt she had been, how sure she had been that he would ask her to marry him.

Yes, he knew Richard was going to finish with her, he had told him the day before, he had at last received a letter saying he was due to go to New York for a year, this had been Richard's dream, he wanted to go abroad whilst he was young, see the world, meet other girls, live life to the full before he had to settle down. For him Rachel would have been the death of any dream, any freedom and she certainly was not marriage material, at least not for him and doubted any other man would be crazy enough to marry her. He had been seeing another girl on the side, someone called Judy who worked on the third floor on accounts. Not a brainy girl by all accounts but nice and shy. Someone Richard felt he could go out and would not take the relationship seriously, she was aware that guys like him were highflyers and if she ever dreamed that someone like him would become serious, she would not voice it, she would keep quiet and accept things and see what happened, nearly always staying as a casual and relaxed relationship. Of course, this did not mean she would not be upset if he finished with her.

Richard had decided to finish with Judy the day before finishing with Charlie. Tim had Judy in his office in tears, she did not know him, but she knew Richard and him were close friends. He had been annoyed that this woman had assumed she could just come in crying to his office, as if they had known each other, he was more annoyed that after all her carefree attitude about a casual fling she was now devastated about Richard finishing with her. He just did not understand. He sent her packing, politely but firmly, he explained to her that he had nothing to do with Richards's emotional entanglements and reminded her that he had work to do. He hated being cruel, but he did not want to be part of this charade, one where all the players involved new the score and the rules!

Why it is that people always thought they could reach out to their ex's friend to dump all their emotional garbage. What gave people the right to do this? He was angry at Richard as well; he should not be left to clean his mess.

He went to speak to Richard about it later, voicing his anger about it. Richard was apologetic; he had never seen Tim this angry and knew he was uncomfortable having women crying to him about his friend's relationships. He promised he would have a chat with Judy and that this incident would never be repeated again.

Charlie had been a bit like Judy was when she was crying, the difference was probably that Judy had genuinely fallen for Richard and had not planned to speak to Tim, it must have been a genuine whim of the moment, to see if Tim could help her. Charlie on the contrary must have planned it, after all, she knew that Liz was going out until late, she must have known.

"I must go to the loo; I will be back in a second." Tim had noticed that Charlie's tone of voice had changed; she had been holding his hand, whilst relating how hurt she had been with everything. Her finger kept caressing it, very seductively, an act he picked up her doing unconsciously and absent minded rather than purposefully, what a fool he was. Within 15 minutes she had been stroking his arm. He liked it, he knew she was flirting with him by then; maybe it had been the fact that he already had 3 glasses of red wine and she was already on her second, even though she had only arrived twenty minutes ago at the most. In any case, he was hooked, he did not have the strength to fight back.

He heard the toilet flush and then no noise. He lived on his own, he hated sharing a flat. His parents had looked at this flat with him and they all liked it, they bought it for him as a birthday present when he started his second year after spending a nightmare year sharing a flat with 'ass holes' as he called it.

The flat was in his name and had 'only' cost them around £55,000, he did not have a mortgage, his mum would have worried, so she convinced his dad to pay for the full thing. The flat was nice and compact it had a medium sized kitchen, a very large living room, dining room large enough for a table and six chairs and a Welsh dresser on the side, a present from his granny. The bedroom had an en-suite toilet with a window and there was a small box room off the living room, large enough for a bed and a small wardrobe, but instead he had a nice desk and his computer gear.

He got up off the settee, feeling a little bit tipsy, drinking the last vestiges left of red wine on his glass and walked toward his bedroom. Maybe deep down he had known that something was up but he still kept walking towards it. The door was ajar, and he could just see that the bathroom door was open and the light was off. He started pushing the door open; his bed side lamp was on, he could see the full bed now, and Charlie.

His heart nearly stopped as lying on his bed was Charlie, fully naked, her legs wide open for him to see everything and she was stroking her breasts giving an invitation that was hard to refuse, too hard. He was hypnotised unable to move, staring. One of her hands ran from the tip of her nipple, slowly down her belly and pass her belly button and disappeared in a mass of curly blonde hair where one finger played teasingly. She was not embarrassed, and he could not move his eyes from that spot, rooted to the spot unable to get his brain in gear and get out, escape. She was staring at him, enjoying herself and she knew he was excited after all, it was unmistakable when a man was aroused.

"Now, don't tell me you don't want a bit of this?" Charlie was grinning like a Cheshire cat, she knew she had him, his erection was visible, and he was not bothering to hide it. Her voice was soft, seductive, very sensual and very inviting.

Tim's mind was going on overdrive, he did not know what to do, he just stood there, something was telling him to back off, but he could not. He was so turned on that his mind was no longer able to make sense, order him to get out and have a cold shower, that this was all wrong, that she was Liz's friend. She was so beautiful, she was perfect, not that Liz was not beautiful, she was, but Charlie had a voluptuousness that called for rampant sex, an orgy, the way she was looking at him held a promise that if he gave in there was more to come.

"Come on now, don't look so scared, I promise I will not tell" She started stroking herself down her legs, slowly, he fingers disappearing into her, she started groaning, one hand has busy in between her legs, fingers disappearing into her moist parts whilst the other one stroking her left nipple.

"Don't you want to help me Tim? do you want me to undress you?" It all proved too much to Tim, slowly he walked towards the bed, his erection was starting to make him uncomfortable, he started unbuttoning his shirt, being clumsy as he was trying to do it rushed.

With his shirt off he knelt by the side of the bed, open her legs wide and buried his face deep in between her legs, she was delicious, wet with desire. He could not believe Richard had finished with her. Even for sex Richard would have kept her surely, maybe promised her he would visit her often from New York. He started moving upwards towards her breasts, savouring every inch he could, kissing her stomach and then each breast at a time and then finally kissing her roughly on the mouth. He could not wait any more, and without bothering much about extending her pleasure, just entered her roughly, moving rhythmically until he came.

He had been lying in bed for ten minutes at least, his mind a blank, not wanting to think about Liz, trying desperately to remove the guilt when he started getting aroused again, he could not help it and turned to face Charlie who had been looking at him with what he had confused as desire but was instead a triumphant smile.

They had made love, if one could call it that, twice after that, the last time, once he had been fully satisfied, reality started hitting him tenfold, he realised the time and started panicking. He ordered Charlie to get dressed and to get out, he had been brutal in his ordering her out, he did not care, told her she was definitely not going to break things up with him and Liz.

Charlie was adamant that she was going to wait for Liz to come; she was staring at him in a threatening manner, daring him to throw her out. He knew she would have no qualms in telling Liz the truth unless he let her stay.

"OK, you can wait for her, but I promise you, I will kill you if you tell her anything. I swear, if she finds out about tonight you are history."

"Don't worry, I will not tell, there is no need to threaten" she was giving him what anyone would call a dirty look. A look that asks what was he so worried about?

"Come on, go to the living room, I will make the bed very quickly and open the windows so there is no sex smell.

"Can I have a shower?

"No, you can't, just wash yourself. Liz is due any minute."

What both Charlie and Tim did not realise though is that Liz had walked in on their third love making and had gone out quietly, her dreams destroyed, crushed by betrayal. Tim's relationship already finished, without him realising it, he had been placed in the past, their relationship shelved forever.

He remembered waiting awake until 4 a.m. and Liz still had not turned up. Jealousy crept up and played in his mind. What if Liz was in someone else's bed, doing what he had just done to her. No, he was trying to convince himself, she would not dare, she loved him. Slowly, doubts crept into his mind, the shadows of the early morning can play more in peoples mind than the full daylight, it was like a horror film, a nightmare where he had been the unwilling main character, his stomach churned, he hated himself. Jealousy was blurring his mind, he had so much anger and hatred towards an invisible man that he did not know even existed, his imagination taking full control of his thoughts and not letting go.

Saturday Tim had spent it really stressed, after the drink at the pub he went back to his flat and stayed at there, his mobile and home number ringing like crazy, only to be the wrong person or it was Charlie trying to speak to him. He did not want to speak to Charlie, in fact he did not want to speak to anyone, he wanted to be alone and think, he decided to switch his mobile off, it was easier, he knew Liz was not going to call him.

The messages left by Charlie changed in mood and tone as Saturday slipped into Sunday; the final message left on Sunday at noon carried a threat. He did not care; he knew he had lost Liz.

He had not eaten the day before and had not eaten on Sunday either, it was now ten thirty p.m. and he did not feel hungry at all, then again, he did not do anything that spent energy apart from sleeping and drinking. His whole body felt heavy, his mind lethargic. He had drunk two bottles of wine since Saturday afternoon, it was not much in two days really but considering he had not eaten anything in those days it was starting to take effect in his body, he felt exhausted and sick, which was also aided by the fact that he was depressed.

His mother had left two messages asking him to call her regarding his father's birthday present. He had ignored it and felt guilty, but he could not call his mum now, she would get worried and get his dad to come round, his mum had a knack of seeing through him. He could not let them see him like this, it was not fair on them. Their perfect son a mess over a woman, not only that, but he had also made the worse mistake ever.

His phone started ringing, he must have fallen asleep, just after looking at his watch, he felt lost, did not know where he was or what time it was. He looked at the machine that displayed the incoming call; it was Liz's home number.

"Hello?

"Hi Tim, it is Liz. How are you?" Liz could feel her stomach going crazy, she felt as if her heart was going to stop any minute, it was pumping at miles per second, her hand shaking, she was desperately trying to sound normal, calm and collected.

"Hi Liz, are you just back, it is one a.m.?

"No, I have been in for half an hour or so, I took one of the last trains from Glasgow. Are you OK?" Liz realised Tim sounded off, way off, he had never heard him like that. "You don't sound very well; do you have the flu or something?" she felt concern, regardless of what he did to her, she still cared and that could never be taken away.

"I am okay" Liz could hear as if Tim was about to cry. "I am so sorry Liz, I love you, you don't know how much I love you. Have I lost you? Tell me I haven't lost you" Tim started crying, begging to be forgiven, wishing he was there with her, wanting to explain.

"Don't say anything Tim, please. We will talk tomorrow, I think we both need a good night sleep" She could hear him trying hard not to cry, his voice cracking, trembling with every word, suppressing it and not being successful, he was very quietly sobbing, she felt sorry for him but there was nothing she could do, the damage was done.

"How did you know?

"I don't think that matters anymore. We will talk tomorrow Tim, I know you have work, so maybe we could meet in the evening, I could either go to you flat or meet in a pub, I don't mind."

"I called Sarah, my boss, I explained that I had some family issues that needed to be resolved, I asked her for the day off which she gave me" muttered Tim, hoping Liz would change her mind and bring the meeting forward.

"You shouldn't't have done that, don't jeopardise your work, it is not worth it, not now, not for this" She felt she had to tell him that, so that he was prepared for tomorrow. She needed him to get use to the idea that it was over, she was not going to take him back, she could not, who would after not only a betrayal like that but with her best friend which was unacceptable.

"I love you; you don't know how much I love you. You don't know how sorry I am. I was not thinking. Can't we try and save us?" His voice trembled with desperation, full of sorrow for a crime that could not be turned back, the deed was done. The hurt too deep to be erased and forgotten. They could probably pretend for a few months but then the hurt would come back and eventually it will start showing in cracks, resentment and doubt creeping its ugly face, it always eventually did.

"We will talk tomorrow; I will be at your flat at 10 a.m. then since you are not at work. Bye Tim" She did not wait for him to say goodbye, she wanted to go otherwise she was going to start crying. She wanted to have it over and done with, but it had to be at his flat, this way she could leave whenever she wanted. She wanted to have the upper hand and not show the hurt and humiliation she was going through.

She had three notes pinned on her door, all messages were from Charlie, one of them, the latest one at ten forty-five p.m. said she needed to talk to her urgently. She was not going to call her, she decided she will call her on Tuesday, she needed to agree things with Tim before doing anything, whichever way she looked at it, she was the looser. She lost Tim; however, she was determined to go out with her head up, she was not going to lose her pride over it.

Liz woke up very early in the morning, still not early enough to meet Lorraine and Kieran, they always got up early and left to go to the library to study for seven thirty a.m. By nine a.m., Liz looked like a million dollars. She had a very casual pair of black slacks, a cream blouse and a pair of black flat suede mules. She had put very little make up, enough to give colour to her very pale cheeks and some lip stick and mascara, of course, the mascara was waterproof, she was not going to be covered in black make up if she cried. She looked natural, which is the look she liked. She left her flat at 9.15 in the morning and walked to Tim's flat. She preferred to walk to recap on what she was going to tell Tim. She needed to be calm and the walk helped, there was a slight breeze which also helped brush her face and bring some colour to her cheeks which were still pale.

By exactly ten a.m. she was sitting in Tim's living room, she had let herself in. To her surprise Tim was already showered and dressed, regardless, he looked as if he had not slept in days and his eyes were red and puffy.

"Do you want some coffee? Tim asked as if he was scared, he said the wrong thing.

"Yes, that will be nice, thanks."

The phone rang, Tim just stared at it.

"Aren't you going to answer it?" Liz knew who that was; she wondered if Tim had told her. Did they see each other on Saturday?

Did they make love again? Did he tell her she was here to finish with him?

"No, it is probably Charlie, she has not stopped calling since Saturday morning, has left nearly twelve messages so far and I guess some threats. Just leave it, I guess I will have to speak to her sometime today or tomorrow." Liz had not told him she knew; however, he knew she knew, there was nothing he could do to hide it, just to be honest and go with the flow.

"Here, white no sugar." Tim put the coffee cup beside her on the little table to her right.

"You know it is over, don't you Tim?"

"Yes, I know, I guess I deserve it" He was looking at her, his eyes full of unshed tears "I am so sorry." A tear just fell down his right eye, running down his check, he turned away to hide it but it was too late, she had seen it, she felt as if she was being torn apart again, why did he have to do it? His beautiful eyes, red with lack of sleep and from crying.

"Tim, please." she tried stopping him, this was not the reason she came here. She got up and rested a hand on his shoulder, it was like an electric current that went through both of them, they both new they loved each other so much, they both felt so much, it must be so hard for her to be doing this, he thought, his hand grabbed her hand gently, he was looking at the floor, trying to avoid her gaze, a sense of resignation flooded all over him, an acceptance of what he had done. Considering it was him that had hurt her, she had so much strength, she was a force to be reckoned with, she was amazing.

"No, please let me explain, please let me tell you how much of a fool I had been." He drank some of his black coffee noisily, tears were free falling down his cheeks, this time he was not hiding them, one of them fell in his coffee but he did not care.

"I don't know how you knew what happened, I just wanted to tell you it never happened before and I never planned it, she came here crying and …."

Tim went into detail explaining what happened, between crying and begging her to stay with him, supplicating. The whole thing started her crying, she could not bear this, she had to stop him.

"Tim, it is over, I am not coming back to you, I can't, not after what you have done. The reason I am here is because I wanted to finish it the proper way, I did not want ill feeling between us and… she hesitated…. I need my pride back."

"What do you mean? Tim looked confused.

"I was here watching both of you when you were making love" Tim suddenly felt sick, interrupted Liz. "No, it was just sex, it meant nothing" He looked so pale, realising that this was not just someone telling her about him, she had actually watched him, he could now understand why she did not want anything to do with him.

He had lusted that night after Charlie, women don't understand when a man lusts, there is no emotion, just animal instinct, she probably thought she had been after her for a long time, that he loved or felt at least something for Charlie.

"Regardless, I would have rather you done this to me for something that meant something to you" she continued, her face hard, hatred filling her heart but fighting not to let that take over her. "I was here and it was not nice what I saw, it hurt, badly. I trusted you and you let me down. I loved you and I guess I still do but I can't forgive you."

She took a few breaths, her heart beating fast and her emotions going all over the place. "I don't want all our group of friends to know, I can't bear it. Charlie will tell everyone and laugh at me, I cannot face that, Tim." Tim's face was clearly showing full horror at the realisation that Liz had watched him, he wondered how long she had watched them, he now understood, one thing is to cheat one someone and then confess, they might be forgiven, another is to have been caught in the act, did she watch all of it or just had a glimpse? He could not ask. It must have been agony. He had hurt her, really hurt her. He knew it was over, her stance and her attitude told him there was no way back, but he was going to make it up to her, he was going to always love her and be her best friend, he will never let her down again, he will always protect her.

"I will deny it, I promise you, I love you; I will not let her humiliate you."

"You don't understand, it is over, I am going away to London, I am moving there to live in a week's time. Hopefully by next Sunday but I need to wait and see if someone could move into my room" Liz watched Tim's face go from hurt to full disbelief and total shock.

"You can't go, Liz, I will never cheat on you again, never. I want to marry you. I am sorry" He knew it was over, but he still wanted to try, his mind and his heart were not connecting "I will do anything for you. I will endeavour to all my life be about making you happy, loving you!"

This went on for one hour, Tim tried his best to get Liz back but eventually he accepted things. He had tried kissing her, gently, then pleadingly, to show her, as if physical affection showed love!

"OK, what do you want me to do?" He looked so down and depressed, but at least he stopped crying, he had realised at last.

"I want us to be good friends, I don't want to lose that. It is not as if we were married. I want you to tell people we are over; I want them to know that it was mutual, that my decision of going to London meant we could not continue as a couple, I want them to think we split up some weeks ago. I don't want to lose contact with you or anyone in the group."

She knew she was rambling, but she wanted to put her point across and then leave "I don't want it to be an awkward situation between all of us, and as you say, Charlie did not mean anything to you; I don't want you to maintain her friendship. I am planning to keep her friendship, after all, most of our friends are in the same group but I don't want the two of you to keep touch, if you do, then I don't want anything to do with you. I don't want to come up to Edinburgh and visit you and find out that I have to go out with our friends plus you and Charlie."

"I don't want to go out with Charlie, Liz. It was just sex, she meant and means nothing to me, as a matter of fact I always thought she was a bit of a bitch and always knew she was not a real friend to you."

"OK, I also don't want her to know why we split, you can make up any excuse so long as you tell me but please don't tell her that I caught both of you at it and that I am hurt and upset. I don't want her to even think that I suspect. It will mean a lot to me."

"Do you still want me to go to John's wedding with you?" Tim was expecting Liz to say no, but he was surprised she said yes, after all, the wedding was in three months and hopefully things will be settled by then. The hurt would not be gone but the wound would not be as deep and some healing would have taken place.

"We can talk about it nearer the time but yes, if you don't mind, I would like you to come with me, I think it would be good for both of us, plus, it will stop the tongues wagging."

Tim and Liz went for lunch together; it was the start of a friendship, a beautiful, stable and fulfilling friendship, which is what they had before but without the sex. She was going to miss him, miss his cuddles and his love making, his kisses when he was trying to cheer her up, his silly comments about her pear shape bum, holding hands, it was all painful, but the pain will slowly fade, at least that is what she hoped and what people told her happens in cases like this. She remembered he liked resting his hand on the small of her back, play with her little hairs there and then kiss her all the way to her neck, God, this was going to be hard, so many memories, so much love and hurt, maybe one day she will look back and think it was an amazing friendship but for the moment all she could think was of the lovers, the hurt and betrayal. It kept playing in her head twenty-four seven, so much so it hurt.

Tim and Liz agreed that they will meet each other three times on the week in the evening before she left, maybe go for a meal and practice at just being friends, after all, the next time she would see him would be in three months in Ireland. He was going to take her to the station on Sunday, if by Sunday she found someone to move into her poky little flat!

# Charlie

*'Real friendship is shown in times of trouble;*
*prosperity is full of friends.' Euripides*

She was getting so angry, she could not believe that Tim had not called her back, it was now Monday, she had tried both his phone and Liz's phone. She wanted to tell Liz what her and Tim did, she did not want their relationship to last when hers has now been finished. She hated Liz, she had a nice guy, not what she classed as good looking but charming and extremely good at making love, it was not fair. "Why did Liz have to have everything and she nothing? Why did she not get the best, why did people only saw her as a man eater"? Charlie was speaking aloud, she had not noticed, she was so engulfed in hatred, her mind was focus on her pain and nothing else.

She knew she had to be careful, if the whole of her university friends found out, she would be regarded as not only a bitch but a slut as well. Personally, Charlie though the only one to blame was Tim, it was his responsibility; he was the one that was cheating, not her. She wanted to keep both their friendships but wanted full control of Tim and Liz, and that meant them not being together. She wanted the upper hand, all humiliation focused on Liz and Tim, not her.

For a guy of only twenty-three, his experience when making love could match a well experienced man in his thirties. She wanted him, at any cost and she certainly did not want Liz to be happy when she was not. Jealousy was eating inside her, she felt sick, she could not cope when someone else was happy or happier than her.

Her phone rang several times, it was Tim's number, she will make him wait, make him leave a message. She will then call him back with an excuse.

"Hi Tim, it's Charlie, how are you? Sorry for not answering earlier on, I was in the shower." Tim could imagine her Cheshire cat smile widening, thinking she had fooled him but she did not, Tim did not care for her, she was a piece of meat on Friday, a piece of meat that cost him dearly and one that he was going to remember for the rest of his life. She was not going to get away with it easily. He recognised the fact that he was also at fault but the fact that she had phoned at all made him sick.

"Hi Charlie, I was just returning your call."

"What do you mean by returning my call, do you mean the last twelve calls I made since Saturday? Don't you think I have feelings too? Don't you think I was worried about everything?" she was trying to be innocent, but Tim knew better, it was all too late.

"Feelings Charlie? I did not know you knew what that meant. As for the calls, I had too much on my mind, nothing to do with you of course." He was the one smiling now, this was going to be the biggest blow to Charlie, it will save Liz's pride and maybe destroy his reputation a bit but who cared, he deserved it.

"Liz finished with me on Friday before you came to visit me, so as you can see I was upset as well but did not want to tell anyone, why did you think I was not out with her on Friday? I am glad you came though because it made me feel better, at least I knew my charms were still in full working order" Tim was smiling as he said that he was really enjoying himself, it had been the first smile since the incident.

Charlie had been silent, for the first time in years, she did not know what to say, she was not only surprised but when she had spoken to Liz on Friday evening, she had not mentioned anything to her. Usually, Liz would confide in her or so she thought.

"What do you mean Liz finished with you, I don't believe you, you are just bluffing because you are scared in case I tell." there was an urgency in Charlie's voice that had never been there before, maybe it was the realisation that people did not need her as much as she thought.

"Liz is going to London next Sunday, she is going to try getting a job there and since I have a job here, she thought it best if I stayed on as a single man, for us not to try and have pressure on us to keep something going when we may find other partners there."

"You mean she dumped you!" There was a hint of laughter in Charlie's voice. She could not feel sorry for anyone but herself, she enjoyed hearing of other people's misery.

"Yes, if you want to put it that way, she dumped me. She feels that London is best for her at the moment as a single person especially because she does not have a job. She does not want to carry the emotional baggage of me being there and she is worrying about me or not being able to afford to visit me." He felt remorse and sadness as he worded this to Charlie. Oh God, what a mess he had made of things and how much he missed Liz. This was something he will regret all his life. He was wondering if he will ever recover, is there such as thing a recovering from this kind of a mess?

"Well, it sounds to me as if she had planned it for a while and fooled us both." Again, she was trying to be catty, never missing an opportunity, never caring, wanting to always be ahead; on top, laughing at people's misfortunes.

"Not really, we have talked about it for a month, it just came to a halt on Friday. We will try and stay friends and I will try and get her back; I am not going to lose her." There was a lot of emotion on Tim's voice, this bit was not a lie he dearly wanted her back, he missed her terribly.

"And me, what about what happened on Friday?" If Charlie expected Tim to be nice she was mistaken. The blow was brutal, short and sweet, her eyes flickered with anger and passion. "Don't you care about me Tim? Don't you think our love making counted for something?" She was trying emotional blackmail, she was sure this would work, it always did! Surely her calculated plan had to work, if he fell for her once he would again.

"What about Friday? you and I knew it was just sex, it meant nothing. If I recall correctly, you were crying for Richard. Oh, and before you think about it too much and get some weird idea, Liz came back from Glasgow this morning. She went to visit her friend Charlotte and say goodbye to her, she knows everything, I told her, not only that, but she was also fine about it since we had already split up by that stage."

"And another thing, I spoke to Richard this morning and he knows about it as well. Again, he was not bothered either, so threatening me would not work and neither keeping up the friendship. If you are out with the group then fine, I will say hi and be polite, otherwise, I don't want to see or hear from you again." The triumph in Tim's voice was unmistaken, he felt as if a giant weight had been removed from his shoulders, he felt free and relieved. The first time in days that he was sure would sleep very well, he had lost Liz, there was nothing he could do other than try and rectify things and remain a friend to her.

Charlie just heard the phone go dead and she could not believe it. This had never happened to her before, what was going on, she stood with the phone against her ear listening to the dead ringtone, she was not moving, she was numb. She was really shocked and her hands and entire body were trembling, nobody had done this to her before. So much in shock she was that she started crying, she did not know what to do, Tim must be telling the truth, he must have, Richard and Liz must know, Liz must have finished with Tim before it all happened, otherwise he would have not told Liz, he adored her. Tim must have meant them not being friends, this was not real, she called the shots!

She realised she had been jealous of Liz, who wasn't. Liz perfect Liz! that is all she heard, nonstop compliments, she kept repeating the words to herself, like a mantra but instead of giving her peace it was eating away at her, the green monster had resurfaced, more powerful than ever before., making distorted faces, rage and jealousy burning in her eyes.

Charlie cried her eyes out in bed for at least the next two hours, it is funny as she had been so spiteful and now that the cards had turned, she felt sorry for herself and still did not care for Liz. She suddenly realised how much she had liked Tim, she felt sick and now she did not even have his friendship. Why did every man treat her like this? They all liked her for a while and then got rid of her. It was only the ones she called worthless adored her or wanted to be with her and marry her, the ones worth something always went for a Liz type girl. Charlie was so blinded by her own self adoration, that she did not realise that she was the only one that scared the guys away, it was her attitude, her will to destruct everyone else, of having fun of other people less fortunate than her, it was always about her and nobody else. Karma was indeed a bitch.

Sitting on her bed, legs crossed, her face swollen and her eyes red with all the crying. Was it her physical appearance, was she overtly sexual, did she appear desperate or too easy? What was it that Liz had and she did not, it was not fair!. All these questions haunted her, wondering why she could not get what she wanted, without realising that she only wanted what other people had, she was never satisfied, always looking for the grass greener something else.

She started remembering their second love making. Tim was much calmer now, having been satiated with her once already. He was more curious of her body, wanted to savour everything, his fingers going everywhere, slowly lingering in certain parts that he knew would excite her, he moved around her with ease, stroked her where she liked and kissed her in a rough but caring manner, making sure he was not too rough but not too easy going either. She wondered if he did the same to Liz, she felt a pang of jealousy. It was not fair, not even Richard knew how to make love like that.

Tim had been mesmerised by her body that Friday night, how it moved underneath him with easy, with ease, like a serpent, slow but lethal. The way he entered her roughly from behind, hurting her slightly but still arousing her, making her cum twice. She was sure she could pull another one again and then Tim would be hers. She could make him hurt with desire, she knew she could, but would that be enough? She did not want to be second best and if it was only sex, he will eventually treat her like Richard. Sex is something most guys regard as something on the passing, it does not mean commitment. Maybe that is why Richard and John had treated her badly. She wanted revenge, she hated them all, but mostly, she hated Liz. She needed to sort things out with Liz and Richard as soon as possible, she was sure Tim would not have gone into detail with them, so she still had a chance of turning things around, make Tim look like the bad one and not her and then he will have no chance but to come back to her. She did not realise it was all too late!

# The Lie

*Sometimes a lie is a necessity, but mostly it is
used by the weak to hide.*

The phone rang for a while; she was ready to hang up when Liz answered.

"Hello?" Charlie noticed that Liz's voice did not sound the usual happy self, maybe because she was going away or because she was scared who the caller might be.

"Hi Liz, Charlie here! How are you?" Charlie was nervous, she had never been this nervous before. She had not spoken to Liz at all since the incident and it had been four days since Tim had called her, it was now Thursday, and she knew that Liz was leaving on Sunday. She was not going to apologise but she wanted to test the water.

"Hi Charlie. I am fine, thank you, how is life?" Liz wanted to go and forget everything, she did not need this, she was stressed packing, someone was moving to the flat on the Saturday, so she was going to stay with Tim on Saturday night and he was going to take her to the station, well, he was going to take her by taxi to the station.

"Liz, I need to talk to you, please. I know you have heard things about me and Tim, but it is not what you think." She knew that is she begged a little, Liz might give in, but she would not apologize, after all it was not her fault.

"Charlie, please, I am really busy." She knew what Charlie was doing and she also knew that she had to face her at one point or another, if anything to pretend things were okay so that they could both get on with their lives.

"I know you are busy but for the years of friendship we have had, please can I come round, I need to speak to you, clear the air. You can't leave for London without us sorting this out."

Liz knew she had to see her and 'sort' things out, pretend the friendship was intact, after all, she had been told by her lecturer a long time ago, don't burn bridges, they could be useful one day. Did that make her like Charlie? Should she really turn fickle and not just walk away? Pretend everything was OK?

"Sorting out? Honest, I am fine with you and Tim being together, I don't mind you two being a couple since we had already finished; honest" she lied, she had to, pride was her worst enemy, not a nice thing to have, she had a fear of making a fool of herself, did not want anyone to feel sorry for her "I tell you what, Charlie, why don't you come round, but make it brief and I mean brief, as I really have to sort out me moving out, come round in an hour and whilst we speak I will have to continue doing my packing and cleaning. OK?"

She had to pretend that Tim and Charlie were now a couple, she did not deny it, the usual Charlie behaviour but she knew from Tim that they were not longer even friends!

"No problem, see you later." Triumph at last! Something was finally working her way, she felt she was going to get what she wanted. The only thing she did not like is that Kieran and Lorraine might be in when she was there. She knew they did not like her; they had seen through her from day one and did not want to do anything with her. This annoyed her, especially since Kieran and her were from a similar background, a rich family, a private school and money to waste. They also shared in certain circumstances the same social circle and friends. They BOTH turned up to the same family balls thrown here and there by their families and friends, so the least he could have done is tried to be friends with her, but it was not to be, they were all so overprotective of Liz that nothing would deter them from snubbing me.

Charlie did not like the tone of how Liz said 'her and Tim' were together. She probably did not know that Tim had rejected her!

However, she will have the last laugh when Tim came crawling back to her! A smirk, crossed Charlie's face, triumph written all over it, so sure that she would get Tim back! She looked ugly, divorced of reality, sick and totally unaware that the laugh was on her.

The doorbell rang exactly at three thirty p.m. an hour after she had spoken to Charlie on the phone.

"Hi Charlie, come on in." Apprehension filled Charlie, scared in case Liz had told Lorraine and Kieran about last Friday and they pounced on her. Then again, if Liz had finished with Tim before it, then it was none of their business. Liz was not going to London because of her or the breakup but because she wanted to find a job. She was definitely feeling much better now, convincing herself that things were alright, that nothing had been her fault, as usual.

The conversation went better than expected, mainly because Liz knew where she stood. Charlie did try to put the blame on Tim saying that he seduced her in her hour of need, but Liz ignored it. She was not bothered, she knew the truth and trusted Tim. Yes, she knew that even though he made a mistake, she knew he was not lying this time. He was strong enough to face the truth and to accept it and he was not a coward and he knew that deep down he still loved her.

Life after this was not great for Charlie, she had stayed in touch with Liz or shall we say Liz allowed her to stay in touch with her, just the odd call here and there and Christmas cards. Charlie's love life was full and colourful but never steady which is what she had craved for, with relationships only lasting an average of six months an either she would move on to something that in her mind was better or she would be unceremoniously dumped, which was generally what happened.

Of course, Charlie never understood why this was so. As far as she was concerned, it was always someone else to blame or they were below her, people she considered so insignificant that they never counted, her favourite statement.

The first few months after 'the incident' were bad. Her own circle of friends was weary of her and invited her to very few parties, but eventually, like everything else, people forget or put things in the back burner and she started being invited out again. They preferred to believe the story that Liz and Tim had spit up before the incident but saying that, people always found Charlie untrustworthy, call it female intuition. Most girls would never leave their boyfriends and partners alone with Charlie, it was something that they felt instinctively. The men of course thought they were just insecure and needed a steady partner, typical male way of thinking! The only other male that knew exactly what had happened was Richard and Liz preferred it this way, of course, Charlie was none the wiser.

Career wise, she was doing very well but then again, she always did. It did help the fact that she was willing to sleep her way up the ladder but in all honesty, she also had the brains to do the job, which is something nobody could take away from her. Charlie was gifted. This point was not argued by many people, even if she got the promotion by going out with the boss for a month, everyone knew that good changes happened when she started a new job. She was good and understanding as a manager, something which is hard to believe in a personal level, she always hated people if they achieved more than her, especially a friend, but if it was a stranger, she was better and some would go as far as saying she was quite humane and nice. Of course, nobody found out her nasty sharp side until it was too late; everyone just saw a very beautiful woman and they all automatically assumed she was also nice.

One of these people was Richard, he had gone out with Charlie, broken off with her and to his surprise she pursued him for revenge like a tornado destroying anything on its path. It had been Richard who had brought the most spite in Charlie, she felt a lot of anger and revenge and blamed the failure in her friendship with Tim and the fact that she had slept with him on Richard.

Once Charlie was finished with Richard, he hardly had any friends left since they all took sides and people did not hesitate to describe him as a bastard which to a degree they were right, however, if they knew Charlie at all they would have realised why.

With Liz it was a different matter though, Charlie did not want to lose that friendship for various reasons, in particular the vast number of contact and friends that Liz had, had proven handy and she knew that in the future they might be so again. She had to keep her sweet from now on and had to be careful of not upsetting her again. Most people found Liz trustworthy, a quality that Charlie valued, she had to keep someone like her close to her, after almost people trusted you if they knew you had a very trustworthy friend.

It had been almost two years since Liz had spoken to Charlie when she got the call from Liz to see if she could stay with her, for years after graduation they had remained friends at a distance, maintaining what was necessary in case one needed the help of the other in future. They both knew that you could not burn bridges in today's society, even though they came close to it they both knew better. Charlie thought her jealousy and sense of insecurity would have disappeared by now, but as soon as she saw Liz coming off the train, she felt it again, she had not changed, Liz looked as beautiful as ever and as calm and confident as she had been when at university. She still maintained an air of shyness about her, but it made her more attractive, men wanted to protect her, and women wanted to mother her. Vile anger hit her; nothing had changed!!

She felt sad for Liz but only because of the passing of her mother could not have come at a harder time, even though it was always bad to lose such a close relative, it came at a time when the job market had dried up and from what she heard, she had not had a partner for years, preferring her own company or just a few friends around her to spend the odd evening out relaxing and sharing jokes and anecdotes.

She wished she were as independent as Liz was, confident and happy with her own company, in her own skin, something she could never do. If she stayed more than two nights without seeing people, she started getting depressed. She started feeling she had no friends, uncomfortable very quickly if she did not see people, she always had to be on the phone, know everything that was going on, good or bad and be the one dishing out the advice, wanted or unwanted. She felt deep down she was always right and if people ever got annoyed with her it was their fault, not hers, she was always the 'good one'.

# John and Jenny's Wedding

*A successful good marriage is not only based
on the power base being equally shared but on
shared minds that recognise they are two different
autonomous individuals constantly evolving*

This was the first time since Liz had seen Tim since she had left for London that Sunday, three months after that dreadful Friday when she had caught Tim and Charlie together.

She had arrived in Dublin on the Saturday, the day of the wedding, wishing to avoid seeing Tim the night before. She decided to take the easiest route possible by flying London to Dublin from Stanstead Airport using Ryanair. It was all she could afford, rather than do what everyone else did which was to drive and then take the ferry to cross over the Irish Sea to Ireland. She felt that arriving the day before would be too much for her; she was already a bundle of nerves with the idea of seeing Tim. It had only been three months since she last saw him and did not know how she was going to react to the encounter. Her emotions were still raw and now and then she still felt the pain of being back stabbed, she could still vividly see Charlie and Tim together, it was too painful.

Her stomach had butterflies, as if she had thousand in it trying to escape. She felt as if she was going to vomit. She 'knew' and understood she was no longer 'in love' with Tim, she loved him of course and they had shared so much, felt so much, dreamed so much, like two lost souls that had found each other, their dreams and fears, all their emotions in the open, their soul naked, yes, she did love him and wanted the best for him.

Her mind was racing, did he have a girlfriend now? Had he forgotten or got over her? Was he as nervous as her? Questions that she knew would never be answered but nevertheless important to her peace of mind. Like all other women, she was no different, she wanted to know, needed to feel that she had not been discarded, that she had meant something, that he still felt something for her to some degree.

Liz arrived at around twelve a.m. in Dublin and took a taxi to Greystones Village which she had been told was just outside Dublin, but nobody warned her it would cost her an arm and a leg. €100 to be exact, the Village was not as close to Dublin as she had expected. The wedding was at a small Catholic Church, which would hold around eighty to one hundred guests.

Greystones was a small town, around 30 kilometres from Dublin City Centre. It was a cute little town by the seaside with the Sugar Loaf Mountains behind it. A favourite place for the sailing enthusiasts, it was a surprise that John had not decided to settle in this picturesque place after all he was crazy about sailing, his favourite sport. Jenny's parents were members of the local sailing club and they practically lived there and since they were retired, they were there at least four out of seven days during the summer months.

Jenny herself was a member, having attained her Skipper certificate two years before. With every summer spending all full three months sailing, not having to work as her parents financed everything for her, an agreement that suited her and to her credit, she was not spoilt, she knew she was lucky and valued everything life gave her, never taking it for granted.

As far as Liz was concerned, this was a mini paradise, not due to the sailing as Liz could not really care for the sport, in fact she did not like getting wet especially if the water was cold, she liked it warm! No, she imagined that during the summer it would be warmish enough to sunbed. She imagined that this area would be popular with walking which was one past time she enjoyed and the beautiful beaches lent themselves to that, the waves murmured in your ear, like a seashell calling, encouraging you, keep going and enjoy the view and allow your feet get wet by the shore. She liked the noise the waves made when crashing against the rocks, it was a peaceful calling noise, it relaxed her.

Regardless, she was pleased for Jonny and Jenny specially when she saw the family make up. She was not jealous but always loved looking into the loves of people, how they lived, longing to have a family like some of the people she saw. Jonny was well liked ad welcomed into a solid family unit, one that would support him and Jenny throughout their married life, you could see form the dynamics they would be there for him. Both were easy going, aware that they were a unit with different opinions, willing to grow and change together, adapt but throughout it, support each other with love and respect. You could tell they would last, it was written and visible, like a beacon stating these two were solid. Maybe she was jealous and in denial, she wanted that feeling, to belong.

By the time she had arrived there, it was already twelve thirty p.m., and the wedding ceremony was due to start at one p.m. She was one of the first guests to arrive to the church, was worried in case she got the wrong church, she checked and double checked the invitation, where was everyone?

Standing there like an idiot for ten minutes approximately, she started feeling like a lemon, did she miss something? Get the instructions wrong? Maybe she should have gone to Jenny's house. Thoughts playing in her mind and making her doubt the clear instructions she was given, when suddenly and out of the blue all the guests started arriving, trickling couple and single, smiling, in anticipation of a happy celebratory day. She did not recognise any of them and apprehension took over her, what if Tim decided not to turn up after all. Maybe he just had enough and decided that even her friendship was not worth it. She was sure John had told her that another three people on her class had also been invited to the wedding; surely all three would have not been able to make it.

Liz had been shaking strongly for the last ten minutes, it felt like a lifetime, stomach clenched, holding the bag so tight her knuckles turned a bluish white. The cold was so intense, she never had expected it to be this cold, then again, it was November. The chill in the air was not the problem; it was the damp wind, which penetrated through her coat and straight into her bones sucking all the heat out of her as it passed. She had prepared herself for this weather, but it seemed it was not enough; she had a very elegant outfit and a very large and warm coat over it which did not seem to be able to stop the wind.  If the wedding did not start soon, they will have to have a funeral instead, her funeral, she could just imagine the newspapers, guest dies of hypothermia whilst waiting for wedding party to arrive.

Around 12.45 p.m. Tim arrived.  To her relief, he was looking his usual charming best but she felt like crying, she really had missed him and felt deep sorrow for their low.  She had not mourned properly and could feel the pang of longing.  He looked so handsome in his morning suit.  Looking around and surveying the crowd, his eyes suddenly rested on her and a smile lit his face, like her, she was sure he had not mourned either and you could visibly see the pain hidden behind the beautiful smile.  He started walking towards her, looking a little nervous, the fear of rejection hanging over him, like a dark cloud ready to pour on a wonderful day.

"Hi Lizzie!  his voice sounded hoarse, as if he had an apple stuck in his throat or had a very bad cold, "how are you? You look great!"  The last comment seemed genuine, his eyes sparkled as he appreciated and savoured her beauty, yes, she did look a million pounds.  "Your hair suits you."  a wide smile appeared across his face, his eyes looking a bit sad, but he was still smiling, appreciating the beauty fate allowed him to once again admire.  The pain of the last three months clearly written on his face. The regret and the loss clearly visible, his voice had hesitation every time he spoke, as if he did not know if he was going to be welcomed.

For the wedding, Liz had her hair cut noticeably short, a boyish style which accentuated her high cheek bones and her big brown almond shaped eyes.  She had dressed simply and elegantly, a silk jacket and three-quarter length skirt.  The very pale green pastel colour suited her complexion very well, it enhanced her skin and gave her a glow.  She also had matching-coloured shoes, a bit of an extravagance on her part but she wanted to look good, to feel good and she had achieved it, just by one basic right accessory.  Her shoes had a very tiny little heel, she felt that her 5' 3" frame would look ridiculous with stilettos, and, in her mind, she would have easily ended up looking like a tart.  Some people liked their high heels and would not be seen out without them, it was part of them. For Liz it was the opposite, she liked comfort ahead of anything else.

Her coat was made of rich soft wool and had a very light camel colour; it reached the end of her skirt and finished her very high-end look. As a final touch, she had hired a sun bed two weeks before the wedding so that it would give her skin a golden colour, just slightly. which in the end meant she did not have to wear much make up as her face looked perfectly natural. Her lips had a very light red/brick colour and she put on some mascara on. Liz had never been a fan of makeup, she felt greasy and uncomfortable but like everyone else, she needed some light colour.

Blessed with good skin and slight tannish colour which needed a bit of sun now and then. Her usual before going out was to just wear lipstick but she thought for the wedding she would darken her eyes a little bit, give it more of an exotic look, which the mascara did perfectly, giving her a mysterious effect.

"Hi Tim, thank you, you look good as well, how have you been?" Looking very confident and composed whilst saying this, her only give away were her eyes, which were slowly flooding with tears. She had to look away and compose herself. She was not going to cry.

She could not, would not cry and she had come a long way from the Liz of three months ago.

"I miss you, I am sorry for everything" Tim took a big gulp "I wish I could have you back." His eyes were not leaving Liz's face, as if looking for a sign which never came, he blurted all this out showing his nervousness, he did not even take in a breath as he talked, he must have thought about what to say thought Liz for the last three months, feeling suddenly a rush of adrenaline surging through his veins, face going red.

"Stop Tim, please stop," her eyes were pleading, if they talk about this she will cry in the middle of a wedding "We talked about this, please don't bring it up again. Let us just be friends, please, you are going to end up upsetting me a lot and I will have to leave" Liz's eyes were pleading at him now, she understood he was hurting, but that is just life, it is the price he would have to pay for what he did to her; she was not going to forget it and therefore there was no point in trying to get back. Anger and pain had eventually destroyed what they had felt for each other, it was better just to try and be friends and move on. The pain he had will ease in time and he will forget, or at least move on.

Tim was panicking, he realised that three months had meant nothing and had not erased the memory of her or the incident and that he had truly lost her, he knew then he had to try and gain back her confidence and keep her friendship, if he kept pushing her, he would even loose that, which he treasured just as much as their lost relationship.

"I am sorry, I understand how you feel" his eyes had left her face, embarrassed and sad at pushing her.

Liz hugged him, a strong hug that covered an array of feelings and unsaid words. It felt good. He felt re-energised, welcomed to the fold, even if it was as a friend only.

"Anyway, how have you been Tim? What have you done in the last three months?" Liz was trying her hardest to be nice, to move the conversation away and make it light-hearted which is what they needed. She wanted to keep the friendship, he was still valuable to her and still he meant a lot to her. Her heart was healing but she still had so much affection towards him as a good human being that sadly made a serious mistake.

"Well, I have been working hard and have just been promoted to Team Leader two weeks ago" Tim had a twinkle in his eye, he was glad the conversation had changed, it did not change the situation they were in or their feelings, but it allowed them space to move on and readjust themselves to ensure they enjoyed this wedding. Allow the healing to truly begin.

"Oh wow! That is fantastic, you have only been there eighteen months and you are already on your way up. Did you get nice pennies with it?" A nice genuine smile came across Liz's face, it showed that not only she had relaxed but also that she really cared for Tim, after all, they were, before everything went wrong, soul mates and she hoped that they would retain that.

She wanted the best for him, she knew he will achieve a lot, he was ambitious and a fighter.

"Well, I received ten grand as a pay rise and I am now entitled to large bonuses, not the same as the fat cats but better than a kick it in the teeth. I guess I am now on my way to riches." He laughed loudly, his beautiful, well cared for white teeth were on display, wow, he was gorgeous! She felt a pang of sadness fill her being, she wanted his big arms to engulf her and make love to her. She felt sad and lonely, this was awful "maybe if I performed to their requirements I could be sent to the New York office for a year."

"New York!? Is that what you want?" Liz was surprised, taken aback, she had never thought of Tim moving abroad.

"I have already spoken to Richard who is already there, he has a two-bedroom flat in Manhattan and so far he is not sharing with anyone." What Tim did not tell Liz was that in the event of him being rejected by her he had decided he was going to accept this offer.

This for Tim would be an ideal opportunity to get away from things, from Edinburgh, which constantly reminded him of Liz and what he did to destroy everything. He had nothing to lose now, he had to get away in order to get over things. He might even settle in the States, after all, he was very young, did not have to settle down, he had not dependents and his parents would not mind, he would only be a 'flight' away from them.

The wedding was lovely and fun, everyone enjoyed themselves. John was delighted that Liz and Tim had made it; however, he had been a little bit concerned about things between them. He had heard they had split up but unlike everyone else who had accepted their version of events, John knew better, he knew something was amiss with the story they were all given, something must have happened to make them go their separate ways, the story was too perfect, manufactured even and both looked so sad, you could tell there were still strong feelings between them but it was good that were both trying to work out the friendship. Both looked hurt and had been hurt and however much John liked Tim, his concern was more for Liz whom he really liked as a sister and only wanted her happiness.

Charlie had gone to visit John at his flat on his last week in Edinburgh. He had been packing when the doorbell rang and Charlie had materialised herself there, unannounced and acting as if they had been best of friends. He was very angry that Charlie was there, he had told her several times he wanted nothing to do with her. Jenny had been very clear to him, she had an inkling that she was somehow involved in the Tim and Liz debacle, not only from conversations with Tim and picking the odd hurt, slip of the tongue and behaviours in general. Jenny had also known about John and Charlie, from gossip but also from John himself. She had warned him that if he ever saw Charlie their relationship would be over, there was to be no friendship between them, which funnily, never really existed, it had always been sexual, Charlie was too empty and selfish to have anything meaningful.

John had decided long ago that Jenny was the one. He would be honest and faithful to her. He had confessed to her that evening called her and told her that Charlie had appeared to his flat uninvited.

Jenny was fine with his version of events however, curiosity got the best of her and demanded to know what the exact conversation between them had been. John, without any qualm started relating it to her, after making her promise that nobody else would hear about it.

Charlie had been honest to John with what happened. He did not feel sorry for her as she had it well deserved and at this rate she would end up with no friends if she kept going like that. The only thing wrong with Charlie's story was the fact nobody knew that Liz and Tim had concocted a lie and she thought that Liz had finished with Tim before the tragic event, it was the only thing that could save Liz's pride.

Funnily enough, this was something that John felt could not be true. He had seen the way they both behaved with each other, how loving they were and how attentive Tim was to Liz and vice versa. They really cared for each other and only a fool would have not noticed. He also knew that Liz was the proud sort, one who would not take well to being humiliated in public. This was in a way a shame, as people would have sided with Liz, spurned Charlie and felt sorry for Tim. Charlie would have been exposed at last for what she was: an insecure cheat and liar who went out of her way to deceive and hurt people for her benefit and sometimes for the hell of it, like a selfish spoilt brat. Did not like to see people happy!

To Charlie, friends were a means of achieving something usually it meant her friends might end up losing their boyfriends to her.

Tim and Liz danced together most of the night laughing and joking, relaxed at last, knowing where each other stood, knowing that their friendship would survive. They were both staying in the same hotel as the wedding reception and because of this, had danced and talked until the early hours, drinking and singing with other people whom they had met that day.

It had been very tempting to spend the night together, or what was left of it but by doing so they were in danger of ruining everything they had achieved. They both desired to make love to each other by a way of comforting each other for their loss, but it was not to be, now or forever it seemed. Each went back to their own rooms, their passion unsatisfied still hungry and starving but with no hope of fulfilment.

The next day they both headed for the airport and left. Not as lovers but as firm friends. Liz had not slept all night, thinking, dreaming, aroused by thoughts of previous love makings, reminiscing, and wishing things had been different. She missed his caress, his cuddles. She thought she had stopped loving him but it was now obvious that she hasn't, she felt so much for him. Sadness engulfed her all night until the early hours and as a result she had only slept one hour.

"Will you visit me in New York Liz?" Tim was looking into her eyes, expectant, like a child who had asked if he could have a sweet from the store.

"Maybe, it all depends on how things go work wise." She stated, her face smiling, relaxed. "Like you, I really want to make sure that I make an impression at work. Anyway, I will try, I don't promise anything, but I would probably be in desperate need of a holiday by mid or end of next year. "You will write, wouldn't't you?"

She had to be honest, she cared so much. One hand instinctively touched his hair and face, longingly, showing him that she too was sorry that she loved him but she could not change things, she could forgive but not forget.

"Yes, of course, what a question! And I will call you as well." After hugging her, his arms strongly embracing her, as if she was going to suddenly disappear, not wanting to let go and savouring their last embrace, he suddenly let go and started walking towards his departure lounge. His flight was leaving in 60 minutes, he was late but did not care.

He could not allow Liz to see tears in his eyes. He was angry, angry that he had ruined the best thing life had thrown at him and this made him feel like a failure, empty and lacking energy. He promised never to do it again, never to cheat, it hurt too much, it cost too much.

# Tim - New Beginnings

*It is because I care that I let you go; I care for*
*you and I care for me*

Tim was not good at writing like he promised. He had left for New York three months after the wedding and after two months, in April, she had only received one postcard which contained his new address and telephone number. However, in Tim's defense, he was good at calling. For the first two years he called once a week, mainly for a short chat, curious about what she had been up to and glad to speak to her and hear her voice.

Tim settled in New York in the end, it had been nearly eleven years now and his calls were mostly once every two months, but he still called which pleased Liz very much. At the start Tim always questioned Liz about her private life quite avidly desperate to see if Mr Right had appeared, shocked to hear that another guy had replaced him. Another man was making love to her. After all this time he still yearned for her, he wanted and needed her, but needed to say goodbye, he needed to bury the past.

In those eleven years, Liz visited Tim three times in New York. Twice were for holidays, just to get away from London and also to see how him and Richard were doing. The third time was two years ago and it was to attend Tim's wedding. He had married a very beautiful doll-like red-head New Yorker called Lisa, who for some reason had taken strong dislike of Liz, but she did care for Tim, it was to be understandable after all Liz knew about the flame Tim carried for her. What Lisa did not realise was that Liz would never take him back. She was probably jealous but deep down probably knew that Liz and Tim were history.

Now she should try and find herself someone, but she knew her 'tick list' for the ideal man would be hard to match, she was too picky and the older she got the worse it would get.

Lisa and Tim had both moved to New Jersey and bought a nice little house which was to be honest three times the size of Liz's flat in London and they called it their 'little pad'. They both now had a two-month-old baby son called Bethan who was the pride and joy of his father and you could tell he had his father's looks and confidence about him. Tim was happy at last; Liz knew that now and was pleased. Both had finally moved away and closed the door to the past.

He loved Lisa, maybe not the same way he had loved Liz but certainly it was love and Betham completed that love, he had the family he wanted and was not going to mess it all up, ever!!

There was nothing Lisa should worry about, she was beautiful, her flowing straight red hair went very well with her tall height which at 5' 6" set her aside from most girls in New York. She was three inches taller than Liz, slightly flat chested with long legs, you could say she had a wonderful figure not curvaceous and voluptuous like Liz's.

Lisa had fallen in love with Tim straight away the moment he had walked into the New York office on his first day, looking tan and full of confidence, nobody knowing that he was hiding heart ache. Lisa had been a PA to one of the partners and she had told all the other girls in the office to not even think of trying to chat him up, he was hers she decided, a task that would take a long time and effort and tears to achieve.

Whenever a new girl started at the office, word got round that: 'The Englishman belonged to Lisa'. It was more a joke than anything else, after all, why would someone in the exec team with so many prospects end up marrying a PA or so she thought but in the end her dream came true. Tim finally took notice.

It had taken Lisa 9 years to net him, and when she did, she made him promise that he would marry her within a year, a promise he kept. He knew he would not find a girl like Liz, there was only one and after all these years, their deep love, which was still there, had just changed to pure friendship and understanding, maybe after all they were not destined to be with each other and he accepted that now, he believed in fate and knew that he had married the best girl for him.

# Richard

Richard, by all intents and purposes was Tim's best friend who had also broken all links with Charlie in view of what she did to Tim and Liz. He had also settled in New York and taken the place by storm, and his over confidence was a great success with the Americans who liked to be with a winner. He had shared a flat with Tim for four years and then moved on to his own flat, his theory being that after a while sharing loses its charm and he really wanted some space.

He married at the age of thirty, a wedding to which Liz had been invited but was unable to attend, which in a way was good, as after only six months his wife had filed for divorce on the grounds of his constant adultery. Something everyone knew would happen sooner or later. The man just could not keep his bits to himself.

Nobody blamed Alexandra for it, most of the female guest at the wedding had been or were in line to be Richards next lover and all knew that it was a very dangerous business, he was so smooth and so full of himself that he really believed Alex would have had him back time and time again, but he was wrong.

He had never met a woman that will out do him. He did not think one existed, but Alex had her plans and like the saying goes 'there is nothing worse than a woman scorned'. Alex took Richard on the ride of his life, as far as she was concerned, he had not only made a fool of her but shattered her confidence and public persona and she wanted revenge, she wanted to get back what she had lost, her pride. She took him to the cleaners and made sure she had the best detergent available!

Richard did not date anyone for three years after this marriage fiasco. Not only his confidence had been dented but his pocket had been pretty much emptied as well. Alex had made sure that she had to hit him where it hurt the most, his pocket. On top of this, Alex's father filed a lawsuit and won making Richard pay back to him the wedding costs and all the expenditures that were incurred by Alex's. His argument to the courts had been that Richard never had any intention of making a go at his marriage, that it had only been a game to him and if he had known of any such attitude, he would have not spent $250,000 to provide his daughter with a wedding deserved by his family status in society. He had been made a mockery and wanted retribution.

The court case looked was straight out of a Hollywood scandal. Every single woman he dated or charmed had a one-night stand or was on his waiting list was summoned as witness. It was a hurtful and humiliating even but also cathartic for both Alex and Richard. For Alex, the act of revenged brough some closure and the rest she knew time would heal. For Richard, it brought reality to his door in black and white. An embarrassing situation socially and for his work. All his business contacts were aware of the scandal gripping New York! There was no escape.

Richard had gone to London at least twice a year since he had left for New York. Soon after his divorce, which was very quick even for American standards, he had spent a weekend in London with Liz, catching up with old friends, thinking of moving back to London. Life had not been the same since Tim had moved in with Lisa and now that they were married and had Bethan and another boy in the way he would end up hardly seeing his friend.

The fun of being in New York no longer appealed to him, he wanted to come back to Britain, be close to family and friends, well, family were not close to London but at least it was all in the same country, his friends however were mostly living in London which would be ideal for him.

He remembered trying to chat Liz up, which ended up backfiring on him and in his mind with nearly the most catastrophic consequences. It is weird because he had never fancied her whilst they were in Edinburgh, it was just an attempt by him to increase his conquest list, but the older he got the more he thought about her, appreciating every curve and classical feature, every skill and talent she had, how clever and hardworking she was, maybe it was to do with growing older or his taste getting better, maturing and appreciating really what was important in life.

The older Liz got the more beautiful and desirable she got, she was no longer the shy girl he once knew, in her place was a woman that exuded confidence and sex appeal. Gone was the puppy fat on her face, her skin was beautiful and silky, touched by a very light tan, giving her a very light olive complexion. It suited her. Yes, she was sexy, now he understood why Tim was distraught for years after they had split, he really had lost a treasure there and he must feel it even now. There was a 'je ne sais quoi' about Liz!

Lisa was beautiful but not like Liz, there was an air of elegance and confidence, a sexual electricity that emanated from her body only accentuated by the fact that she was unaware of this. He wanted to bed her, but he knew better than to try but the wine had got to his head and he had lost control, he felt powerful as if he had a chance. What had he been thinking of!

All four of them were out that night he recalled. Liz, Tanya, Damien and him. Liz had just lost her mum and had too much drink, by the time they had all got back to the flat, Liz had done her share of vomiting in the taxi, she could hardly walk and was slurring her words, even like this it made Richard fill with desire, he felt horny, he felt the urge in his loins, holding Liz up, his arm felt her left breast which sent a shiver through him. He wanted her, more than he had ever wanted anyone. The thought of being a traitor to his friend crossed his mind but the urge was stronger – 'Fuck Tim!"

Tanya and Damien were off to their bedroom, like rabbits that had not made love in years. Richard was left to help Liz, which he did and added a fair dose of groping which Liz was not very aware off, she was far too drunk to notice.

Liz sat on the brown leather settee, in her drunkenness she still tried to make sense of everything but was not successful at it.

"If I vomit, at least it is leather and I can clean it easily" She giggled nervously, her sixth sense warning her that not all was quite right but too drunk to make sense of it. Her eyes moving all over the room, like trying to make sense of things, trying to focus on one thing but everything was just to dizzy. Her stomach felt weak, like a washing machine on spin cycle!

Suddenly and without warning, Richard was all over her, groping, pulling, kissing her with such force she nearly vomited on him. Her mind was racing, could this be happening? Has the world gone to pots? Suddenly from nowhere her mind stood still and sobriety hit her or as close as sober as she could be under the circumstances. She backed off and shouted at him furious whilst trying to stand up.

"How dare you!!" Shouted Liz "what in the devil drove you to do that?" Her beautiful hair was all over her, in complete disarray, covering part of her right eye, making her look sexier than ever, more alluring if it was not for the absolute anger emanating from her. She was so loud, Damien and Tanya peaked their heads out of their room, shock in their faces, not knowing what to make of the situation but realising it was not that bad that they had to interfere.

"Sorry" Muttered Richard looking suddenly very sheepish "I thought, I don't know what I thought, I am sorry Liz, I thought you liked me." He was completely embarrassed, his hands covering his face and looking downwards to the floor, he felt lost, beaten! He had miscalculated everything, assumed just because they were having fun that she was up to all this.

"In all honestly I don't know what got on to me" He lied. "Sorry Lizzy I really only wanted a kiss, I was not going to hurt you or anything" He was ashamed, he knew it. "I" His voice trembled "I did not mean to scare you" Complete embarrassment filled him. Even him suggesting a kiss which was an unwanted trespassing was unacceptable and realise his colossal mistake.

It was at that point that he suddenly realised how much he liked Liz, really liked her, not just physically, how much he admired her. This in his mind was not another conquest, he actually felt something. He was intelligent enough to realise he was not wanted, but deep down he felt he could make her change her mind, like most men do when they think of themselves above most fellow men. Most people liked him, the only reason his ex-wife didn't it's because he got caught 'in fragranti'.

Tanya and Damien retreated to their own room, giggling but conscious that if the situation got any stickier, they might have to stop their love making for some serious confrontation, something they did not want to end the evening with.

"That is mega embarrassing" Muted Tanya, her beautiful body just being covered by a loose sheet, which she dragged from the bed when she heard Liz shout. Tossing it on the floor as she went back to her bed, Damien staring at her, admiring her beauty "Why on earth did Richard think he had even a remote chance with Liz? I thought most guys knew straight away when Liz was not interested" Damien's face showed confusion, how could someone get ot so wrong "And they have known each other for a long time." He made a face and jumped in bed, excited at the anticipation of what awaited him.

"I know, I think he was just chancing it to be honest. I think the drink must had played a part on it" added Tanya from the bed, Damien had already lost interest on what had happened or the conversation, he wanted to go back to the fun, to the wonderful love making that awaited him "Don't worry about it, it will all be forgotten by the morning." Other than the initial embarrassment, my guess is that it will all be all right" His eyes were glistening, staring, hungry in anticipation of something wicked and delicious.

Liz put a hand on Richard's shoulders, to steady herself and also to show him that she was in control, or at least it made her feel as if as he was in control, which she was, without knowing, since Richard had his tail between his legs.

"Let's just call it a day Richard." Liz was looking into his eyes as he lifted his head "Maybe tomorrow we can talk about what happened or we can just forget all about it, I think you know at the moment I am not interested in anything or anyone, my life is crazy lately and to be honest, I see you more as a friend than a lover. I am sorry." Liz felt she needed to apologise, for what, she was not quite sure, all she knew is that unless the right words were said to night, it would be more embarrassing in the morning and the damaged would be irreparably. She had to have a steady head on.

Richard was sitting in the cream sofa, he relaxed, his arms were spread across the back of it, looking more as if he was trying to support himself, in fact, he looked and felt defeated, as if someone had just slapped him in his face which they had, with words which were just as powerful as the act itself.

Liz was standing right in front of him, legs separated, her arms were now firmly on her hips, she realised that maybe putting her arms on his shoulders was not quite what she should have done. He looked so vulnerable, she looked not only pissed but majorly pissed off.

"Come on Richard, we are friends, we have been friends for years, I don't need this." As she said this she walked off to her bedroom. "Go to sleep, let's forget about it and start again tomorrow." She closed the door, stumbling to her bed, hardly being able to stand unaided. She was desperate for a glass of water but was too tired, too drunk and too confused. She will get up later to drink from the bathroom tap.

The next day her head hurt, she was hardly able to stand, vaguely recollecting what had happened. She slowly went to the toilet, she was just wearing her G string, her slim legs looking rather pale than her normal tan and healthy skin. She was sick. This was a mess, her hair looked a mess, she had bags around her eyes. She stared at herself, was this what had become of her, was this her life, where were the people that loved her, what was the point. Thoughts just crossed her mind as she brushed her teeth; the tooth pasted leaking from the side of her lips, dirtying the sink and some dropping on the floor where her toes caught the drips.

Everything she did was automatic, after brushing her teeth thoroughly and removed the furry white gunk on her tongue she rinsed her mouth, feeling as if she was going to vomit again "Please

God don't let me vomit again, I can't face this anymore, I promise I will never drink this much again". Tears were streaming down her face as she sat down on the toilet, she had been bursting for a pee but her mind was too slow to react. She needed breakfast she thought, that will keep her going and settle me, remember everything in the last 24 hours.

As she walked slowly towards the fridge, her silk robe, barely covering her body as it clung to her figure. Liz was battling with the belt as she approached the fridge, mindful that Damien and Tanya may be already up and about and that Richard was fast asleep somewhere. As she was about to open the fridge, she noticed the note and Richard's signature.

As Liz read it, she robotically started towards the kettle, one eye on the letter and one eye on the kettle leaver.

*Dearest Lizzie,*

*'Sorry about last night.*

*I guess that my feelings had finally surfaced with the help of the wine. I am sorry that I have offended you for which I am very apologetic and regretful and wanted you to know that I have greatly admired you from a distance for a long time. I have great admiration and respect for you and my behaviour last night was not how I would normally behave, and it does not represent how I feel about you. To me you are not only a friend but also someone I greatly connect with and love.*

*Maybe when things cool off a little bit you may give me the opportunity to convince you that I am not a bad person and give me a chance to prove it to you.*

*I am planning to comeback and live in London soon, and hope that you give me the chance then to prove to you that I truly care.*

*Again, my intention was not to offend. I am truly sorry for my behaviour.*

*Richard x*

*Ps. I have put the bed linen on the dirty washing, hope that was OK.*

This was crazy Liz thought, this had to change and she had to change and had to make sure Richard clearly understood that she was not interested in him. She could only regard him as a friend, a good friend and nothing else. He was a lovely guy and extremely good looking but there just was something missing there, she knew that what she had had with Tim had been close to it, so she definitely knew that she felt nothing for Richard.

She also knew that Richard's behaviour was out of the ordinary, he could gauge when someone was interested in him and her guess was that the court case and divorce had affected him. It made him look like a sad guy who could not get satisfaction or control his sexual urges. He was shown as a weak man, which she knew he was not, he just should not have settled down, not until he was at least 50!

# Part 2

## The Shaping

### Christopher

*"Waste no more time arguing about what a good man should be. Be one." Marcus Aurelius, Emperor of Rome.*

Life had slowly started getting better and better for Chris, two years ago he had been promoted to Director of Corporate Services at a prestigious bank in the city, this not only meant an increase in his salary and bonus to millions of pounds in the last year but also it meant that he had achieved the credibility and respectability he had yearned for so long and for which he had sacrificed all these years by working until the early hours in the morning, not attending parties like most people at his age did. His habits and demands he imposed on him were punishing.

His life was starting to reward him for his hard work and like his work, his 'private' affairs were also doing extremely well, and by this he did not mean the romance front, which has always been OK, but it was his 'house purchasing scheme' he had started twelve years ago that was doing extremely well. It had all started with one flat which he purchased a couple of years after graduating which he bought in Edinburgh very cheaply during the recession in the late eighties had been unlucky for some but certainly not for him. He did not have to have an extortionate mortgage and the rent he received from it more than covered the monthly mortgage repayments and left plenty of money for him to invest elsewhere. Focusing on very high-end properties in London and catered for the very wealthy, renting some of his property for a week for people that only wanted a short let.

At the start, he did all the work himself. Forcing himself to learn how to plaster and do the carpentry, leaving the gas and electrics as well as the water to the professionals. He never messed up with those.

Since he had been a young boy, he always dreamed of not so much being rich but achieving something that he felt could be described as an achievement. He knew he was good and was out there to get it. He wanted contentment, not ever to worry about money but also wanted to show he did it. He wanted to have proof of what he had achieved.

Within the next seven years after graduating, he had not only increased the value of his investment property portfolio; property prices were going through the roof, rising rapidly, but he had managed to purchase another four properties before the market shot up in value, which again were providing him with more income. Yes, Mayfair and central London properties were doing pretty nicely, he knew he had nearly achieved all his dreams, he had plenty of money in the bank, earned a lot from his day job and his 'hobby' produced quite a nice pile of money which he just invested in stocks and shares which again had turned very well. This took a lot of his concentration as he had to work and keep an eye out on the stock market in case it crashed.

It had been twelve years now since he had started doing this and he now owned thirty-three properties of which he rented them all out, apart from the one he lived in. Three properties were in Edinburgh, two in Glasgow and the rest spread about in the West London areas like Ealing, Acton, Turnham Green and Richmond. His main reason for buying in west London rather than in Central London like Mayfair was intuition. He knew west London was not 'the place to be' eight ten years ago, but he predicted that there would be a shift in people living in a relatively small flat that would start moving further afield in search for new areas where they could get a bigger house for the same price as in the centre of town, he noticed that families in particular valued gardens.

He could buy a large double fronted house in Acton and precited it will quadruple in price in 10 years.

His personal life was slightly different but also good. He had never fallen in love, but he had been very fond of some of the women he had dated however none of them made him desire to walk down the aisle. All the women he dated had not only been extremely beautiful and fun to be with, but they were also very bright and intelligent in their own right. They all were very successful professionally, the only problem he was starting to encounter is that most of them irrespective of good they were at their job, they were desperate for him to propose in order for them to become a housewife and fulfil their life desire of having a family, or so they hinted.

Their manipulation and machinations were sometimes too obvious, other times there was just a hint but all the same they led to the same conclusion, they wanted marriage and kids.

He liked women, respected them, but he never felt he had found 'the one'. He wondered if that 'finding the one' was the concoction of one romantic nomad a millennia ago, who, disappointed with love decided to write about it as a way of fulfilment, making everyone think that love did exist, giving them false hope. Chris's opinion was that it might, if you were lucky, you would fine 'the one'. He felt that his parents had that luck and he certainly was not going to settle for second best, it was 'it' or nothing and since 'nothing' happened in years he just forgot all about it, never searched for it, just accepted it as fate. His lot in life to be alone.

Janine, his latest 'flame' learned as much as she could from him regarding the property industry. She had invested her inheritance, that her grandmother left to her two years ago, purchasing four properties in London, two in Acton, one in Chiswick and another one in Hammersmith. She still lived with her parents, so she had no requirements for a flat for herself, at least not yet. She had successfully refurbished all four flats and sold two of them for a 200% profit which was practically unheard of, however, she had been a good pupil and had house hunted for a long time before making a decision, she knew what she wanted, Chris had taught her well.

Janine was, out of all the women he dated the one that knew and understood that she would never become Mrs Christopher Wandsworth. She knew from day one that he was a man that either would stay a bachelor or would fall in love out of the blue to someone different from his usual 'type' of girlfriend. She was slightly bothered after all, one does become attached to one's lover, even if one had not intended to.

Chris always went for very tall brunettes, even though he admired blondes and many of the ones he met were beautiful, but his weak spot was for the Amazonian type, long dark hair, dark eyes, tall, with a large inviting mouth and very white teeth. He disliked people that could not take care of their teeth, saying that he did not like the false perfect look either which was currently favoured by the superrich or the LA set. He preferred to know that people managed to take care of their own teeth and keep them, he did not like the idea of kissing someone that only had capped teeth, for him that showed him that they did not take particular care of their mouth and teeth and oral hygiene was important. He also liked mischievous eyes, simply because he enjoyed flirting and one sure way to tell that someone was enjoying themselves was by their eyes. Glimmering eyes, dark and mysterious, he liked flirty eyes, very deep brown or black.

Janine was all this and more, she had been a model for some years, never achieving any major fame but always managing to socialise with the very famous and wealthy thanks to her father's connections. Regardless of who she met, she had always maintained her old self, her beauty and self-respect. She was not the typical skinny model, no, if someone did not like the way she looked then it was their loss, not hers. Her figure was perfectly built with enough flesh and fat to set her apart from those skinny models desperate to achieve fame and recognition that only ended up with minor fame and major anorexia and drug problems.

Her height helped a lot, Janine could afford those extra pounds and still look amazing, her size 36 c bust looking perfect, just the right size. Janine valued the fact that life was too short and she had to enjoy and savour everything life threw at her, it was not all about money as she wanted to enjoy herself and be happy, she did not want to get to be eighty years old and realised she had not had any fun.

Because of her sense of humour, she had been the longest girlfriend to date that Chris had ever had. She knew how to make someone laugh and feel happy. She made everyone feel as if they were the only ones in the room, the only ones that mattered. She was good and very down to earth and of course, extremely good in bed which mattered a lot to Chris, and he knew was sometimes hard to find. She was not a selfish lover, she wanted to please and was very clever about it, because by doing so, she knew she would make anyone please her, maybe not in bed but in other ways. Chris was probably the only one that was not fooled by it, but he had so much gratification with their lovemaking that he would always make a point of ensuring she was happy with him.

He was always grateful of the love and care she provided him with, not that he was the only one he was aware, Chris knew that now and then she would sleep around, making up a lie for him not to find out but he knew. He had always known, not that he blamed her, after all, he had always been honest with her and his lack of commitment to her. She had every right to keep on looking for Mr Right and he was very grateful that whilst doing so she was still warming up his bed.

Janine was young but not as young as she wished at twenty-nine. She wanted to settle down and have kids. She knew that it may be hard to give up on Chris, but that was life, she had to watch out for herself. You had to be number one.

It was not 'looks' that made Chris attractive even though he was exactly that, a very good-looking man. His charm and generosity set him aside from the rest, he did not need to convince anyone of who he was and what he had achieved, and he did not have to prove anything to anyone. He was a nice man who appreciated that life at its best is tough and one had to make the best of it. He had never looked down at anyone and people went up on his estimation if he found out they were hard working, honest, and generally good, however, if anyone wanted to take advantage of him they would find a side of him that was still very fair but not so nice, if you wronged him the doors would shut and would not open again for you, there was no second chance. Christopher would reduce even the hardest of men to tears and would sack anyone without any qualms. He did not give friends a second chance and made it very clear to his direct reports that if anyone played dirty the repercussions would be worse than they had ever anticipated. Sorry was not something he accepted with ease.

In 1998 he had been voted 'best employee' at the bank and his team themselves had voted him the most popular, liked and fair member of the team; this accolade meant more to him that anything else. To achieve riches is one thing, to achieve respect and recognition is another. His achievement and wealth did have a significant effect in his life though, sometimes he did feel lonely and travelling all the time was not only hard and tiring but also a very lonely journey as it deprived him of companionship, which is what he missed the most. He had lots of friends but sometimes he would seek being alone, even though deep down he yearned for company. Sometimes he would spend a week or so on his own just working and not seeing any close friends. It was as if he wanted to distance himself between the people that mattered. He knew that and knew why but he did nothing to rectify it.

# A Perfect Marriage

*For it is only perfect by human standards, but*
*never the less, perfect it was*

His parents had what he called the perfect marriage. His dad, John, an accountant with his own practice and his mum Natasha a housewife. They were born to be with each other, they adored each other and their children Christopher and Jonas.

John and Natasha had been married for nearly twenty-five years, Chris was then twenty-four and Jonas twenty, when everyone started noticing the changes. Their loving mum, who increasingly, as the years went by had become more and more hard of hearing had also started losing her memory.

It was not just a case of being forgetful but worse than that, one had to repeat things four or five times only to discover that you had to repeat it all again. It was exhausting and not matter how much you loved her, it proved a challenged and created frustration and resentment. She could not remember what she had done the night before but the most basic tasks like putting on the kettle, cutting an onion or even getting dressed were alarmingly hard for her.

"Come on mum!" Christopher said, trying to be as nice as possible to her. "Dad is going to be back from the supermarket soon, it is now 10 a.m. you know."

"Oh, is it, I did not realise the time, I thought it was only 5 a.m. which is the time I had always got up at. I wonder what is wrong with me." Her eyes were looking at Chris not understanding what had been going on, lifeless, searching, trying to understand her confusion, they were desperate eyes, frightened, the prospect that she may be going crazy. Natasha had been up at 5 a.m. as usual but was not aware that she had on all her clothes but her trousers and been walking around the house as if nothing had been wrong.

If john went out, one of them had to look out for Natasha in case she left the house half dressed.

"Try and put one leg through, yes, that is it." Frustration sometimes got the best of Chris but he was trying desperately not to show it, he was upset that his mum, whom he adored and had been so clever and full of life was losing her memory, she was too young, it was not fair. It is not the same feeling one had when someone dies, this was different, it was worse, they are there but at the same time they are long gone, the living dead.

Guilt kept eating at him, every time he lost his temper, he felt bad but he was exhausted.

"I really don't know how you can do this dear; I find it so hard you know; did someone teach you how to put trousers on?"

"Yes, mum, you did, however, it is one of the hardest things to do, so I quite understand that from time to time we all find it difficult." He was so caring, tenderly speaking to her and he seemed full of patience, a patience he knew sometimes would be tested to the limit, in his mind he was screaming. Even his dad was struggling to keep his patience under control at times and it hurt him. He was riddled with gilt when he lost it as he knew Natasha would have been better if it had been the other way round.

Chris had noticed his dad had started showing early signs of depression, something most carers who were family, went through at one point or another. He had to start thinking of how to help his dad so that he did not have to take the burden of it all himself, it was not fair, after all he was not young. Even trying to get someone to relieve him for four hours a day would be helpful, he would be here every weekend trying to give him some respite. Dam, he was angry, why did this had to happen, his mum was a good woman, this was not fair. Why did God have to hand this to his family?

He had made up his mind, he would call the Council and find out what could be done in terms of helping his dad and if that did not work, he will finance one or two nurses to take care of her whilst her

145

dad could still maintain some life and still be near the woman he loved.

"Oh really, but I can't do it now, it is too difficult, just so complicated. I think I am going mad Chris; I am frightened." Her pale blue eyes looked so sad and remote, lifeless, it broke Chris's heart, it made him angry.

"It is OK mum, you used to be good at it but if you don't do it often one forgets." This silly but sad explanation seemed to have appeased Natasha and never questioned Chris, who had at last managed to put her trousers on. All she wanted was confirmation that she had not lost the plot and those words were enough.

"Come on, I think we'd better get ready, dad is going to take us for a drive and then we will go for a walk in the park."

"But we need breakfast; we can't go out without feeding ourselves."

"It's OK mum, we had breakfast at 7.30 a.m. you just can't remember."

"Chris, you don't think I am losing my memory, do you? I don't want to end up like my mum with dementia." This had been Natasha's biggest fear since the day her mother died of dementia. She had been terrified that it was a hereditary illness and that either her or her bother Thomas would get it.

"No mum, you are OK, don't worry about it. We all forget a little bit sometimes." It was the least Chris could say, there was no point in upsetting her which can be easily done when in that state. The only thing he could be was as loving and supportive as a son could be, especially when it came to his dad, whom he knew was taking it all very bad. There was no retiring in the sunset for either of them, this was the life they would have, moving forward, one of carers, frustration and sadness for what was and could have been. It was all gone.

"Chris" said Natasha, looking at the distance "Sometimes my head feels as if it's full of fog, I just feel lost, it is very weird. I am so worried Darling. I really don't want to be a burden to you or your dad, I don't want to end up like my mum."

"Don't worry mum, everything is fine." He kneeled beside her, his hands on her knee "I love you mum, you are not ill, whatever is making you feel uneasy we will help you sort it out, we will go to the doctor soon." Natasha had already forgotten that they had been to the doctors at least ten times, all of which she cried when more and more diagnosis were done, forgetting four hours later what had happened.

Chris cuddled her, like only a son or daughter could, his strong arms around her. There was n embrace like the one full of love, this was not a friend hugging, it was pure love and the feeling is different, the energy being released is different, it felt like home, it was welcomed. He loved his mum so much, she had been one of those mums that children never fought with, she was strong and fair and even the unruliest of teenagers realised they were on the wrong. She had been so easy going, always ready to listen, kind, but ready to give honest and brutal advice. She took no prisoners and teenagers don't like that but respect it later in life. Whilst cuddling her Chris felt that this may be the last time that he may have a reasonable conversation with her as she was deteriorating quite quickly.

John, who was desperate to cure her, had taken Natasha to several top consultants for a diagnosis, only to be baffled by their responses. Nobody seemed to understand how out of the blue, what seemed a very advance stage of dementia be affecting a woman who a month ago was reasonably okay.

This did not deter John and he kept trying to find an answer and possible solution, which he knew deep down did not exist. The answer came from a consultant based in Edinburgh, one of many he went to see desperate for a different diagnosis and the hope that what was happening was something else that was curable. This consultant not only told John of how everything happened but what would happen next, the latest was something he already knew and every consultant in London had already told him so already. He is the one that force John to see and accept the reality of things. There was no cure and he had to prepare for it. Once he was told how it had happened, you could only feel pity and sorrow for this family whose nucleus had been its matriarch. John was desperate to try and fight to keep it together. He knew he could not survive without her. She was his life; she was the very ticking bomb in his chest that kept him alive and going.

Natasha and John, who were based in Godalming, Surrey for most of their lives, had purchased a country house in Le Touquet in northern France, a small commune of a few thousand of people, where they spent two to three weeks every summer and two weeks in winter there. Most Christmases were spent there, surrounded by nature and peace and it was good for the boys to practice their French.

It was three weeks after Natasha's operation on one of her ears (she had a viral infection that rendered her left ear deaf) that John and Natasha had decided to go to France for her to convalesce in peace and without being disturbed. They had flown to Dinard in Normandy and then hired a car and drove to their destination. They drove for five hours to their secluded and idyllic cottage.

It was there that the first sign that something was not quite right was just after landing at Dinard Airport. Natasha for some reason did not want to get off the plane, she was under the belief that they had not taken off from Stansted and kept demanding to be flown to France. It was more providence than luck that John had been there with her, the original plan had been for him to go ahead and get the cottage ready for Natasha's arrival. Natasha had been a bit nervous and fidgety and had asked John to fly with her, this was unusual since Natasha enjoyed flying, it was John the one that hated it. On top of all that, Natasha had always been very independent, she would not do something just because someone was not there with her.

It had been John's persuasion and calming words that had convinced Natasha to leave the plane. Once in the car, Natasha had slept most of the way, waking up now and then crying and confused, she did not know where she was and where they were going.

When Mr Connaught, the consultant in Edinburgh saw John and Natasha and asked them of any unusual events. Natasha could not remember anything unusual, which was not surprising, but John had remembered this episode and related it to him. Apparently, Natasha should have not flown for at least three months after surgery. The operation had not been in itself something difficult and life threatening, but they had to operate in the head which meant it was a very delicate operation where arteries or veins could easily burst. It seemed that the wound, after the brain operation, had just sealed, however, the flight had made the seal break slightly, blood seeped and coagulated into parts of the brain which deal with the memory. This was confirmed later on when several head scans showed clotting in various parts of Natasha's brain which have covered, sadly, quite a large area of her brain.

He also informed them that this memory deficiency was likely to have happened to Natasha later in life as her mother and grandfather had suffered from it which pointed at a hereditary condition., but the process had been speeded up by other events like the hemorrhaging and then blood clotting.

Life after that had never been the same, the family tried it's best to appear happy, but it was nearly impossible. Chris caught his father crying several times on his own, damming everything and everyone, feeling pity for himself, for having physically the woman he adored but whom mentally had left them a long time ago.

Natasha died three years after it had all started, Chris was barely twenty-seven, but the worst of it all is that she had died exactly one week before his twenty seventh birthday which was on the ninth of May. A catastrophic hand of fate that had forever changed the meaning of his birthday for him, especially since the funeral was held the day before his birthday.

The effect this had on the family was indescribable, devastating to say the least, emotionally it had ripped the family from its bowels, destabilising it to the core. They were all left scared and scarred, its scar going deeper than anyone had imagined. John, due to severe depression and loneliness hanged himself in the garage barely three months after Natasha's passing. He had planned it all so carefully and methodically. He had left all his affairs and will in order and two letters found at the bottom of the stairs, one to Chris and the other one to Jonas.

*My Dearest Chris,*

*I know that while you are reading this you are hurting and maybe you are hating me as well because of my actions, my intention was not to cause pain, I just want to free myself from this terrible pain.*

*Your mother was my soul mate, my saving angel. She came into my life and gave it meaning. She was the one that helped me achieve everything I have, but most importantly gave me the contentment that most of us look for and sometimes never find. She also gave me the two most wonderful sons. Both you and Jonas were a blessing*

*I am sorry that I am leaving you this way, but you and Jonas will have to complete this journey alone without me. I don't want to be a burden to you but I am also aware that there is no point continuing this alone. Your mum and I have brought you up to be the best, to fight for what is right and yours, to be honest, hardworking and above all loving.*

*In time I hope that you will find it in your heart to forgive me and to understand why I had to do this. Maybe one day you will feel the same for someone else, and if you do, then you are a lucky man. My life finished when your mother passed away, yours and Jonas is just beginning. Achieve all your dreams, and always be fair, don't let pride and arrogance blind you, which I know so far it never has. Most importantly, take care of Jonas, he is still young and impetuous, guide him and always be a family, don't let work rule your life.*

*I will always be with you and I am sure one day in the distant future we shall all meet again and be a family.*

*All my love,*

*Your loving dad XXX*

That was the event that hardened Chris, we all have one in our life that shape us in such a way that there is very seldom any return from it. He was suddenly scared of losing anyone again, anyone he loved. He adored his mum, her laughs, her cooking, her zany sense of humour, it matched his character. It had hurt him so bad and it still did, it left him desolate when she died, and now, losing his dad, the man that had taught him everything, how to cycle, play rugby, his dirty jokes (which his mum had disapproved of), his wisdom and guidance, it was all gone, it was too much to bear.

Who would have thought that at the age of 27, within 3 months him and his brother will be left orphans, alone? Whoever says that you feel only orphaned when you are a child is wrong, losing a parent, hurts at any age, it devastates you and leaves a sense if incredible loneliness.

For three months after this, Chris, went into severe depression, he hardly got out of bed for the first two weeks but he knew he could not keep this up, his company had given him one weeks leave and he took another one as a holiday, he now had to go back to work and he could not face it, see people giving him their condolences, so he ended up burying himself in work, not going out for lunch, avoiding seeing anyone. He did not want to know or accept reality; he did not want to see his surroundings, after all that would be accepting things.

Friends had asked him to see someone about it but he refused saying he could cope, that there was no question about him not getting over things.

Chris had been the one to find his father. He had been staying with his father that weekend as he had done for most weekends after his mother died and as usual had woken up at six thirty a.m. He had showered and gone down for coffee only to find two letters and the bottom of the stairs. He sensed straight away that something was wrong, the house was silent which was an unusual thing as his dad always got up early and went straight into the garden to pick up leaves and then have breakfast with Chris at around 8 a.m. It was now seven a.m. and the silence was deafening, not even the radio was on. He started opening the letter, but threw it halfway through, opening the front door and running to the front garden, screaming: "Dad, dad... no, please don't let it be true!" The next thing one of the neighbour's saw was Chris heading towards the garage, running with only his robe on, screaming like a crazed man.

It was seventy-year-old Clarisse Rutherford, a next-door neighbour that saw John hanging from the garage ceiling and Chris embracing him and crying loudly.

"Why? why did you have to do it? we would have worked things out. Why dad?

For her advanced aged, Clarisse had poise and standing, she was very old stock, stiff upper lip, her eyes showed kindness and pride at the same time.

She had been talking care of her beautiful garden, which had very matured and had the most unusual borders. Her favourite plants were her Agapanthus Headbourne Hybrids, the long stem carried a cluster of blue flowers, full of colour like pompons in the wind, she also had some Alacea Rosea Nigra, a holly hock whose cup shaped blooms were almost black. Clarisse liked her violets, blues and whites mixed with pinks, very much a cottage garden, her Achillea Stephanie Cohens were everywhere, rich pink filling the garden, such reliable perennials which so obviously favoured alongside her Allium Globemaster which has huge flower heads up to 9 inches big, made of tiny star shaped flowers.

When she saw Chris running towards the garage and had the unluckiness of witnessing such a sad event, she really felt for him. She had known John had been very depressed but had never imagined it would go as far as this.

As soon as she had seen John, she had gone into her house and dialled 999 asking for the police and the ambulance. She had then gone back out to the garage and held Chris's hand, whispering words of comfort and telling him that his dad was now in a very happy place, beside his mum.

Chris could not remember her words of comfort, he only had a vague feeling that Clarisse had been with him all day, making tea and then lunch, giving him the support only a neighbour like her could, after all, she knew him since childhood.

The police and ambulance had arrived barely five minutes later and had tried taking Chris into the house which had proved impossible, he kept holding his fathers' hand. He had stopped crying but was in a state of trance. The medics brought the body down and had repeatedly asked Chris to leave the scene, but he did not listen. The moment the noose is released, the body, through spasm released its bowels and urine. Chris was sure that if his dad had known this he would have never done it, then again, he was set on killing himself and was obviously not worried about what anyone else thought of him once gone

Chris remembered very little of the whole episode apart from embracing his father before they brought him down. He had for some reason a very clear picture of what his father had been wearing that day. It had been one of the first things he had noticed after realising he was dead. Chris felt the reason he remembers this so clearly was because of the clothes his father wore, his kilt, ghillie shirt, the whole Scottish apparel. An unusual thing to wear when you kill yourself, but I guess he was very proud of his roots and was in his own way saying to his sons, bury me this way or so they though, unless John believed that you appear in heaven the way you are dressed, which somehow sounds a little farfetched. One thing for sure is that John was not in his right mind, the depressing had left him a shell of him normal self. He was obviously not thinking straight, grief blinding him from everyone and everything.

A year later, Chris was back to his old self, with a difference, nobody could touch him emotionally; it seemed he had run out of emotions when his dad died.

He had never forgotten Clarisse's kindness; and would call her often and four times a year he would make sure to visit and take her out for lunch or dinner. He did this for four years until the day she died at 74. He felt he was losing everyone he loved, slowly, all the faces, smiles and smells that can sometimes help you remember someone, all the little details started becoming hazy, the only face that remained, vividly, smiling, always encouraging was his mothers. How much did he miss her, her strength and vitality. Life was so hard and unfair, he had loved all three of them and they were all gone now, Jonas was the last one left.

He sat there after he had received a call from Clarissa's youngest son Jakob, whom he knew well, to tell him the news. She had died peacefully in her sleep, it had happened at 11 p.m. at night, luckily when her oldest son Jonathan was visiting.

As Chris sat down in his flat after hearing the news, his mind started wondering, remembering his mum, how she cuddled him and Jonas all the time when they were kids, even when he was sixteen, Natasha Wandsworth had her own way of showing her two boys how much she loved them, she kissed and cuddled them telling them adorable nothings.

She would never embarrass the boys in public by cuddling them or kissing them but in private, she made sure their lives were filled with love, kisses and compliments as well as encouragement. God how he missed her, even when he had left home, he had made a point of always visiting her at least once a week, sometimes even staying overnight. He wanted to be home, yearned for home. He felt protected and loved. A feeling he had not felt in a very long time.

He had always enjoyed himself being with his parents, he watched rugby with his dad and helped his mum cook a roast for Sunday or sometimes just watched her. Natasha always made sure that her children's favourite dishes were done when they visited. Chris liked chocolate macaroons as nibbles whilst watching a game or floating island as dessert, whilst Jonas enjoyed Black Midnight cake or Danish Pastry and lots of custard.

Natasha was, in her children's mind, the best cook and baker in the world and she really enjoyed it and felt it was no effort for her to have lovely dishes made for her family. She also enjoyed eating what she cooked. She enjoyed having dinner parties and also organised some charity nights where she could sell her desserts to give to her favourite charity, cancer research. She also believed that if you were feeling down, the best way to cheer you up was to serve you some of her delicious food or dessert with some lovely wine.

Natasha was also good at listening, calm and non-judgmental, an empath with a code of when to walk away and not get involved. She could tell a mile away if someone was down or feeling out of place. She had a gift. She knew this life, this trial period on this earth was hard for everyone and firmly believed in 'live and let live', on the same token, she always believed that if we all did something, there was no reason for people to suffer. She was good Chris believe, not just an opinion of a son but someone that looked from the outside in, yes, Natasha was an Angel brought to this earth to help and ease the pain of this journey, and now she was gone along with his dad and Clarissa.

Only Jonas was left, Jonas, who needed him as much as ever.

Jonas was at last admitted into a clinic for detoxing in the USA. After John's death he went into decline, trying every drug possible, drinking all the time until he lost consciousness and not caring for the world, not even his brother.

He took a year out from his economics degree at the request of the Head of Department at his university who had also called Chris really worried thinking there was something seriously wrong with him. This was Jonas's saving grace as he would have died had it been otherwise.

It seemed that the one person Chris reacted to and cared for, beyond the call of duty was his little brother Jonas. As if his life depended on it he was determined to help Jonas get over his addiction. Chris had been aware that Jonas had been having problems like very mild depression however what he had been faced with when he saw him was something he had never imagined, it was beyond comprehension. Jonas had never touched drugs until his parents died, he was very anti them actually. With drinks, he would have one or two beers but never got himself paralytic. He had lost nearly three stones in weight, his hair was long, greasy and filthy, there were bits of something stuck on it, it was disgusting.

His body was emaciated, due to the abuse he had put it through with drugs, alcohol and lack of eating properly, his face gaunt with a blue/grey tint around his eyes and mouth. He looked old; his lips had lost its natural colour, as if he had put grey lipstick on. His nose was dribbling. Jonas looked like a corpse!

Chris was angry at himself for not having visited his brother lately, he only spoke to him once a week on the phone and he had always sounded as if things were okay, he felt awful, but neither of them had tried seeing each other is the last eight months, he should have known. He was after all the older one. When Chris saw him, he just hugged him, so hard, scared of losing him, tears in his eyes but not outwardly and loudly crying, a run of emotions taking over them.

"I am sorry Chris, I am so sorry" Jonas started crying, holding onto Chris as if he was about to slip into oblivion. "I swear to you, I don't know how it all happened, I lost control! I just missed them so much, I am scared, I hate this life, this fear, I miss mum and dad so much, I just don't I can cope." He was sobbing, barely holding Chris as his strength was ebbing. Jonas was so weak and now that it was all out in the open, he had finally relaxed and all emotions poured out of him, wanting only to be cared for by his older brother. Desperate to feel 'home' to feel 'loved'.

"It's OK Jonas, don't worry" Chris could hardly talk, it was as if his throat had suddenly dried, he was in shock, he did not want to lose his little brother as well. "We will sort it out, don't give up, we can do it together. I promise you2. His throat felt dried and painful. "I am so sorry I did not come sooner; I am so sorry."

Jonas was crying, sobbing, shacking violently, letting months of hurt and pain flow out of his system.

"I miss mum and dad. I am so lonely Chris, they meant everything to me." Jonas stated between gulps and sobs. "It is OK to be scared Jonas, I am. I don't like the idea of death, but life goes on, we have each other and for each other's sake we must be strong."

"I did not want to call you, I thought you might get annoyed, I thought I was being childish."

"Don't be stupid now" Chris said those words with tenderness on it, a loving telling off, still holding on to him, even though his voice was soft, his eyes were hard, annoyed that his little brother would think that. "We have each other, so we have to make sure we are both OK, do you understand?" He looked deep into Jonas' eyes, trying to see if he understood what he was saying. "Promise me that if anything bothers you from now on, you will talk to me, call me wherever you are, it does not matter the time or the place, I will be there for you, yes?"

"OK" It was hardly audible, more a whisper, one of relief, a sign that he understood, he wanted to understand.

They held each other for what seemed an eternity, but it was in fact seconds, seconds that changed their lives, they both realised it and cherished it, they each had someone to rely on, someone to help them and guide them, they were not alone, they had each other. The just made a new discovery, they had both been ill and both faced their 'illness' with bravery and courage, Chris his loneliness and Jonas his drug addiction. It was all going to be OK; they had found each other.

Chris was the one that decided to send Jonas to the USA for treatment of his addiction. He believed that the UK had very good institutions, but he wanted to make sure Jonas was away from his so-called friends, the pushers and those people who encouraged him to keep his habit. He also felt that it was best for him to be away from England, he needed to be away from the pain, from areas which constantly reminded him of his parents.

Jonas had spent all £250,000 of his inheritance and was about £10,000 in debt from loans which Chris had no option but to clear, he had also been served a notice of eviction for not paying rent for the last six months.

It had taken seven months of treatment for Jonas to be given the 'all clear' but he was to be supervised for at least the next twelve months to make sure that he did not have a relapse and went back to drugs. The doctors said he did not have to be a tea total but that under the circumstances it would be advisable, at least for the next 6 months or so, but if he wanted to drink, he could have only one-half pint in the evening and if he had any urges, he had to leave the pub or restaurant or just drink a soft drink.

Jonas moved in with Chris at his West End flat as a temporary arrangement for the next year or so.    He had also transferred universities so that he was based in London and was able to complete his degree which he did successfully.    This arrangement had not only proven good for Jonas, but it had done the world of good to Chris, who made an effort to come back home and prepare dinner or take Jonas out for a meal and/or the cinema.    It was a re-discovery trip which they both deep down longed for and made them closer to each other than they have ever been.    They had lost their parents, but they still had a family, they were still a family and this was their home.

Jonas's graduation took place two years after coming back from the States, he was now cleared and ready to face the world on his own, in the knowledge that Chris was always there, and vice versa, he was there for him as well.    He got a job with an insurance company and moved three blocks away from Chris.    The flat he bought was with the help of a mortgage as he would not allow Chris to help him financially anymore, he would make it himself, he knew he could and would.    It had been his fault that he lost all his inheritance, he would get it back, he would make it up.    Hopefully his parents were watching how he turned his life around, he will not let them down again.

"Well, what do you think?"    Jonas showed the flat to Chris, "I know it is small, but it is all I can afford and need for the time being."    By the way Jonas kept opening and closing drawers, showing them to Chris, you could tell he was proud, at last he was doing it himself and even though it was a very small way of starting, it was a start.    He was beginning to be happy, content with his lot and realised that he had not lost everything, he had his brother forever.

"Why don't we go out for a meal to celebrate, get some champagne and maybe after that go to a late movie" Chris was happy, he felt comfortable with his brother, with whom he was close even though four years separated them. There had never been any animosity or competition between them, which is how things should be.

# Tanya

Tanya had known Liz for five years at least whilst they worked together as permanent employees for a large software house. They had hit it off straight away, liked each other's character and sense of humour, or lack of it, as Liz could only laugh at her own jokes and most of the time people had to explain jokes two or three times before she got the punch line. It did not bother either of them that nobody understood them or had their particular sense of humour, they thought it was funny and that was all that mattered. They clicked.

It was after eighteen months at this company that they both decided to give contracting a try, their drive was money, they both felt that they really did not enjoy work very much, that they only did it to get decent money in. Both being perfectionists, meant they were generally successful in their field, they were methodically and very time conscious, so project management was their ideal job. Liz had already been a project manager when she met Tanya and she had convinced Tanya that she had the right attributes to be one, a good one.

Liz would say that Tanya was her best friend alongside Charlotte. They were completely different, Charlotte was crazy in a funny way, she would always do what she wanted, a free spirit with a conscience. She was very softly spoken, well brought up, she was your idea of a posh hippy yummy mummy. Tanya on the other hand was very elegant, business-like kind of way, fun and formal mixed together, she knew how to enjoy herself, but she remained reserved to a degree until she got to know you. She was shy but not when it came to business, when extremely assertive, cool headed, she had to be. Her 'problem' came when it was to do with meeting people in a personal level, always having her guard up and only the ones she got on very well eventually got to know the real Tanya, the fun, crazy but on control woman. A kind and warm individual with so much to give.

Tanya was extremely beautiful in an exotic way. Her parents were settlers from the Caribbean, her dad was black, tall and well build, her mum was a mixture of white with Chinese, petite with beautiful green eyes and very slender figure, the kind you generally achieve with a lot of work.

Tanya had taken the height from her dad, her skin was a dark olive colour, her eyes were a deep green, like her mums and her body was slender and curvy. The hours working at the gym had paid off as well as having inherited amazing genes, her stomach was flat and her bum firm and perky, no trace of cellulite or fat. She was two years older than Liz when they met. Tanya had thought Liz was very shy like her, but when she got to know her, she found a very funny and warm person within her with a very special sense of humour, her kind! They both had a wicked sense of humour, they both joked and called names to each other, when they just had each other as their audience, their attitude and guard went down. Always making a point of sitting down and having wine twice a week and would talk about anything and everything under the sun, resolving the world's problems in a few hours. Their conversation always ended with them laughing so laud and sometimes falling of the sofa, hoping that nobody from the flat below could hear them.

Tanya and Liz had shared a flat for two years now having met three years previous to that. Tanya had met Damien a year ago and of course as soon as she met Damien things had started changing which for Liz was fine, sad but she knew things had to move on and evolve, time did not stand still. She loved her friend and wanted the best for her.

They started making time for their friendship once every two weeks. The rest of the time they either spent it either with Damien or coming and going meeting each other in the corridor of the flat as sometimes Tanya spent it at Damien's.

Damien was a charming guy, easy to be around and of course it made her friend very happy. More often than not, he would do the cooking and always leave a portion for Liz as he knew she sometimes came back from work around 10 p.m. This was something that both Liz and Tanya appreciated as neither was a good cook, yes, they could survive but the nice stuff was usually produced by Damien, who enjoyed cooking a lot of French and Asian food.

Fridays with grilled Asian chicken was their favourite full of garlic, ginger and honey, sprinkled with lots of sesame seeds and plenty of soy sauce. Sundays it was a little less heavy and generally smaller portions with a side salad, which was Liz's job. It was the one thing that Liz enjoying, cutting all the veggies and mixing them all into one bowl and adding bits of pomegranate or grapefruit and lots and lots of green or black olives.

If it was a 'lucky' day then Tanya would surprise everyone with dessert, something easy to make like Eton mess or chocolate macaroons and sometimes she would push the boat out with floating islands or apple crumble. It did not always happen but when it did it was a feast. Everyone had something to give and offer and was received and accepted with friendliness and no assumption it would happen again.

"Tanya, Tanya, the oven!!!" Shouted Liz.

Tanya's baking was fantastic, it relaxed her, the aroma lingering across the flat, it reminded her of her childhood, her mum had been a wonderful mother and friend, never judgemental and always full of praise for her and her brother, she had created the perfect life for them and loved cooking, for her, a housewife had a duty and one of the tasks was to create the perfect home, full of love and care, it made you want to say home and not leave. She loved baking; she was always baking. Every day had a dessert. Chocolate pudding being a common one at home.

"Shit" Tanya was annoyed with herself. "I can't believe it has burned already; this is the second time in as many days." She started laughing, as was expected. One thing Tanya was good at was forgetting, she put something in the oven and then started watching programme or reading a book or just started nattering without a care in the world, forgetting she needed to look after the baking.

"Girls, what is going on." Damien had shouted from the living room, asking a question of which he knew the answer straight away. "Are you two not concentrating again?"

"It is OK." Shouted Liz. "It is just a slight accident" She lied, winking at Tanya. The giggles that came from the kitchen a mixture of laughter and the intoxicating effect of wine, making them laugh more than the occasion warranted. Damien shrugged his shoulders as he sat on the sofa, he knew it was one of those 'you had to be there to understand the funny side', or at least you had to have had three glasses of wine at least.

Tanya and Liz had both drunk a bottle of wine on an empty stomach. It was already six in the evening and they had decided to leave Damien watching television, enjoy his Sport, whilst they tried their hand at baking. Liz watching and chatting whilst Tanya did the hard work.

One must have thought that something simple would have worked treat, but the girls were too drunk for that. The chocolate biscuits in the oven, Liz's favourites, were burnt as the girls forgot all about them being in the oven and talked and tried floating islands which without them noticing had already turned to scrambled egg.

"I have not had this much fun in ages Liz" Muttered Tanya, a big grin on her face, feeling as if she was back at being 10 years old "We seem to work all the time, I forgotten what it is like to have fun, it had been ages."

"Yes, isn't funny", Liz voiced, more a whisper, we have forgotten for a while to have fun. Life seems to have become too serious" Her eyes were looking down at the wine, her eyes focused, a crinkle had appeared between her eyes, concentrating, as if a fly or a bug had fallen on it and was desperately trying to climb out of the glass. "The older we get the more we question why we are doing certain things rather than concentrate on what makes us happy and feel good." Liz's eyes were trying to focus, how on earth did three glasses of red wine had made her so drunk and she was still standing? She did not have a drinker's stomach, could never hold more than two glasses and that only when her stomach was fully lined with some greasy take away like fish and chips or kebab from the corner shop.

Tanya had just finished opening the second bottle of wine, red again, a Gevrey Chambertin 1998. She had already opened it not bothering to ask Liz if she wanted some, just assuming it would go down well. She refilled the glasses, letting her friend continue talking, not worrying about the fact that this indeed was an excellent burgundy, they were too drunk to appreciate it.

"You know Tanya, I think we need to inject more fun into our lives, we have become a bit stale, don't you think so?" Without waiting for an answer, Liz's continued as one would when to drunk. "Let's try and do this more often, you know, baking, maybe gardening next time or let's just learn how to do an oil painting." As she talked, she pressed the CD repeat button for the song to start again for the 5th time Faith Hill: 'It Matters to Me'. Liz was the only person Tanya knew that would play her favourite music again and again, it drove people mad and it drove Tanya mad but she was drunk and was oblivious to how many times the song had been played.

Damien, drinking his beer in the living room, was trying to ignore them but it was starting to prove impossible. Only women could play one song so many times and still think it was wonderful, it was doing his head in. He could actually hardly hear the music or their drunken conversation but because he had already noticed it in the background, he found it impossible to ignore it. It was bothering him like a niggle at the back of his mind and now of course the whole house smelled to burnt biscuits. Usually, he would be desperate for the biscuits to be ready, Tanya was an exceptional baker but when drunk, her mind was just not in it.

He tried sitting right back on the sofa, his head back, looking at the ceiling and closing his eyes, listening to the television in the background, he opened his eyes when he heard the crowd roar, a goal, only to realise it was the opposite team that had scored. He had been following his favourite team, Chelsea, for years, he wanted them to win but it was proving harder and harder each time and then

165

out of the blue they scored, he was screaming, jumping up and down, suddenly forgetting his annoyance with the girls, unaware that the whole room had become smoky, and it stank of burnt.

He was in a high, that day they ordered a takeaway and had burnt biscuits, beer and wine. It was a short evening, Tanya and Liz were drunk they were fast asleep by 9 p.m. which mean Damien could watch the re-runs quietly and not being bothered. Total and utter bliss.

At the next day, grateful that it was Sunday, nobody other than Damien was up, Liz made an appearance at 11 a.m. feeling as if she had not slept and her head hurting as if a lorry had run over her. Tanya on the other hand, woke up at midday as if she had the most wonderful sleep ever. Damien had not only been up at six in the morning, but had gone for a jog, showered, had breakfast and was already halfway through the newspapers.

"Well, you are up at last Tanya, I thought you had died." muttered Damien a pretend angry tone but smiling as if he had won the lottery. His beautiful smiling eyes were shinning, showing how much he loved her, with just one year of going out together he already knew she was the one for him, a keeper as they say, he had known the day he had met her, after all he had dated enough women to know the difference between lust and love and this was it, he knew it.

Tanya had picked up the toast with honey that Damien had made, still half awake and half asleep, sleepy eyes barely opening, her hair all over, sexy curls in front of her face which she blew away with a puff.

Liz had already gone swimming with a friend, the house was quiet and there was an air of anticipation in it, suspense, Tanya could not quite put her finger on it, maybe it was the half smile that Damien had on his face or the fact that she was still under the influence of alcohol from the night before.

Today was their first anniversary together; she had a sip of coffee and bit another piece of toast that had butter and strawberry jam, her favourite. As she did that, she noticed something shiny sticking on it, something she had not noticed the first time she bit the toast and panicked thinking it was a piece of glass. Shock in her face, full of various expressions from panic, surprise, smiling and finally understanding as the realisation sank in, a beautiful emerald ring was sticking from the toast, the actual platinum part of the ring was buried in the toast, its head sticking out of the jam, the green shinning surrounded by red and she could only see the stone, her eyes homing like a seagull eyeing a fish in the sea. The cabochon cut stone was surrounded by 8 lovely small diamonds, she must be dreaming!

"Oh my God, oh my God!" Tanya started crying, the toast had fallen on the table missing the plate, crumbs scattered all over the place, toast right side up. Her hands were covering her face, the ring in her little pinkie finger, holding it with the tip of her French manicured nails. There was so much shock and emotion on her face, her eyes were the size of giant saucers, tears streaming down, she had got up and cuddled Damien "If it is what I am thinking, the answer is yes, yes, and as soon as possible."

Tanya was shrieking with excitement, this was an amazing day, best day ever! Damien kissed her full on the lips, savouring coffee and sleep and the remnants of alcohol, his love for this woman who was a mixture of shy, extrovert, confident in some things and insecure in others "I hope the stone is to your liking my dear." Damien was smiling, knowing fine well that having been born on the 15th of May, her stone was the Emerald, he also knew she loved platinum and diamonds. He had initially wanted to add some blue sapphires but decided against it, he felt it was too much. He wanted simple elegance, just like Tanya.

"I love it, it is so beautiful, I must say I have never seen an Emerald this size before." Her eyes still watery with emotion, her mouth open, still surprised "I love you; this is so sweet." She kept placing the ring on her finger and taking it out, like trying to convince herself this was not a dream, it was real, something physical, tangible, she was not in an alcohol induced state.

"I am so glad you said yes," whispered Damien, scared to break the moment, savouring all that it was, ensuring that this moment was recorded in his memory forever. "Otherwise I would have had to take you back to the bedroom and subjected you to various titillating positions until you said yes, then again, I could always make up an excuse to do that anyway." His beautiful smile lighting up his whole face. Damien did not recall any other time when he was as happy as he was today, he truly felt he had found his soul mate, his love and companion forever, he was grateful, very grateful. His parents had been lucky for a short while, his dad died very young, but he had peaceful thoughts as he knew his dad had been a happy man and he always wanted to make sure that if this happened to him, that God will at least give him the grace to allow him to meet his true love.

"I love you" Tanya was already in another world, daydreaming, her big day, kids, grandchildren, houses, baby rooms, as usual, she was way ahead of time, but she did not care, she was happy, light years away from reality, she was dying to tell Liz.

"I wonder," she thought to herself. "If Liz knew already, if Damien had told her or if she had guessed it?." Liz was good at guessing if something was going on or about to happen, especially if it was good news, she could pick up on the good vibes. Sometimes her amazing friend could appear to have psychic thoughts or just an amazing and well-tuned sixth sense. Regardless, she was going to text Liz and tell her the good news.

They would be married in 2004, in the summer. Damien had said, June or July, her pick.

Tanya was already dreaming of wearing the beautiful Ivory wedding dress she had designed years ago. The dress was long, with Mother of Pearl buttons from the top of the back of the neck all the way down to the lower back. The train, which was part of the dress, was a very light embroidered piece with beautiful tiny river pearls on the edges. There was no veil, she hated veils, they hid all your emotions, she just wanted a dress, something that highlighted her colour and he figure, something simple but elegant.

Her mum's friend Vivien Sheridan was a dress maker she could retouch the design and make her the dress, this way, it will be exactly what she wanted and not too expensive. Vivien could have been a designer, she had talent, she oozed of it, but unfortunately, she was not motivated enough. Her favourite word was: "I can't be bothered", however, to get her by and for a very small and reasonable price, she produced amazing designs and dressed for friends. These designs were accurate, the stitching and cut were of a high standard, as if the gowns had been produced in Paris or Milan.

"You shall be my matron of honour." She said to Liz in a regal sort of way with her eyes shining with excitement "You must." Tanya was holding Liz's arms as if scared in case her friend disappeared or run away or just gave her a plain "No."

"I can't Tanya, I would love to, but tradition states the Matron of Honour must be married. I can be your Chief Bridesmaid if you want to?" She could see disappointment appearing on her friend's face, her downward lips showing. She quickly took a sip of the gorgeously delicious Drappier Champagne they had bought to celebrate.

"Who cares about tradition Lizzie, let's just make our own rules, I hate it when rules stop us having all this fun."

Damien was out and the girls took advantage of it and started designing and planning, the whole wedding, from who was coming to where people were sitting, the venue and the food. It was obvious that poor Damien was going to have little to do with it, and he did not seem to mind, in fact, he was quite relieved of it, he hated all of it, all he wanted to do is get married, he did not want to be part of the planning, he just wanted Tanya to be his, officially. He wanted the world to know she was his woman. Tanya had been on the phone all afternoon, she had been so excited, planning and talking to as many people as she could, spreading the good news., her excitement being contagious, everyone was texting or calling, offering help and ideas.

"I told you I was going to go down the aisle before you cow!" Tanya was laughing, her voice was coarse with so much talking and of course by then she had drunk nearly three glasses of Champagne.

"Hey, watch it, I have not given up yet, you never know, I could meet someone out of the blue, someone wonderful, rich, gorgeous and romantic, just when we think it will not happen, so until you have said I do, I don't think you should write me off just yet, you bitch!" The whole evening continued like this, in between jokes and serious wedding talk and coming to an agreement of Liz being the chief bridesmaid.

"Men don't marry just like that Liz." Tanya looked serious, considering what Liz had just said, men need time to think, rethink and rethink the rethink, they are scared of commitment, so even if you want to convince yourself that you may find Mr Right and he may want to marry you before I get married, I think the odds are stacked very much against you." Tanya wanted Liz to marry, find her soul mate like she did but she was aware that the reality of life was different and on top of this Liz was very careful, too careful. She had heard of the Tim period and was aware he had hurt Liz, but time had healed her heart and even though she had relayed the event o her, the hurt had gone, buried itself and leaving a scare in her heart. She knew her friend too well, she was not going to give her heart away that easily.

"Rubbish, I dare you someone marries me before you." Liz put the challenge back on the table, very aware that she was speaking a load of rubbish, not really believing that someone would meet and marry her that quickly, especially since she was so fuzzy about men. Tanya was right, once bitten twice shy and in her case three times shy!

"Well, said Tanya "you sound so confident, I guess you will not object to me making it into a bet of let us say £1,000 pounds?" She was having fun, her voice wavering a little bit, Liz was beautiful, and men did want her, the problem was her, she was too fussy, so hopefully she will keep being fussy for a little bit longer.

"I could do with £1000 for my wedding you know, my shoes alone may cost that at this rate."

"OK, we are on!" Liz knew that she will very much loose the bet, men found her threatening and those she let into her world, were generally strictly friends "Maybe we should just make it £100? What do you think?

"Oh!" Tanya said, her voice laden with sarcasm. "Not confident at all Lizzie dear, worried about losing? Maybe I should just claim victory now?"

"Listen you silly bitch, I know I can win, so it is on £1000 that I marry before you! I will win, I was just being kind to you as I know you really wanted to get married first, but now I don't care. Bet is on! And considering I will be winning; the position of Matron of Honour is now filled!

"Now, on an important note and moving swiftly away from the subject," Liz's voice turned serious, "let's talk about your dress and the bridesmaid's dresses, are both of them going to be empire line? I am not sure if that style would suit me. You would look amazing on it, but my figure will need a different design."

"Sure, I want you to be comfortable. Why don't we go through different designs and if you find something that will suit you better, so long as you stick to the colour I want, I am fine."

# Brotherly Love - Luke

Luke was four years younger than Liz, a very happy, go lucky and easy-going boy. Liz had always felt responsible for him, as the older sister, she wanted to shield him from the bad things that happened in the world, not realising that her brother was more than capable of understanding and taking care of himself quite well. This was the usual and typical mistake most older siblings make, generally unaware they are doing it, but nevertheless annoying and disruptive.

As usual and like most older siblings, Liz had underestimated her younger brother. He was more than capable than she gave him dues for. When their dad died, Liz tried to over protect him but to her surprise, he dealt with it with calmness and maturity that was a total shock and surprise, he worried more about the wellbeing of his mum, who he realised had lost the love of her life, he knew he will be OK in the long run, he would miss is dad and adored him but he also knew he had to move on, he was young and there was a life ahead of him that he could not dismiss or push aside, he had no choice but to harden up and help his devastated mum.

He knew Liz was going to see Charlotte a lot for support, exhausted from being a shoulder to their mum on a daily basis, a drain to anyone in particular a teenager and knew women tended to rely more on women. He knew, understood and sensed as a brother, Liz was getting emotionally and physically tired. Because of all of this going around, unlike a normal teenager, he promised himself he was never going to be a problem to his mum or sister, he will make a monumental effort to make their daily lives easier and if one less worry would help, he made sure he was not the cause of one.

He had promised his dad, in one of those weird conversations that happen once in a lifetime that if anything happened to him, he would make sure he was good to his mum and sister, he would be supportive. He may not have been able to contribute financially or emotionally, but he would by being good, and that is what he did, he was exceptionally good, some say, too good and everyone worried that as a teenager he should have some scrapes here and there, but he did not, and he certainly did not mind missing on them.

Life had been good as far as he could remember, other than his dad passing away, he had what some people considered a 'happy' childhood. It had been sad at times, especially if he fancied someone and they were not interested in him but generally life was very good to him, his step-dad was a good man, a nice, quiet man, but nothing could replace his dad, his hilarious and contagious laughter, his interested look when someone talked to him, his love of life and his step dad knew that and did not mind that, he knew what was not to have a dad and realised that Luke should treasure and protect those memories of his dad as much as possible.

He hated and annoyed him the fact that some people believed that just because you marry into a readymade family that you have the right to force the children to call you mum or dad.

People forget that these children have a mum and dad; just because someone is divorced or they died, it does not mean they did not have a parent. Today's modern world assumes that a child should be emotionally free and accept the 'new' stepparent and called them mum or dad, which is wrong, these children have or had a parent and that should be respected and never be denied their history, their link and their connection to the being that they recognised as their 'original' parent. We all have emotions, and we cannot erase them just to please someone else's insecurity or worse still, to please society which more and more has become conformist to the liberal ideology of what 'they' consider acceptable. A difficult or insecure step mum or stepdad thinks that by trying to call themselves mum or dad will get them the respect they deserve or mark their authority, it does not, it creates hatred and resentment, it should not be forced upon.

In his mind and as far as Luke was concerned, his stepdad will always be that a kind man but definitely just a 'step'. He recognised him as an authority, same as his mum, but he was not his dad and the good thing is, this was understood and accepted and contributed to a good, happy environment.

He remembered Liz and his mum quite well when his dad died, they both went into shock for around two years, they did not realise this of course as it was their coping mechanism that had kicked in and Luke was sure he must acted oddly or at least become withdrawn to a degree, but nobody mentioned anything, everyone tip toed around him. His mum went into severe depression, she had lost nearly 12 kilos and was looking very pale and gaunt, grey around her eyes were now her signature, the light had stopped shinning in her, she was hardly sleeping and was prescribed antidepressants within two months of her husband's death.

Night times make everything worse exponentially, initially, to help, Luke slept a lot with his mum, he and Lizzie took turns, not to try and force her to sleep, as they knew she was awake, but more to keep her company, chat to her if she needed a chat, reduce her anxiety. It worked both ways and was therapeutic to all. Night times tend to be the worse time and they both thought talking, if she wanted to, would help or maybe not, the important thing is they were there for her and for each other, supporting everyone, like one unit!

They were both so worried about their mum; they were scared in case they lost her too, he knew neither of them would cope losing her as well, it would be too much. They hoped God would not be this cruel to them, it could not happen, they prayed, never telling the other their fears about her but each knew, they were scared, their eyes showed it, their paleness, gauntness that surround them each of them for the next two years and two a degree, never lifted of him.

At only 13, he was quite a mature little boy, he would watch his mum sleep, comb her hair, cuddle her as much as possible as he knew she needed that, kiss her when she was asleep. He really missed his dad, his laughter and even temper; he very seldom worried and was always down to earth. He missed going to the rugby games with him, it had only been a year, but he felt the lack of his presence, he could not understand why he had been taken, at such a young age, it was not fair. He was angry, quietly angry at home for having taken his dad away from him and making his mum and sister so unhappy. He wanted to scream and tell the whole world he was angry, but he knew he could not, it would only worry and upset his mum more, he had to behave. In a way to was good he had made that promise, otherwise, he knew he could easily have gone off the rails.

He remembered at weekends he would go and play rugby, he would ask his mum to go with him and stay, he wanted her to watch him, not only because he wanted a parent to be present like the other kids, but he wanted to be near his mum. He was scared in case he went to play rugby and came back home to her having done some harm to herself. This way, he kept an eye on her, felt as if he had someone there who loved watching him play rugby and his sister had a break, a time to recharge her batteries. It was through this weekly routine that Bethan got to know Keith Certes, Luke's rugby coach and as far as Luke was concerned, a God-send. Even though he felt his mum only belonged to his dad, he knew that something had to be done to restore her life, even if it was just friendship.

Keith was a funny character, old in attitude, outlook and mannerism; he was only 50 going on 60. He owned his own software house in Edinburgh, had lived there all his life and enjoyed it but had now decided to give something back, he left the fast life behind and decided to do something for the community and since rugby was one of his passions, he decided this would be the way to give back and went for it head on teaching it at weekends at his local rugby club.

Bethan and Keith slowly got to know each other and within three years of first meeting, they were a proper item, marrying five years later to the delight of her children, who felt it was about time their mum had some happiness. Luke was then 18 and ready to go to university and Liz was twenty-two.

Both of them have been pleased with their mum. Luke, in particular, as he got to know Keith quite well and realised that his mum could not give up sharing a life with someone at the age of 36, she was far too young when his dad had died. He was also always aware that him and Liz would not always be around.

Keith also assured both kids that he was only a friend and not their dad and they were very proud of their mother when she became Bethan Stanton Certes, she had kept Samuel Stanton's name in his memory and to honour their brief life together. That made Liz and Luke happy, they did not want all of him erased, they wanted him there, present in one way or another, sharing in their mother's happiness a second time round and sure that he would be happy his wife had found some happiness.

God, he missed his dad. When his was sixteen, his first love, proper love, his first stab at sex, he had nobody to talk to about it. He knew he could have counted in his dad, but he was not there and he was not close enough to Keith to share this or ask things, not that he had anything really to ask but he could have done with a father-and-son chat. Regardless how close we are to someone else; nobody replaces a parent or the void a parent would leave if absent.

Everyone imagines someone else can, in time fill that gap, but the reality is that this very seldom happens, we all romanticise what we believed would have been if that person had not been absent and nobody and nothing is there to validate or crush this presumption. Our reality is the belief that things would have been different, better, simpler, easier if the absent parent would not have been gone.

He remembered that period of his life so clearly, etched in his mind, not as painful but as a funny, fanciful period in his life when everything was confusing, blurred. Looking back, he remembered everything even though then he was confused and sad. He looked at it as if he was someone else, detached, looking to a film of himself.

Carly was her name, she had just started at their school, she was six months younger than him and was hot, oh yes, so hot everyone wanted to be the lucky one, he remembered so clearly, how both of them looked, how odd it was, it had only lasted 3 months but it felt like a lifetime and he felt crushed when it was over, over and moving on to the next, Carly, beautiful and sexy Carly.

She had been at the school barely three months when a group assignment had been due, Jonathan Stewart, one of this mates, decided the best place for this to take place is for all of them in the group to go to his house and when the time was right, we could all leave but Carly, he had it all planned, had voiced his interest first in her so none of them could say they fancied her, but Luke knew, he knew everyone wanted her, they had, three of his mates confided in him.

They had left the house two hours after they had arrived, the assignment finished with him having the task of typing it up, which he accepted, after all, at least he could make sure it would be done. They had all left, leaving Carly in the clutches of Jonathan. They had all taken their bikes, so there was no excuse of giving anyone a lift.

He had arrived back home, straight upstairs to his computer, hardly able to contain himself, he had to have a distraction, fast, he could not concentrate. He was amazed nobody noticed his permanent erection which seemed to happen every time he saw her or thought of her, what a dammed nuisance, why did God have to give us uncontrollable penises when we are young! He decided he will get rid of his frustration and went for the toilet, his mum and Keith were out, and Liz was at university, so the house was all his. In his mind he had her in every position possible, which as a virgin he had never tried in real life, but who cared, he had fun, it is a shame it was not the real thing, wondering how she would feel, his hands on her breast, firm small breast that drive every guy in the class crazy.

Shit! He noticed he had semen everywhere and the doorbell just rang. He was desperate, he had to clean himself fast, was rushing to get a towel, clean himself up, compose himself, shouting "Two secs, be right there!"

Breathless he opened the door, feeling as if he had run a marathon, exhausted, his heart racing like crazy, even more so when he realised who was standing there.

"Carly! What?" He stuttered. "What are you doing here?" He sounded like an idiot he thought, an idiot caught in the act. "I thought you decided to stay with Jonathan for a while?" Did he sound curios? He hoped not, shit, he was acting weird, he was sweating.

"I kind of left soon after you, I wanted to speak to you" Her beautiful melodic voice playing with his mind, her eyes were staring at him, she was flirting, she knew what she was doing but then Luke did not pick up on it. "I wanted to come with you, but it was kind of awkward with Jonathan, so I left after, he thinks I am back at my mum's".

She was staring at him, her mouth so close, oh she knew fine well what she was doing, Luke did not realise that he did not have any hope in escaping, not that he wanted but had he been an unwilling victim, he would not have been able to save himself.

"What? Sorry I was thinking. What did you say?" He said flustered, blood rushing to his face and head, his hands in his pocket, trying to conceal a new erection that was fast becoming too big to hide.

"I said may I come in?" Her eyes were laughing, she knew, oh God, she is laughing at me he thought.

"Yes sure" The words came out shyly, as if he was being taken to be questioned by his mother over an incident, and then he felt it, as soon as the door close, she was kissing him.

His mind went blank at that point, his arms incontrollable, touching, pooling, like a naïve boy that he was, feeling the win, yes, she wanted him, not Jonathan, not anyone but him. He let her feel him, was not ashamed now, they were all over each other, pushing, savouring, going crazy.

"Mum is not here" He muttered in between kisses. "We can go to my room if you want, or we can stay here?"

"Here is fine" Her eyes were laughing, she knew she had won; he was hers, just as she had planned it. Luke was so young an inexperienced, he had not realised how hot he was, how good locking and what a gorgeous body he had, he was lovely she thought, she had liked him from the start, from the moment she walked into the class, she had picked him. She kind of knew he was a virgin; he was also very shy and was at the age that everything was awkward.

"I got condoms if you want." she said, as if it was the most normal thing in the world, a statement that made his eyes flicker, too quickly for her to register, he was surprised but at this point did not care, he wanted her and it was being served in a plate, this was great.

"Yes," he said, "Are you sure?" Why did he say that? he told himself to shut up, he did not want to put any doubt in her head, not that she would have any, he did not realise it was him that had been hunted, not her, she knew what she wanted, she had come to get it and unless he was a very strong character, he would not say no.

The sex had been great, clumsy but great and he remembered it clearly, they had made love four times that day in the living room and then hid in his room with the pretext that they were typing the assignment. He was over the moon, he was not a virgin and had got 'the' girl, he felt like a superhero, a million pounds, he felt in heaven. If it could just had lasted a little bit longer, or at least ling enough to understand what had happened.

They dated for three months, maybe three and a half, he could not remember, he just remembered coming to school one day, everyone looking at him funny, as if feeling sorry for him, especially the girls, they looked at him with a hint of embarrassment, pitied him, the last person to know. He knew something was up but could not put his finger on it until it was in front of him, Carly had decided she wanted a new model, a new toy, "Jonathan." He was angry, he had sussed her out a month into their 'relationship' that she was a 'go getter', she did not care who or what was in the way, all obstacles were removed, she targeted her prey and went for it, but he never thought he would do it to him. They were just standing there, holding hands, Jonathan had not realised Luke had arrived at the school, so his face registered shock when Luke saw them and tried to jerk his hand off her, only to be glared by her, too late, Luke had seen it.

As far as he was concerned, this was the incident that lost his faith in women but in particular because it was a friend that did this to him, someone he considered a close friend, whom he respected. Men did not do this to each other, there was a rule, male friends did not 'shit on their friends' turf." Just the night before, him and Carly had made love, it was the usual and she appeared to be in love, however he had learned since then that is one of the easiest thing's women can fake on top of orgasms and a list of other things. Yes, Luke the cynic was born that day.

Jonathan had been sorry, he was desperate to make amends, but Luke never forgave or forgot what had happened, what is the point? They did it once they will do it again. It was the end of a friendship and the beginning of a 'new' him, deciding he would only have fun from now on, he promised himself that this was to be the last time he will give in to any fancy such as being in love, his parents had been but that was it, it was his parents and as far as he was concerned perfect love very seldom happened and he doubted it would to him.

Luke kept to his word, he never caused any problems to his mum and sister and got on extremely well with Keith that there was never a problem there. He did extremely well as a student and sportsman, so good that he went to study journalism at Napier University and became involved with the Students' Union where everyone knew who he was.

After graduating he decided to concentrate on his first love, Rugby. Sadly, due to a severe back injury he had to give up the sport he loved and had to retire from the game at only 25, however, his passion continued and watched from the bench as much as possible. Eventually he became a freelance Sports Journalist, a hobby more than a job, as sport was his passion. He liked any sport, the human spirit, the passion, the resilience of individuals drive to win, to sweat blood and years of effort and training for a medal, a cup, the glory of being crowned a winner and recognition that you have achieved the top. He loved all that, the smell of sweat, the hard labour performed by muscles pushed to the edge, probably wrongly but determinedly.

# Mother's Love

*There is no denying, there is no love so honest
and real as that of a mother*

Sitting in her flat back in London, it was raining, Liz had nothing to do or more to the point, she was not in the mood to do anything and Tanya was out.

Her second glass of red wine must have slowly been affecting her senses; sadness started filling her whole being as she remembered what it was like before her dad passed away. She had been 17 when he died, he was only 52 years old, a young man by all accounts, full of life and conviction, always encouraging her, making her want to achieve all her dreams, telling her that everything that she wanted and dreamed of could be a reality of she worked hard. He always reminded her though that money and success was not everything, she had to be happy with life and the only way to fully achieve that is through love and respect.

We had such a happy family, most people would not believe Liz if she said how happy they were, as it seemed almost unreal. Liz's mum was the unifier of the family, she held everything together, showered them with love, hugs and kisses. She was so affectionate, it was great. She used to chase the kids around the house saying she wanted to give them a big sloppy kiss. Of course, they used to run and run until she caught up with them. Luke was always giggling everywhere they went; mum would make faces at them or make us laugh when we needed to be serious. She could always bring some humour and lightness to a serious situation and of course, the fact that their dad adored their mum and them, made the whole environment a happy one.

Of course, there were some tense moments when both, Luke and Liz did know things were not quite all right. They had overheard whispers late at night, where I would hear their mums voice, trembling with stress, worried of the future and their dad trying his best to reassure her. Both their words laced with fear, one for fear of losing it all and the other fearing the assurances were nothing but a thin plaster on a bigger wound.

It only happened a couple of times and as a child neither Liz nor Luke, who was younger than her, did not understand what it was about but Liz knew it was bad as mum never worried for just something trivial, it had to be major, something very bad.

"Mum?" Liz asked, it was 7 in the morning and they were all getting ready for the school run.

"Yes sweetie." Her mum looked cheery, as if last night never happened; Liz wondered if she had dreamed it. After all, she did not know what exactly her parents had been talking about.

"Is everything OK? I have heard you and dad talking last night and you sounded so worried and upset". The last words came out more as a whisper, she was embarrassed and was not sure if her mum would be upset for her asking.

Bethan, as Liz's mum was called, did not believe in lying to a child. White lies to protect, maybe, but this was too big for a lie plus if she heard something that meant she knew she was being lied to and it would destroy the trust and love they shared. She was only 9 years old but mature for her years, she deserved the truth.

"Sit down Liz, I am going to have to be quick and brief as dad and I have to take you and Luke to school, however, when you come back home later on today, we can have a longer chat. Saying that, I don't think Luke ought to know, he is too little and might end up worrying unnecessarily."

"Do you know what an embezzlement is?"

"No" Replied Liz wondering what that had to do with mum and dad being worried.

"Well, it is when someone has taken money illegally; in this case, someone has taken money from a company illegally. As you know your daddy is a lawyer, one of the best if I may say so and he has had his practice for nearly 25 years which he has shared with Uncle Richard who was a friend. Unfortunately, because of this we are going to have to tighten our belts a little bit and watch the pennies. It means not going on holiday abroad, unless it is camping in France and it also means I might have to get a job myself."

Liz never picked up on 'was a friend'; she was more concerned with the fact that it sounded as if they were broke. Like any child, she was worried, what will her friends think of them, was her first thought?

"Also, Lizzie, people may talk about your dad and Uncle Richard and I want you to know your dad did not do anything wrong. The embezzlement was done by Uncle Richard, who you may have to point out to people, is not really related to us." Bethan knew children could and would be cruel, they never measure their words or worried that there may be an explanation for things, they just went, invertedly for the kill.

"What are you saying mum, what has exactly happened? "Liz's frown was a clear statement that she could not believe what she was hearing that kind man, one of dad's best friend had done us so inconceivable harm?

Bethan never really elaborated in detail as to what exactly 'Uncle Richard' had done but she later found out that he had embezzled clients' deposits from property to feed a gambling addition which had steadily been growing throughout the years, it had started soon after his divorce and it spiraled out of control when his ex-wife married a mutual friend of theirs, which not only hurt dearly but it hit him the hard when this man moved in to his previous marital home and not only too reside there but ended up sharing this with his kids who were only 10 and 12 then.

His money issues were only discovered when a very wealthy client purchased a £1.5 million property near Ravelston, which was quite a sought-after area in those days before people split their houses up into flats. He had put the deposit down before the contract or agreement pending the survey was sealed only for the buyer to discover that the property had severe subsidence. Richard was counting on another seller putting his deposit down that week for his tracks to be covered and to be able to return the deposit as well as hoping that finally he will win some money at the Casino, only to realise that he had been unlucky at both again. When the client did not get his money back and he eventually did 3 months later, it was without interest, prompted an immediate investigation, leading to his arrest and subsequent incarceration.

Poor Uncle Richard was now serving two years as a 'guest' in HMP Saughton in Edinburgh a high security prison, and her dad had to borrow large amounts of money to cover all the losses incurred as well as having to say goodbye to two of the junior lawyers who had joined the practiced only two years previously.

"Are you saying we are broke?" Liz was trying to digest all this information, worrying first, like any child, what are all her friends going to think of her.

"No, I am not saying we are broke, because your dad still has clients, not as many, we have a lot of savings and we own outright the house and the car. Do you know what I mean by owning outright?" The problem with telling a child too much is they don't generally understand and then the inflate the problem and focus on one thing and it damages them for the rest of their life. Children should be children.

"Yes. So, what are you going to work as?"

"Well, as you know I am a qualified nurse, I have not practiced for years but I could retrain, I have already information on that. If I need to work now, then I can certainly be an auxiliary just to bring extras. Now, before you get carried away with your imagination, we have plenty of savings and you will continue to be at your school. We have money enough for both you and Luke to finish your education, so don't worry about it." Bethan had the money on her savings account, so if anything, it was untouchable by the authorities, they will not be left destitute.

"Lizzy darling, I mean it, please don't worry about it, we are working on resolving it" Too late of course, she was worried, in fact she was terrified.

Of course, Liz was aware that she was in quite a prestigious private school in the outskirts of Edinburgh and that it cost a lot to be in it, she also knew that not losing face was very important and that some of her friends might never speak to her, but she was always aware that some people were good and some people were just mean and selfish and would not understand., nevertheless, it was something she would rather not experience but it seemed life was not going to grant her that wish. The school of life lessons were hitting her hard.

Liz remembered thinking as she was taken to school that mum and dad knew best and the fact that they told her meant that it can't be bad, plus her mother would not have lied. She felt empowered and she also knew that she had to be careful as she really had to start saving her pocket money, yes, pocket money, was she still getting that? Would Luke? It was only £2 a week, which she knew it was a lot of money as most of her friends got £1.

Nothing happened after this and nothing was ever discussed again with her parents, which brough a degree of relief to Liz, she could not get her head around the problem's adults had, she was too young, she could understand just, the implications of going to jail and stealing money but the actual meaning of embezzlement and the loss of pride for her parents, she could not understand that, but she followed her mums advise, deny, deny, deny, to the letter.

Liz never knew if the situation got resolved, but it must have as holidays were back to normal within two years. She had never heard her parents talk about it again and family resumed its happy tone. Her father reputation was slightly affected, the practice suffered mildly as the story had been spread in the tabloids which meant some of their clients had left them unceremoniously, the long-term ones had stayed faithful, knowing that sometimes this happens, it is not necessarily everyone's fault.

Uncle Richard never visited us again after he was released from prison, in fact, he emigrated. Mum mentioned he had met dad several times before emigrating, making amends and apologising for all his failing, their friendship was never resumed which was sad but in dad's eyes he had nearly destroyed the family.

# Part 3

## Friends and lovers

### Jonathan

*Love has different layers and expressions, not*
*all of them are for man and wife*

London had grown into Liz's affections; she enjoyed the anonymity. It was not a village where gossip would spread anything and everything, the fact that people did not know who she was, she could go shopping in various areas without bumping into someone that knew her, unlike Edinburgh or any other small city, she was not stuck with just Oxford Street, which she hated, she could go to the Kings Road, Kensington High Street, Knights Bridge. It was great, there was so much choice, loved the buzz and the constant change in environment. She was not a great shopper, but she enjoyed the variety and the buzz that London provided her with.

The restaurants were fantastic, her favourites were Thai restaurants. There was one in Acton High Street that she loved and the other one on the Uxbridge Road was good, where you had to take your own wine and lastly a Greek restaurant, a couple of blocks further up on the Uxbridge Road from the Thai restaurant. This was the ultimate party restaurant and she would say 'my favourite', they had a singer and the atmosphere was fantastic, after ten o'clock you were given a maraca and some noisy instruments and then be expected you to join in the singing. Of course, it was extremely friendly, very relaxed, it was the talk for weeks every time they went to this restaurant. Everyone always drank too much, the last time nearly fifteen bottles of their house red Greek wine between 11 of them, it was an absolute hoot, at the end of the night they had walked home as unable to take a taxi due to lack of funds. It took them nearly an hour but it was worth it and it sobered them completely, however, not enough to make the hangover disappear at the next day. All restaurants were walking distance from her flat and that to Liz meant a 30-to-50-minute walk. Not something everyone agreed with but as far as she was concerned it helped specially after eating a hearty meal.

She had been in London five years and loved it, had made a new circle of friends, moved into project management and dated several people, none too serious. Then again, after Tim, she wanted a more relaxed relationship, she did not want to be hurt again. Her most long lasting one was with Jonathan, yes, the wonderful medic student that she kissed when she had stayed with Charlotte in Glasgow many years ago.

He had rung her several times and after not being able to get hold of her, called Charlotte and asked her for her new number in London. He came to stay with her on the second weekend she had been in London, he was wonderful and did not push her at all, he seemed besotted and would do anything she would say. He knew about Tim and how much he had hurt her, what he had done to her and the fact that we were still friends and she cared for him, but she could and would not go back to him.

The first weekend he stayed they did not do anything; he took her out for a meal at a rotisserie in Shepherds Bush and then they went for a long walk. It was very nice and relaxing even though then, Shepherd's bush was not exactly the safest place on earth, but they enjoyed ourselves.

The feeling of safety and belonging took over her, she could relax with Jonathan, talk to him and share her fears, her dreams, yes, she was very comfortable with him. Unfortunately, something deep inside her was very distant from it all, it could not quite fully connect with what Jonathan was offering. She could not understand why she felt like this, she was safe, more than she had ever felt and have been in what she would call her longest relationship and of course, Charlie was not there to destroy things.

Charlie was nowhere near her, in the last two years they had only spoken on the phone a dozen times, every time she came to London, she made sure she was in Scotland or on holiday or 'busy'. Maybe the reason she felt like this was fear of Charlie getting to close again and taking what she loved, she was not going to let that happen.

After two years of travelling back and forth between London and Glasgow, it was Jonathan that brought up the dreaded subject. He was just one year older than her but so much more mature and serious. He wanted to settle down, start a family and continue carving his career. He had graduated as a doctor and planned to progress to be a surgeon and then a consultant specialising in Cardiology. For some reason he did not want to be just a partner in a practice, he felt that any doctor could do that, no, he had higher aspirations, he wanted to be the best and prove to everyone he was the best in the field. He wanted to be the top cardiologist in Britain.

Liz would say he was as passionate about his job as he was about her, Liz knew that one day he would be recognised in his field, but she also knew that she would not be standing beside him when the praises and the party invitations came along, she knew that she would not be the one mentioned as his wife, it saddened her but it also made her happy. She knew he was not the one for her, he deserved better, someone that loved and adored him.

Liz loved him and still did, not like a brother but certainly not how a wife should love her husband. There was definitely something missing. That connection that made things click was absent from their relationship. The 'love' was one sided.

Physically and mentally, they were more than matched, their lovemaking was not only powerful and energetic but also passionate, they worshipped each other's bodies and after two years they would still get turned on by the thought of seeing each other at the weekends and making love. Mentally they were more than matched however, because she felt life was so serious, Liz tended to avoid having too many serious discussions like politics, she enjoyed light-hearted banter and jokes. They were both incredibly well read and always talked about books that they had just read, encouraging each other to borrow swap their books and read them.

Jonathan was very good looking in the traditional classic sense. Any mother would be proud to have a son in law like him. His face and features were perfect and his face, with a square jaw line, perfect skin and teeth and tanned meant everyone was always after him. He had 'charisma' and was, the moment he engaged you in conversation, completely focused on you. On top of this he enjoyed sports, which made most of my friends jealous. His favourite sports were tennis and swimming, which meant they could do this together. You could tell that everyone not only found him very attractive but also engaged. After they had finished with each other, they had remained friends and Tanya, who had only met him a few years ago, always wondered how is it that Liz had let him go.

None of these comments she minded. Liz was more than aware that she had hit the jackpot and had lost it and it helped not being the jealous type, or at least that is what she thought.

"What do you mean you don't want to get married? Don't you love me?" You could tell by the sound of his voice that Jonathan was struggling, you could see he was desperately trying to stay calm, but his eyes gave it away. He was shocked and trying not to cry. Struggling to comprehend the meaning of it all. He had assumed so much and never once doubted this was not as perfect as he had assumed.

"You don't understand Jonathan, please let me explain" Liz was urging him to listen, but he just kept talking.

"For the last two years, we have seen each other practically every weekend. We have called each other twice a day and spent all our holidays together, all this togetherness and now this? What are you looking for if this is not enough? All I was asking is to make our relationship and commitment to each other officially, for you to share my life and you turn me down. Would you have just dragged me along for years if I had not asked you to marry me?" His eyes looked beautiful, rage and passion and some disbelief had taken over them, tears were swimming on the edge wanting to escape and run down his cheeks, but he kept them in control, he knew he could not and would not cry. He was angry and dissapointed at the same time, if this was not love, what was it?

"Jonathan, please." Liz's voice was pleading "I love you, but not in the way you deserve, you deserve better, someone that would adore you, be with you all the time, one that would put her career aside and give 100% for you."

"That is an excuse and you know it." His voice turned hostile, angry slipping through each word., each of them sharp and hard, as if stripped of all emotion, understanding suddenly being erased and replaced with a passionless monotone. "I would give you 100%, my career is not as important as you are, but if you feel that your career might come in the way, then that only means that you do not love me at all."

"That is not true, I do love you, but I just feel I am not ready, you are more than a friend Jonathan, I need you." Liz took a breather, conscious that this conversation was deteriorating by the second, she was losing her friend. "I don't want us to break up, I am far too young, I don't want to be married yet." She was looking for a sign that he understood. "Why don't we wait until we are on our late twenties." Liz knew herself, she was bluffing, buying time, she did not want him to know that he was right, he was not the man for her. She did not think that she could change her feelings, she still cared for him, but it was better that he was with someone else and something deep down told her that that would happen next, after all, they had been arguing for nearly two hours now.

"Well, if that is how you feel, then I am afraid we will have to call it a day. I know that I have just arrived, but I would like to collect my belongings and leave." Just like that he got up, determination in his stance, realisation he had been wasting his time. He had to just get on with it, not waver or he will lose his resolve and stay in a loveless relationship only to find out years later she had found someone else.

"Jonathan, you don't have to leave, why can't we enjoy the weekend and be friends? Come on, please?" This is something that

Liz was not expecting, yes, break up but not finish the friendship. She was really shocked that he seemed to finish and erase everything that they had been, finish the relationship and the friendship in one go.

"Maybe we can be friends in the future but not now, I can't, I want to be alone and need space" Jonathan sounded sad but was very much in control, he had regained his composure within seconds, the moment he realised Liz did not love him. He seemed to have quickly accepted things.

Liz remained very quietly waiting in the living room, hearing him going about the rooms and the bathroom, picking up all his belonging that have slowly ended up staying here since he was down here more often that she had been in Glasgow. Their goodbye was sad if maybe non-existent but maybe it was meant to be. Jonathan left with the promise that he will be sending all her belongings down by courier and that he would soon call her. He was polite but formal in his good byes, wounded but not making war, he was too educated and fair for that.

# Moving on

*One good, honest friend is worth 1,000 therapists*

It had been six months since the split, Liz had not been dating anyone and had certainly not heard from Jonathan, but then again, she did not expect to hear from him for at least a year. Maybe Christmas would be a time that he would call, then again, it was only November now. She missed him but she could not go back, she had to be honest with herself and let go.

The phone was ringing, for a dream it sounded real, too real, her eyes opened sharply, nearly fell out of bed, what was going on. It was nearly two a.m. on a Tuesday. I had not only been fast asleep but angry that I had been woken up, tomorrow it was a 'school' day and had to be at work at eight in the morning.

"Hello! her voice was sharp; it had an edge of anger which she was desperately trying to hide but too tired for it to be successful.

"Hi Liz, it is Charlotte, how are you?"

"What? What is wrong? Is it your mum or your dad? Is your job okay?" A sudden panic hit Liz; this was unusual to get a call like that out of the blue.

"No, nothing like that, I just could not sleep." Charlotte sounded worried, scared even. "We need to talk, Liz."

"Sure. I am sure you realise what time it is, so I am assuming it is something bad. Go on, tell me what is on your mind."

"You sound so calm, I had not been able to sleep and every day it gets worse, I just can't keep this to myself any longer. You know I love you, don't you Liz? You are and have been my best friend, since we met at school." She heard Charotte intake to massie gulps of air. "All this has been playing on my nerves and need to own up."

"Of course, I know you love me, what is the matter Charlotte? you are starting to really worry me now." Charlotte had never done this to her before, this was very unlike her.

"Tell me, what is wrong." Liz's curiosity and worry got the best of her, why did her best friend needed nerves to speak to her?

"I am sleeping with Jonathan" That was all Charlotte had said, there was silence on both ends of the phone, nobody saying anything, just waiting.

Liz froze at the mention of this, it was not pain or jealousy, it was more confusion. Yes, confusion is the only way to describe it. how can a man profess deep and undying love six months ago and then be shagging one's best friend, it was weird, unthinkable, unless of course they had both been laughing behind her back.

"Did you hear me Liz, are you okay?" worry oozed from every word Charlotte had said, conscious that this could break a friendship, even one as solid as the one her and Liz's friendship had and even though Liz and Jonathan had broken up with each other by then.

"Yes, no, that is fine, I am happy for you, how long?" Liz needed to know before the conversation progressed any further. She was desperately trying not to get upset or sound upset, which in all honesty she was, even though she did not understand why and she did not love Jonathan and they had finished with each other good and proper.

"I know Jonathan finished with you six months ago." Charlotte kept speaking but Liz was no longer listening, her mind went into overdrive, Jonathan never finished with her, it finished by her saying no to marriage. "He said he did not love you and that it was best to end it rather than string you along the way for years."

"Hello?

"Yes, I am listening Charlotte!.."

"Honestly, we did not start going out until four months ago. Jonathan told me he wanted to tell you himself, but I just could not longer sleep anymore not being able to tell you. Are you mad at me Liz?" Desperation lined her voice and each word. "Please tell me you are not mad at me or at Jonathan, I could not bear it you being upset with either of us."

"Not at all Charlotte, I love you, you are my best friend, more than that, you are like a sister to me and you are right, Jonathan and I were finished so there is no problem, no reason for you to feel guilty. I just wish you would have told me earlier." Liz took a deep breath, her heart pumping a 200 miles per hour. "I hope you are really happy." Liz meant what she had said, she was happy for Charlotte.

"Are you sure? I mean, you never told me much about your split with Jonathan so I guessed you must have been very upset by it and maybe that you still were upset. I was going to bring it up and then one day we just started dating and things just got messed up."

Charlotte was going on overdrive, talking nonstop like a charlatan, Liz stopped listening again. She realised she never spoke to anyone about Jonathan, not even her little brother, Luke, someone she confided on all the time, there were no secrets between her and Luke. She must have been more hurt that she had realised or anticipated. It was her fault, she should have told charlotte, then Jonathan and her would have been able to date without being worried, more to the point, without the lies Jonathan had given Charlotte.

Was Jonathan trying to get her jealous? Surely he would not dare try such a cheap plot and have the audacity to do it with her best friend? Did he love Charlotte or was he just on the re-bound? Why did he lie to her, why did he just not tell her the truth? After all, they were friends in their own right, why could he have not confided in her at all, Charlotte would have listened to him and they would have probably gone out together regardless.

"Oh Liz, you are so nice, I love you too." Charlotte sounded as if a big weight had been lifted from her shoulders. "How about if I go to London this weekend to visit you?"

"Hmm, I am actually going away to Cornwall." Liz knew she was pushing it with a lie but she did not really want to have to face things early, what if he came down as well? That would have been horrific, all happy families with them shagging on the room next door. Liz needed to think and put her thoughts in order. "How about the weekend after?"

"Yes, that sounds good, maybe we can go out for a meal or got to the pictures or both."

Charlotte and Liz talked to each other for over two hours, both of them wanting to make sure the other was okay with things and also realising that their friendship went back years, too long a way and not worth destroying it over a man. After all, she did not run off with Jonathan, he was free to go out with anyone as he pleased. Regardless of it though she was determined to make sure that she talked to him about his 'little' lie, he was not going to get away with things that easily.

# The Peace

*To clear the obstacle in our mind, is to pave the
way and give permission to new flows, without it,
we remain closed and in darkness*

As expected, it was nearly midnight when Jonathan called that evening, worried in case Liz let the cat out of the bag. He had either been sitting by the phone thinking how to approach this or he had been busy doing additional work at night like paperwork or Charlotte was with him and he was waiting until she went to bed. Whatever, Liz did not know and did not want to know, the idea of him worried about this whole thing made Liz feel tremendously better.

"Hi Lizzie" He called her Lizzie when he was either in deep trouble or trying to get or give affection, but since not a shred of affection had passed between them in six months, any guess was that he was feeling extremely guilty and a little bit scared.

"Hi Jonathan, long time no hear?" A smile crossed her face, revenge was so sweet. "To what do I owe this honour?" Liz knew why he was calling, but there was not harm in making him suffer a little, after all, he owed it to her to have told her and to have been honest, she wanted him to stew for a while. "How are things in Glasgow? How is life as a doctor?" Sarcasm dripping off each word, knowing he was uncomfortable.

"Well, I guess you know why I am calling. Charlotte told me she called you" It was very much Jonathan's style; he did not beat much about the bush and ignored her questions. "I am sorry about everything."

"So am I." Liz felt sad, they had not only been lovers but the best of friends, she had deserved to know for all times sake, after all, just because you don't go out with someone does not mean you do not care. Charlotte should have also told her about it, but she was not annoyed at that. "How are you? I hope Charlotte is not within earshot."

"No, I am in my flat alone, I just came back from the hospital, we had an emergency and have been operating since eight this evening." Jonathan sounded sad, tired and stressed. "Liz, I did not want to lie to you, I am sorry, it just happened. If you could just understand, I loved you and still do! I guess I was looking for some affection elsewhere, I was so hurt"

"Jonathan don't, please don't say that. Don't say anything you might regret, please remember that you are going out with my best friend and I don't want to hurt her." Liz said all this in a hurry, desperate and scared of what a moment like this could do, the harm it would cause. She did not want her relationship with Charlotte to be ruled by lies.

"I wanted to talk to you for such a long time, I needed you for so long. The number of times I tried picking up the phone just to hear your voice and could not, and now, all because of this mess I have to." He took a breath, exasperated, it was all too much. "I am not in love with Charlotte, I just wanted to feel loved and since we have been friends for so long, I went to see her one night. I thought she had still been going out with Rupert. When I got there, she told me what had happened between her and Rupert and one thing led to another and …"

"It is OK Jonathan, I don't mind, I" Jonathan cut her off.

"But I do because I still love you."

"Well, I am sorry, but I cannot love you back in the way you want me to. I care for you a great deal, but you deserve someone better, someone like Charlotte who loves you and thinks you are the most wonderful man in this earth."

"Shut up, you are making me sick." Jonathan's old sense of humour started coming out, which was good as it meant that he was accepting things.

"I love you, even if I end up caring about Charlotte, I still love you and I will always love you. You mean everything to me."

"Jonathan, I know it hurts you and I am sorry, but one day you will be fully over me. Please be careful and don't go and destroy something that I think will end up being very precious to you."

"What can I do?" His voice had an edge of desperation to it.

"Please don't tell Charlotte the truth, it is too late for it now. Let's just all forget about all this. Let's just assume that the truth is what you said to Charlotte. If you are honest now, you will destroy not only Charlotte but what you have with her and you will make it impossible for us to keep a friendship as I will have to make sure Charlotte is okay."

They were on the phone for around one and a half hours and spoke of everything, their feeling, thoughts, fears, back to the old ways when we shared our inner thoughts. The fact that they shared this secret made them closer, but Liz was still cagey. The call was wonderful; it not only sealed their friendship but also buried their secret forever. They promised to call each other every two to three weeks and promised that nothing would destroy their friendship but most of all, they had to protect Charlotte, it was not fair on her.

It was very sad that things had turned out the way they were, but Liz knew she was right, she did not love Jonathan and he had to accept that and build up his life again with someone new, which is what he was doing, even though he did not admit to it but hopefully he would be careful as to how he achieved happiness.

Such was her luck, she was now twenty-three and love was eluding her as always and again, she was let down by another man. At least this time she was not cheated on!

Charlotte came down to see her the weekend after, as promised and agreed. When she had picked her up from Heathrow airport, she had flown from Glasgow Airport, she had looked so beautiful. She looked in love, her cheeks were rosy, and she had an aura of happiness about her. Her hair had grown very long, and she had it very straight. She was wearing black boots, green velvet trousers with a sixties style short sleeve polo neck with olive and white horizontal stripes which was made of wool which went very well with the black wool coat she was wearing on top. She looked stunning, then again, Charlotte always did, even if she had dressed like a bag lady, she would still look stunning.

Charlotte was smiling but looked nervous, a scared rabbit that saw the car headlights and froze.

"Hi Charlotte. How are you? You are looking great." Charlotte's smile suddenly beamed and she visibly started to relax.

"Hi Lizzie, it's been so long." She said this as she hugged her. She could feel her embrace getting tighter and knew that she did not mean to hurt her and that she was still worried.

"It's OK Charlotte, don't worry, I am more than happy about you and Jonathan, as a matter of fact, I am hoping that in a couple of years you will have good news for all of us." Tears appeared on her dear friends' eyes, a sign of true friendship, she had done well.

The weekend was great, they went shopping, ate out, lunches and dinners, had lots of coffees but most importantly they talked about everything, like they've never had since her dad had died. They even talked about poor Rupert' fate, yes, the medic student she was really crazy about nearly three years ago.

Rupert, who went out with Charlotte for nearly two years had gone to Somalia to do some aid work as a doctor only to catch cholera less than two months later. Even though he had taken precautions, sometimes some diseases would take the victim anyway and Rupert was one of those casualties, nothing could be done to save him and within two weeks of catching the decease he was dead.

He barely knew by the end that he was going to die and when the time came it was swift, he probably thought he was in paradise already, having hallucinations, imagining things, the high temperature robbing him of any normal or coherent thought. His body was sent back to Glasgow where his parents lived.

Charlotte did not attend the funeral as she was no longer his girlfriend, another medic student, who went to Somalia, went to the funeral, she heard she was beautiful. Not that she was jealous, after all, Rupert wanted her to go with him, but she declined, hence they finished, it was only one month after he had arrived in Somalia that he had sent her a letter of his adventures and also to tell her he was going out with Kathleen.

She still had deep feeling for Rupert and shock ripped through her when she heard of his death, after all, she hoped that once this crazy idea went of being a doctor in not only deprived countries but some of them dangerous, that Rupert would return to her and marry her. She felt he needed this time for himself, to find out what exactly he wanted from life, she also knew that whichever 'friendship' he had with anyone else would not last as she knew he loved her more than anyone else.

But it was not to be, maybe it was fate that Rupert died, we will never know. Would he have married Kathleen, maybe, after all they both shared a passion for travel and also for going to remote desolate and desperate areas in the world that were crying for aid, for doctors to sacrifice their life for a good cause. Maybe deep-down Charlotte knew and was fooling herself. Maybe it was just as well she will never know for sure, deep down she knew she would have been broken hearted.

Charlotte left for Glasgow on the Sunday night; Liz drove her back to Heathrow in order to catch the eight-p.m. flight. It was a sad goodbye, but they knew they will be seeing each other soon, more still, they knew that if they did not, their friendship would always remain the same, unaffected by all the trials that life brought upon one and still as strong as when they were kids.

# The Wedding

Monday for wealth
Tuesday for health
Wednesday the best day of all
Thursday for losses
Friday for crosses
Saturday for no luck at all

It was exactly two and a half years after that fateful call that Charlotte married Jonathan in a beautiful April day. Charlotte had been so nervous for the last six months, so much so, that all, including Liz were desperate for the wedding to be over as soon as possible. Nerves had been flying all over the place, Charlotte scared in case Jonathan changed his mind, which of course he would and had not.

The day of the big day, which was a Wednesday as Charlotte was so superstitious, was a beautiful sunny day, they were all nervous, but it had been worth it. In front of 80 guests, Charlotte walked down the aisle flanked by her bridesmaids Liz and Suzy, Charlotte's younger sister. Charlotte looked radiant; her beauty accentuated by the gown she was wearing.

The gown was a sleeveless pearl colour dress which touched the floor. The top half was made with a satin material and the bottom half, which was a flowing skirt, was made of rough silk. There were three rows of pearls arranged as beading around the neck and sleeves. She wore no necklace but had on two small pearl earrings. Her hair was up on a chignon style on which a beautiful translucent veil rested. On top of it resided a small silver crown with pearls. The veil only went down to the waste as Charlotte hated long veils and trains. Her shoes were ballerina type slippers with a tiny little heel and a small bow just before the tip. In them, she had placed a one penny coin for luck and wealth.

Jonathan was very smart in traditional Scottish regalia, the kilt with sporran, a sheriffmuir doublet, a very pompous and flamboyant lace jabot and the final touch, a Sgian Dubh, the traditional Scottish dagger. Jonathan's had an amber stone encrusted at the top of the sgian Dubh and a thistle crest on the handle. He looked the picture of happiness standing relaxed and proud as his bride walked down the aisle to the beautiful tune of Canon by Pachelbel, the usual wedding march, played on the organ by the overly excited and dutiful ministers' wife, Rosalyn Docherty.

The bridesmaids wore the same as the bride but without the veil. Both had chignons and a small diadem on their head with smaller and less pearls than the bride but just as impressive. Both looked beautiful and happy for the bride, who glowed and glided down the aisle.

All three, bride and bridesmaids carried the same type of bouquets, the bride carrying an exceptionally large and flowing version of the same. The bouquet consisted of an arrangement of lavender hydrangeas mixed in between a waterfall of peonies and lilies, which had cost Charlotte £80 for hers and £40 for each of the bridesmaid's ones. The effect and beauty it provided was worth it, all looking a million dollars.

The church they married in was in Edinburgh, a small church in Morningside, which was a well to do area. The decision for this was because Mr and Mrs Farrell, Jonathan's parents, lived in Edinburgh and because Jonathan's mum, who was wheelchair bound after falling from a horse would have found it uncomfortable to go all the way to Glasgow.

"Dearly beloved, we are gathered here together...." as the minister, the Reverent Johnny Docherty started with the wedding ceremony, you could hear a shuffle, everyone was moving and whispering, looking to the right of the church. The minister was trying to concentrate on what he was saying but could not help also looking and then slowly, a smile appeared on his face, a smile which slowly turned into a grin.

On the right-hand corner of the church, two chimney sweepers in what could be called their traditional attire of the Victorian times which included brooms, sat quietly in one corner, trying desperately not to smile, their lips playing with the corner of their mouths where you could tell a smile was desperately trying to form, desperately pretending there was nothing odd with their appearance.

Jonathan and Charlotte sensed that something was going on, and slowly, fear in their faces, they turned around to look at whatever it was that was baffling the congregation. Their faces showed not only surprise but confusion, she could not remember inviting chimney sweepers. She looked up at Liz in confusion, wondering what to do and noticed the grin on Liz's face. Liz winked at both her and Jonathan and silently she said: for luck.

On the way out of the church grounds and following tradition, everyone threw confetti on the newly married couple, whose smile was contagious and their happiness touched everyone. Charlotte moved away from Jonathan and shouted calling all single woman who wanted to be married next, she took off one of her shoes and turning away from the crowd threw it behind her, towards all the single girls who were screaming in anticipation.

Shock hit everyone suddenly, silence took over, nobody knew what to do, they did not know if to rush and grab the shoe or run away from it in case it landed on their face. Shock was on everyone's face when they suddenly realised that the traditional bouquet throwing was replaced by shoe throwing. Once this realisation sank in, which only lasted less than two seconds but felt like a lifetime, they all started battling their way to win and grab that shoe which could mean any of them walking down the aisle next.

What nobody knew apart from a few elderlies was that traditionally, it was a shoe that had to be thrown and not a bouquet. One wonders why this tradition had changed over the years. Maybe in the old day's shoes were so cheap; people could afford to get rid of one of them in such a manner. Nobody knows.

The whole event was unforgettable, marked by unusual forgotten traditions and mixed or changed with modern ones that set this wedding aside from the general ideology that weddings were all the same. This one was fun, more than that, the bride and groom thoroughly enjoyed themselves and every guest left feeling they had taken part in an unforgettable journey.

The reception, consisting of eighty guests were mainly very close friends or members of each other families. It was held in one of Edinburgh top restaurants under one the bridges which for the first time had catered and entertained a wedding at their premises. Usually, they would do outside catering for such an event. The restaurant was just off the Grassmarket and it was one of those places that if you did not know about it you would not have realised it was there. It had been beautifully painted for the occasion and the manageress, and the catering team had excelled themselves with the menu which was beautifully and timely served.

The Catherine wheel of sole filled with a light Scottish salmon mousse which was served with a light citrus mayonnaise as the entrée, and it was 'to die for'. Very light and inviting and the salmon melted in your mouth. The main course was sliced breast of duck served with a classic orange and Cointreau sauce. Even though Charlotte was not fond of Cointreau, she loved it in this dish as the bitterness and sweetness of the oranges and the liquor made it a match in heaven.

Dessert was Cranachan served with boudoir biscuits. The cream and the raspberries were delicious.

The whole wedding had little things that reminded all the guest of where the bride and groom met and their love for all things Scottish. Very small but meaningful reminders, some traditional and some modern of the country. Most of the guest would have missed it as most of the guest were Scottish and they were probably not noticing the small details.

The wine list was Dame de la Vallee sauvignon 1996; for red there was Gran vino cabernet sauvignon 1996, for the toast Drappier champagne, Grand Serendre 1989. This was a champagne that Liz introduced to Charlotte and Jonathan and both loved it. It became tradition that for every celebration, they had to have Drappier as the champagne of choice.

The band used was a ceilidh band called 'The Hooters' which nobody seemed to have heard of, not even the bride and groom, but who had so much liked the name that they had decided without even thinking twice about it to hire them. This was something that paid off tenfold as it was an unexpected success.

Jonathan and Charlotte left the restaurant venue at around 1.30 a.m. to go to their hotel in the Grass market and pack as quickly as they could as they had a taxi coming to pick them up at 4 a.m. to take them to Edinburgh Airport for them to fly to their honeymoon destination, the island of Aruba.

On the way out, Mr Robinson, Charlotte's father, handed Jonathan, and noting his daughter's surprise and guests utter disbelief, a pair of very old and dirty shoes that had belonged to Charlotte and which she had forgotten excited at the back of her wardrobe. Charlotte never wanted to throw them out as she had been attached to them. As Mr Robinson handed the shoes, he said, very loud for everyone to hear "Like tradition calls, my handing you this pair of shoes, which are to say the least extremely smelly, I am longer responsible for my lovely daughter Charlotte. The full responsibility of her happiness and wellbeing lies on you Jonathan. I hope this is a task you take on seriously as she means the world to me."

Charlotte could not close her mouth. This was not part of the wedding ceremony, independent Charlotte, who herself and only herself was responsible for her wellbeing. She knew why he did it behind her back she glared up at him, just as her dad raised on finger on the air, put it on his mouth and made an invisible line on the air and then went back into the restaurant laughing.

Charlotte could only smile; she had lectured her dad for the last six months, telling him exactly what to do and what not to do, making sure he did not embarrass her. He knew he had been up to his head with this wedding and wanted revenge, sweet revenge. This was it; he freed himself from his daughter's orders just like she would have done if on the same circumstance. They were so alike.

All the guests had not only been laughing at this scene but also at the fact that outside the restaurant was 'Lulu', Charlotte's old and faithful car. They all knew the hotel was round the corner, but they understood that they wanted to go off in style.

Lulu had white paint on the back window that said: 'just married'. There were lots of old shoes attached to several strings which in turn were tied to the bumper of the car. It was a hilarious sight, the car was a wreck, not even for the wedding did Charlotte fix poor little 'Lulu'. Rust had touched every piece of metal exposing it and making it look brown and it had not been washed for at least a year, very much a Charlotte statement. Just as well they did not have far to go!

Four years later, Mr and Mrs Farrell were blessed with a lovely baby girl whom they named Beth, she was absolutely gorgeous with massive hazel greenish eyes, probably from the grandparents' side and also possessed very beautiful large eye lashes. She was born blonde, but as the weeks and months passed by, her hair turned more a dark caramel colour than blonde. You could tell a mile away that when she grew up, she was going to be a stunner, even more beautiful that her mother as she also inherited the height from her father.

Exactly two years after Beth was born, Jonathan and Charlotte were blessed with twins who were called Charlie and Christian, very traditional names, which was no surprise since both Charlotte and Jonathan were both quite traditionalist, but I am sure they would be extremely upset if this was suggested to them as they looked at themselves as quite an unconventional couple.

Charlotte never found out the truth about Liz's breakup with Jonathan and true to his word, he always called her office every two to three weeks just for a chat which would normally extend easily from a quick 15-minute talk to a half an hour chat. Their friendship remained the same which along with Charlotte's friendship, one of the more lasting and solid ones Liz have ever had which she not only treasured but respected dearly.

It was funny, the more and more Liz thought back to her youth, she remembered what the medium once had said to her. She called herself 'Lavender' and told Charlotte that not only she was to marry in five years but that she would have four children. What Charlotte never told anyone is that Lavender had told her she would have twins, two little boys.

So far everything had come true, including Jonathan who had the initials RJ as she had predicted. Charlotte and I never realised that Jonathan was called Robert Jonathan Farrell, RJF, we only knew him as Jonathan Farrell, so it was quite a surprise when we were both talking to realise that she had told us both about the same man. Luckily, Liz never told Charlotte that Lavender had told me that Jonathan would always be in love with her regardless of whom he married in the end. Liz knew this would be something nobody would ever know as she knew Jonathan would never tell and with time, he probably would only love Charlotte in the end. Saying that, Liz did catch him looking at her several times when she stayed with them and he always seemed to have an excuse to do something with her like food shopping or washing the babies. Hopefully Liz was wrong. He never attempted anything but had a sad look about him, as if he was trying to say something to her telepathically. Liz did not approve but one could order their emotions and feelings a certain way. Liz had never loved Jonathan in the way he wanted and that was good enough for her.

# Part 4

## Back to The Grind

## The Present - March 2001

The Sunday of the weekend they had first met, Chris decided he had enough. Charlie was in an appalling mood in the pub, even refusing to make polite conversation, she had been so bad that she made it impossible for anyone to enjoy themselves.

Due to this Chris left first thing in the morning that Sunday, he had not even bothered to have breakfast, he caught the eight-a.m. plane back to London.

He had sent Peter a text message as he was leaving the house at six in the morning. He had tried telling him the night before, but Charlie never left them with an opportunity to be alone, which was very clever because she knew she had overstepped the line. Chris had put a note through Liz's door wishing them to keep in touch and promising to call.

Liz had got up early that Sunday but after seeing the note decided to stay in bed reading until ten in the morning, she did not even venture out of her room to get coffee or breakfast as she knew hell would break loose soon and did not want to be part of it. She needed a distraction and her science fiction 'supernatural angel' book 'Angel Demon' helped, she was glued to it normally and she was not on book two. As usual her penchant for supernatural romance books was as strong as ever, nothing like a good romance to help overcome a challenging day!

At exactly nine, the shouts and screams had started, Peter was obviously very angry and had seen Chris's message. Peter had been so angry he had finished with Charlie there and then, called her every name under the sun, packed his bags and then left the flat slamming the door. In the background you could hear Charlie's hysterical cries and screams accusing Chris of ruining her relationship, this was at nine forty-five, Liz knew that soon Charlie would come sobbing to her room like she had always done, she did not feel sorry for her, she never did, not since Tim. Their friendship was superficial, on a need when required basis but by all means not a true friendship.

"To be honest" thought Liz, if anyone accused her at this point of being two faced, she would very likely not deny it. Liz felt Charlie deserved everything that was coming to her and to a degree, Liz had been expecting something like this would happen; she also had to be realistic, she needed a place to stay, a cheap bed until she sorted al her problems and Charlie provided her with that.

"Why Liz?" Charlie asked but it was more a rhetorical question, she knew the answer and did not really want Liz to say anything. "Do you think I am not beautiful enough for him?" Her eyes were red; she had now been crying for nearly an hour. As usual Charlie never understood that a relationship required more than just looks and she really needed a full makeover and lobotomy to change from a beautiful Franken Bitch to a lovely person, someone that people would want to spend time with.

"Charlie, maybe you just pushed him a bit too much, I mean, you hinted yesterday at things." Liz decided a little honesty was not going to hurt her, after all, she also had to learn "You were extremely rude to his best friend. I knew you wanted to spend time with Peter yesterday, but girls and guys are different, after all, he invited Chris here to visit him for the weekend and you treated him like dirt. I am actually surprised he did not leave before."

"I know, I just felt that there was something weird between them, as if they had some kind of agreement or pact I was not part of." Charlie was looking at Liz with innocent eyes, but it was too late, Liz had learnt the hard way. Charlie noticed Liz did not seem to feel anything, she was like an ice maiden. "Okay, what if I call him and apologise to him, if I tell him that I will also apologise to Chris, I will make an excuse that I am having a hard time at work or something?"

"Charlie, I don't think that would work." Liz got the same impression as Charlie, Chris and Peter were on a mission, maybe Chris was meant to give Peter his opinion on Charlie before he decided to propose or not but the way Peter finished with her meant to her that he had planned finishing with her regardless.

Charlie called Peter a lot the week after, by the sounds of it nearly driving him nuts, at one point he had threatened with the police unless she stopped. It ended up very embarrassing at two in the morning, two policemen knocking at her door, giving her a strong talking to, quite something.

In the end, affected by her own poison, she had decided to bad mouth him to anyone that would hear her. She did this to the point that most people would end up avoiding her and Liz decided to take this opportunity to go to Aberdeen and visit Kieran for a week. Aberdeen for a week was a better prospect at having peace and quiet than Edinburgh with Charlie.

"What do you mean? just when I need you the most you decide to leave?"

"Come on Charlie, it has been four days since Peter finished with you, just move on. My being here means nothing, there is nothing I can do, I have already said and done all I can."

"Well, if you put it that way the same could be said about your mother, I mean, she is dead, get over it."

The shock of what Charlie said hit her like a bucket of cold water; this was definitely below the belt.

"If that is how you feel, then I will go and not bother you again" Liz started to get up from her chair.

"I am sorry, I did not mean that, that was awful, I am sorry." Charlie suddenly realised that Liz was the only one that she had as none of her friends were there, they had all moved away from her one by one as the years went by. As soon as they discovered how poisonous she was they left. Why had Liz not left?

This was something that Liz did not understand herself. She had been betrayed and treated like dirt but had always kept a polite friendship with Charlie, maybe deep down she thought she had changed, but she had not she was worse. She decided there and then that she will go back in three weeks' time. She was going to have fresh start and remove all bad weeds that surrounded her, and this meant Charlie, who was the only poison in her life. She would go for a week to Aberdeen to spend it with Kieran as he had suggested weeks ago and then a week with Charlotte, it was probably her that brought up the excuses not to visit Charlotte as she had the twins, but now she was sure that she would not think of it that way, she would be delighted to seeing her again. She would come back from Glasgow, spend a couple of days with Charlie and then leave and that would it, she had to remove her from her life once and for all.

Liz had left for Aberdeen that same day, she had called Kieran at work who had been more than delighted, he sounded like a little boy when promised his dream toy. Time with him was exactly what she needed, why did she not go there in the first place, why was she adamant that she wanted to be in Edinburgh, was it because she had been so happy there as a student? The realisation that it was not the place but her dear friends that mattered made he feel more at ease with her decision. She had gone to Edinburgh with the expectation of finding peace and even though she had met Chris and Peter who were lovely people, the whole scene had disappointed her because of Charlie.

After Aberdeen, she decided, she was going to Glasgow and spend more quality time with Charlotte. Just have a relaxing time and reconnecting with her best friend. Trying to find that elusive peace she felt she would never achieve now that her mum was gone.

# The Hook Up

"You were lucky to have contacted me yesterday, I just came back from Glasgow an hour before you called, I had been toying with the idea of staying a couple of more days there as I was having such fun."

"Sounds as if I am a lucky guy, or maybe you just got this urge to come back to Edinburgh without realising it was your inner self pushing you to meet me, you know, fate." His eyes were glinting with double meaning and wickedness. He was flirting and it was nice. She felt a connection, something special stirred within her. Familiarity and calmness enveloped her and a warm that you feel when you are at home content.

They laughed nonstop, the conversation was a mixture, some serious some very stupid but that was what made it fun but afterwards they felt relaxed enough to be absolutely stupid with each other.

It had been nice to receive Chris' call, she had enjoyed that first weekend they met he was an easy-going guy with lots to tell. He was not only interesting, but he seemed so confident and she felt relaxed which is something she had not felt with anyone in a long time, actually since Jonathan.

"What do you think of the food?" Chris asked worried in case she did not like it; he was looking for a sign that she was enjoying herself.

"Oh, this is great, thank you and thank you for inviting me again." Liz was conscious she kept repeating this and she realised she needed to get a grip.

The food was nice, it was a fusion of traditional French and modern European cuisine. This lovely tiny little restaurant in Leith and gave them the cosines they needed to develop more of an intimacy through enticing conversation by providing the right ambience.

The salads were amazing, simple but ideal and the marinated chicken she had was soft and delicate. Every bite she took was enjoyable. This, plus the company was perfect.

"Good, you are welcome. I have been wanting to see you since that weekend at Charlie's, how have you been?" His smile was easy and it was a compliment it was easy to tell he was being honest. He was really happy to see her.

"Fine, I feel much better about things now and I am thinking of going back to London. I know it has only been four weeks rather than 2 months, but I feel that I am ready to go back and face things. I feel stronger, I don't know why since Charlie is quite a nightmare, but I guess it helped me to think of other things rather than my parents and having self pity."

"I re-did my CV." Liz just kept talking without realising she was talking nonstop. "I have also called Tanya and told her I would be back in London next Friday so that she can start arranging things."

"Are you sure that you are ready for things down there?" There was concern on Chris voice, he knew from his own experience that sometimes getting over someone's death is not as easy as it seems, then again, neither is running away from it.

"I will be okay; I need to get away from Charlie and do my own thing. I miss my flat, the cleanliness of it, the fresh smell. I feel trapped when I am in that horrid flat."

"Yes, I can quite imagine, it must be very hard living with that selfish woman. She was really a right bitch to the three of us that weekend." Chris's look was intense, he was obviously reminiscing that horrible weekend. "I really don't understand why, what was her end goal? To antagonise us all?."

The restaurant they were in was beautiful, it was situated in a very quiet area in Leith, tucked away hidden from the passers-by and off in an alleyway but close enough to the water. How did he know about it I was not sure but my guess is that since he loved is whisky, he must have known the area quite well. He did mention that him and Peter used to visit there frequently when very young.

Liz had heard of the restaurant but mainly because she had spent her university years in Edinburgh. Generally, if you keep your ear to the ground, you know the 'nice' places to go if you wanted something special and by 'special' I meant somewhere elegant and expensive.

As you went into the restaurant it gave you the impression of going into a very small room, an inn in the old days with candlelight making shadows and giving the place a more romantic and cosier atmosphere. There we six tables approximately in the first room which also housed the bar where you could see people busy opening champagne bottles or squeezing oranges for real orange juice. Through a small room where you had to slightly duck you head if you were taller than 5' 11".

The room was plainly decorated, when they were seated, the waiter informed them that the whole restaurant was a protected building, which to be honest did not surprise Liz. There were a lot of hidden gems by the old docks. A lot of the buildings were converted warehouses which sold for a pretty penny.

This small but beautiful room contained around 10 tables of different sizes to cater for all groups, the walls were washed in a white/creamy colour and there was candlelight everywhere.

Memories suddenly started flooding Liz, as if it were yesterday. Thoughts that had not been revisited in a long time but were welcome, times gone by that brough sweet memories of a time when innocence meant everything was exciting and surprising.

The whole restaurant was very impressive, the last time (and only time) she had been there was to celebrate her twenty second birthday. Tim said he was going to take her out for a meal, just the two of them to celebrate but once she walked into the next room, she recognised six of her very close friends. She remembered that day clearly, she did not see how much the total bill came to, but she was sure it must have cost quite a bit with the Champagne, Drappier as usual, and the cake which Tim arranged the previous night. The cake was a strawberry sponge cake, which was covered, in beautiful creamy meringue and had several strawberries cut in half dotted around the cake. She now clearly remembered how happy she had been that day, she loved and felt loved, a feeling she had not felt since.

"So, you have been here before?" Chris had noticed her mind wondering, like you do when you remember something nice.

"Sorry, I did not mean to be rude. Yes, I came here around eight, nine years ago, for my 22$^{nd}$ birthday. My then boyfriend gave me a surprise birthday meal and invited my best friends to it. It was beautiful."

Her eyes were sparkling, yes, she had been happy, she had been at peace and she had enjoyed her life, this period was just a hiccup and Chris was, without knowing it, bringing back that sparkle and hope back to her. Giving her the confidence to try again and not let hardships bring her down but face them head on. She needed to celebrate her mum's life and not allow her death to be the destruction of hers. She needed to move on.

"Seems I have awakened old memories." He stated matter of fact, no malice, only curiosity. "Hopefully, they were very nice memories I would hate to think I have revived horrible ones!" Chris was staring, his beautiful eyes focusing on her, an amazing connection and desire ignited by common likes, tastes and most of all attraction, the amazing magic that made us feel attracted.

"Yes, it was a beautiful birthday, it is a shame we were finished four months later."
Chris was looking intently at her, as if trying to read her mind and realising it must have been a painful break up, one that she still

remembered for some reason. You can tell just by the reaction on their eyes if something had hurt.

"What happened, do you mind telling me?" He asked, not pushing or prodding, just curious but aware that he was not wanting to hear if she was not willing to tell.

"Oh, not at all, it was so long ago, I actually have not thought about it for a long time. It doesn't hurt anymore." Liz started talking slowly about Tim, smiling at funny memories and drawing a frown when it became sad, Chris listened enthralled, not because it was an interesting but sad story but because Liz related it as if she was reading a story book. She drew Chris to her voice making him want to know more. "So, there you go, I had no choice but to finish with him. He now lives in New York and has a lovely wife. We still keep in touch, does not call often but once every two months I am sure to hear from him which is really nice." She looked down at the table, looking at nothing, her fingers running across the table, not feeling, distant but reminiscing. "He was a nice guy, you just got to be strong sometimes and let go, somethings you can forgive, with this one I forgave him, but I knew it was over then. I knew it would not be the same again and I would live with the resentment and anger. You can't control those feelings and I know myself and what I can put up with. It would have been a plaster for a wound that would take more than that to fix."

"The only thing I don't understand is why are you're still friends with Charlie?" He was not accusatory, but it was one of the things that had played in his mind since first meeting her. Why would an accomplished woman run back to a nasty viper like Charlie? It made his mind boggle.

"Well, it is a long story, but she does not know that I know what happened and that she was the reason we split but besides that, I don't like falling out with people. I just drift apart from them which I did with Charlie for a while, just having the occasional chat with her and not seeing her much. I came to Edinburgh wanting to get away and not impose myself on people, especially as I was rather down and since I knew Charlie had a spare room, I thought why not.

I just did not realise it was in such a bad state and that she was worse than before."

"Well, I hope you are not sad now that we came here tonight and I am glad to hear that you are going back down south soon, you got to get away from Charlie, she is a bitch and does not really like you, you can tell by the way she looks at you, she is jealous."

"Of course not, on the contrary, I am happy you brought me here, I should have made an effort to come here more often, it too much of a beautiful place to just let go, as for Charlie, don't worry about it, I know what she is like and will be leaving in a week."

The conversation had flown so easily as if they had been best friends in the past who have not seen each other in years. Just before coffee had arrived, Liz got up and went to the toilet, on her way back she could feel his intense gaze staring at her, suddenly very conscious of what she was wearing.

She wore a beautiful wrap dress in dark blue, intense like the colour of sapphire. The beautiful jewel tones enhanced her curves and turned her body into a very flattering silhouette that belonged to an exotic and entrancing beauty.

She walked slowly towards Chris, nervous and unaware of how attractive she was. Her kitten heels clicking as she slowly moved towards the table, a nervous smile, full of anticipation played on her lips whilst her eyes scanned the hungry man watching her move closer. He would not move his gaze away from her, starting at the plunging neckline and then continuing down to the discreet but unmistakable thigh split in the dress, showing just the right amount of skin.

She was never someone who spent her money in clothes but was very partial to quality and had her own favourite boutiques, one of the Kings Road in Chelsea and the other in Ealing, both in total contrast of each other an equally alluring in the clothes they sold.

Once coffee was finished and Chris had very politely insisted on paying for the meal, they left the restaurant. The night was lovely, perfect for a stroll. Chris had gently placed her arm in the crook of his, walking slowly, listening and savouring her. Her rose scent was so light but with the still night he could smell it. Drinking slowly its entrancing scent.

"Shall we stop in one of the pubs and have a digestif?" He pointed at the pub beside them. "Come on, I want to hear more of your stories." as if he needed to convince her. His fingers had curled up and laced in between hers, slightly pulling her to this place. She was happy to spend more time with him, in fact she did not want the night to finish. All the ghosts from the past had finally crossed over and, in their place, only peace and contentment remained.

"Sure, that would be nice." Her heart beating, knowing he wanted more time with her. It was so nice to have someone that interested on her. Wanting to listen to her.

The pub was gorgeous, dark blue, floor length velvet curtains framed beautiful cosy alcoves with elaborate bright pink sofas and gold leaf lamps with dim lights. The effect of all this was a very intimate but at the same time very relaxed environment. Opening its arm to the visitor to use more than just their visual senses, calling for closeness, luring the mystery of the unknown and taking you back to times forgotten.

"This looks very nice, I love it." Liz was mesmerised, her stomach doing summersaults as well as feeling like hundreds of butterflies were trying to push through her stomach walls. Chris had been holding her hand as they walked into the pub, electric shocks being sent through her whole body. The excitement of the moment, the discovery of a soul mate of finally clicking at a spiritual level, she was finally home.

How could she feel this closeness to someone she had just met, she was not a particular believer in love at first sight, but she was a believer on fate, on a predestined path or at least part predestined path, after all, she had always been a spiritual individual. There was more to life than science, she was convinced and deep in her heart she knew this was it, she had found her other half.

They were kicked out of the pub at closing time, having dissected both their lives to a detailed almost microscopic level. They both talked nonstop, sharing passions and believes, histories as well as stories arriving to a common understanding that neither wanted to let go of each other.

They had a wonderful time that evening, an unforgettable even, no subject was out of bounds, no criticism or judgement laid, just understanding. Both their souls laid bare.,

As they walked back, Liz had told Chris that Charlie was not aware she was out with him, she told her that Kieran was down for the evening from Aberdeen and since both disliked one another, there was not a worry that Charlie would invite herself out.

At the end of the evening, Liz and Chris walked all the way back to his hotel the long way so that they could have a view of the water of Leith at night. They stopped staring at the shadows the lamps created against the water and the murmur of the water as it hit the walls of the canal.

Just before their destination, Christ stopped, his blue eyes piercing and intense, focused desire intent on one person only. As he held her hypnotised, he bent his head slowly and kissed her. Initially tender and probing, the hunger increasing as he savours every moment of it. He had dreamed of it from the moment he set eyes on her.

His arms locked her, determined not to let her go but gently in his hold, as if he was holding and protecting the most coveted and fragile treasure in the world.

"How about a nightcap at my hotel?" Chris looked at her with dreamy eyes. "I promise you it will just be that if that is what you want."

"Okay, a nightcap would be nice." She was hoping it would be more but knew that if it was not, it was because he was being polite, buying time, not pressuring her.

Her stomach was still doing butterflies, the first time since Tim, such a long time ago. This time though the excitement and anticipation were different but equally strong, too strong, she was hardly controlling the urge to jump on him. That feeling of anticipated love. She knew this was something special, she felt it in her bones, in her core, this was a special man, a special moment.

To Liz's surprise that is all that happened that evening, once they had a drink, Chris did not make a move towards her apart from to kiss her a couple of times, he was watching her curiously, as if he wanted to talk the whole night through but was not sure of himself.

What Liz was not aware of is that Chris felt the same. He wanted to get to know her, for him this was something special, she was a keeper and for that he knew he would go slow, thread carefully, savour every moment to remember in the future, keep them as treasured memories to reminisce one day. He felt lucky, knew he was lucky and knew fate will help to achieve his aim. He drank her beauty and the feeling of the now which is what mattered, he had not felt like this for anyone in a long time, it was refreshing, as if he had been starved of affection for 100 years and had suddenly felt it. He drank her slowly like a 50 year old whisky, savouring every different taste that came to him.

"Well, I'd better go, I am a little bit tired and it is now two in the morning" Liz said very quietly, as if scared to crash and destroy the moment.

"Let me walk you to your flat" Chris stated, casually, an easy smile, nothing implied by it other than ensure her safety.

"It's okay, there is no need for that, Edinburgh is very safe." She wanted him to walk her but she also wanted to think, rejoice on the fact that this night was an amazing night, she was alive and wanted to feel it, relieve the night in her head as she walked home.

Chris did not push her, he understood "Okay, if you insist, can I get another kiss before you go?" his eyes shone in anticipation, enjoying her uneasiness like a child playing with his favourite toy.

"Of course, as many as you want!" If Chris noticed mischievousness in her eyes, he pretended not to notice, he instead kissed her roughly, his hands pressing her buttocks and moving upwards towards her breasts and then suddenly stopping, he wanted to leave an imprint, not in the shape of a mark, no, more of an emotional imprint of where he had touched her and felt herself shiver in anticipation and sexual excitement. He wanted to tell her how much he liked her and what she meant to him.

"I will give you a call when you are back in London, it would be nice to meet up again and hopefully continue on from here." His eyes never left her face, desire etched in every muscle movement and crease, his beautiful eyes savouring and saving every memory of this moment and what she looked like. He was falling hard, very hard, in love and he knew it. He also knew it was too late to back off, this was him, he had fallen. "I do want to see you, I like you a lot which I am sure you have noticed by now, it would be nice to keep going, if, likewise you feel the same as me" He was so honest, sincerity in every word which he had carefully said, he did not want to appear desperate and scare her but he wanted to ensure she knew he really did like her.

Liz was back on her bed by two thirty, exhausted since she had met Chris at six in the evening, she had not realised the time had passed that quickly and it only felt as if she had been out for only a couple of hours. She felt happy, confused at Chris's reaction but happy and she knew he liked her, liked her a lot.

# Unclouded Mind

It was so clear now, life and everything that surrounded her, the actions and reactions, the path she had taken and where it had taken her, her destination and detours that she had during the last 8 years, the bumps and crashes the sadness and happiness all entwined together, made her what she was, give her the enough resources and strength and experiences, even if negatives, built the Liz that was now in the present. Life had given her the necessary tools and experiences to be able to survive in this world. She understood the lessons she had painfully learned. Most importantly she had learned that the best path in life is a simple one, we complicate things too much and even though we forgive friends, family, colleagues, there are times that one must walk away. In fact, by walking away you build strength within yourself and send the message out that you want and need to be respected. Certain things you can forgive a friend, no everything, but there are lines one should not cross.

There is nothing wrong with walking away, it is sometimes the only and healthy option and that is one Liz had never done and she kicked herself now but admitted it as another lesson. Always forgiving, always a friend, always understanding and it was time to draw a line and think of herself.

She needed to hold her head high. Politely explain the whys and move on and move up. Whoever said that you were only a friend if you forgave a friend, even if that friend was constantly mean or absent, was probably the bad one in the relationship.

# London - May 2001

Liz had gone back to London one day after seeing Chris, she had made the decision when the day after, Charlie came back from her work in a foul mood. You could tell by her eyes that she was looking for an argument. She had not seen her when she woke up at the next day as at nine in the morning Liz was still asleep.

"Well, how was your date last night? Don't tell me, you have decided that after all you fancy Kieran and want to shag him." Poison was coming out of her mouth, jealousy written on her face, annoyed that she did not go out that night.

"Charlie, I don't know what is wrong with you, but I can tell that you are looking for an argument and I am not in the mood for it. You know fine well that Kieran and I are just friends." Liz's face was red with exasperation and anger, she had enough, wanted out of this toxic friendship once and for all.

"F F Friends?" Charlie stuttered, taken aback and surprised. "You said he was here for the day, the last train to Aberdeen must have been at nine or ten in the evening, you came back home at half past two! To me that means that you found a nice cosy place to shag and what I don't understand is why did you not just stay there for the rest of the evening. I mean, I would have, unless of course he was not functioning." Spite and poison came out of Charlie, which took her by surprise, in fact both of them, Charlie and Liz were surprised to the level of vitriol coming out of her. You could only come up with that if a lot of negative feeling had amazed itself slowly throughout the years, this was not just a by the by comment, this was a build-up erupting. Lava and magma all in one go, spitting it anywhere and definitely burning!

"What is wrong with you?, if I shag him or not, is none of you damn business, so what is bothering you?" Liz's voice was raised "come on, spit it out?"

"Well, let me see, my friend asks me for a place for two months to recover from the death of her mother, she comes here, within two days of her being here my boyfriend dumps me and I get threatened by the police for harassment. Have I missed anything else, like maybe he was in cohorts with my boyfriend or his friend? You did not seem incredibly supportive from what I recall?"

"Hold on a minute." Liz tried interrupting, knowing where this was leading.

"Let me finish, you ask what is wrong and I am telling you. If you would not have come, I would have had a room for Chris. Peter would not have finished with me, I did everything for you and ended up paying a high price, on top of this, when I needed you the most you bugger off to Aberdeen and Glasgow, leaving me depressed." Liz was taken aback, what an odd logic and definitely a 'me, me, me' syndrome for sure.

"Charlie, you know that is not the truth." Anger started rising again on her, she knew she was getting to the point where she had enough. This woman, a monster child that felt the world owed her, had nothing on her. That as it.

"Shut up!" she cut Charlie as she opened her mouth to utter probably more dribble.

Charlie continued with the interruption "You are selfish, I am depressed because of Peter and you don't care, no, you flaunt the fact that you had a date last night and don't bother with my feelings."

"Right, if that is how you feel, then I think it best that I leave, there is no point of me staying any longer here."

"Oh, so when things get hard you just leave?"

"No Charlie, I don't 'just leave'. I should have stopped all friendship with you years ago, I just kept giving you too many chances, you are a selfish bitch who thinks everyone owes you something when in fact you owe an apology to everyone. You don't care for anyone but yourself."

Liz had all her stuff packed within ten minutes of the argument, it was five thirty in the afternoon and she knew she could catch a train to London if she hurried, even if she had to stand the whole way it was better than this.

Charlie tried stopping her, apologising for everything but it was too late, everything that had to be said was said, Liz asked Charlie not to contact her again.

Liz had managed to get to London at around midnight, called Tanya telling her that she was going to be there earlier than expected but she would take the spare room until the weekend when her and Damien could move their things. The journey in itself was a cleansing experience and she felt good that finally she had let go of Charlie. She would tell everyone in their group that she no longer wanted to hear from her in any level, good or bad news. As far as she was concerned, Charlie was as good as dead to her.

It was lovely coming back home, Tanya and Damien stayed up and we all had a glass of wine to celebrate her return, it was good to be back, she felt she had a good time away, well, as good as she could have, considering the circumstances, but good in the sense that she had a break away from things. A change of scenery is as good as an amazing holiday, regardless off the drama.

"Well, what is new?" Liz looked both and Tanya and Damien who looked at each other suspiciously.

"Well, I got a place at a fashion school to do textiles." Tanya was grinning, a Cheshire cat smile across her face, gorgeous white teeth in display.

"Wow, that is good, congratulations! Hold on, but don't you want to keep up with Project management?" Liz was surprised since Tanya out of the two was very career oriented and was money conscious.

"No, you see, Damien and I are expecting a little baby" The Cheshire cat smile continued and got bigger, she was giggling now. The cat definitely had drank all the milk.

"Ah this is great news; I can't believe it. How long have you known, why did you not call to tell me?" Liz was so pleased, her best friend being a mum was something amazing, with the love of her life and starting a new career, Tanya had definitely landed on her feet. Great times for great people and she could not be more pleased for both of them.

In between laughs and cuddles, everyone was trying to talk, still unable to believe and digest the enormity of all this fantastic news.

"Actually, you are the first to know I am only 6 weeks pregnant, so I am not really meant to tell anyone until at least twelve weeks." Even Damien looked over the moon, it was surreal. A baby! Liz was not jealous, but she hoped one day she could look forward to this with the right person in her life.

"Oh, what does this mean, you are not leaving, are you?" Liz suddenly realised that Tanya would probably move out, a friend she had shared a flat with for years, it was weird, she would be moving to the next stage in her life whilst she was still trying to decipher her, something she knew she was starting to do.

"Well, I am glad you brought it up, yes, we are moving out, but it will not be right now, it will take around four to five months as our new pad needs a lot of repairs."

"Oh, so you have put an offer down, I did not even know you guys were looking!" She felt guilty but the last two months she had focused on herself only and never thought of anyone else or to even ask how they were doing.

"We have put an offer on a house just round the corner from here, we did not want to be too far from you, we are so excited."

"Actually Liz," interrupted Damien "it is more than just round the corner, it is in Acton, in poets' corner, a nice quite area there. It is a lovely turn of the century cottage, small and compact but ours!" He looked at Tanya, proud and excited, so many unknowns but proud he was going through those steps with Tanya.

"Okay, don't be picky." Muttered Tanya pretending to be annoyed. "What I meant is that we can visit each other often. Anyway knowing me, I will be round here all the time." A secret knowing looked crossed between Liz and Tanya, yes, they would be spending lots of time together, buying mummy's clothes, kid's clothes, etc.

Neither of them had mentioned wedding, so Liz guessed that they were quite happy as they were and as long as they stayed together, nobody really cares now a days if you are married or not.

Liz went to bed around three in the morning, another late night but another good night. It was good to be home surrounded by friends and being in her own house, her very clean house, she had missed that. She had told them about Chris and how she felt about him and the date they had. She poured her feelings and emotions and could tell what Tanya was thinking, this was it for Liz, the end of the road, she had finally found her soulmate.

# Moving Forward

*'The unexamined life is not worth living' —*
*Socrates.*

The next time Chris had called her was exactly one month after the time they saw each other in Edinburgh, she had been feeling very down thinking that maybe he did not like her and just felt sorry for her or that maybe when he came down to London, he met someone else, some glamorous highflyer. Her mind had been thinking twenty-four seven about him, severe overdrive, she was exhausted and so worried in case she had missed the only opportunity to find true love.

Chris called half an hour after she had an interview at a software house for a two-year contract as Director of Operations for a Canadian company trying to set up an office in the United Kingdom. This was her third interview which was a conference call with the Managing Director who was based in Canada. The rubberstamping call. She had got the job offer there and then, which to be fair it was good after all the hurdles she had gone through.

She had been sitting sipping a green tea looking out of the window, admiring the view, excited about everything and for the first time not having Chris at the forefront of her thoughts.

Liz's thoughts were distant, thinking of the whole journey she has had for the last 10 years, what she had learned, the hurts, loves, let downs, the good jobs, amazing jobs, her brother, her lovely little brother whom she adored, her mum and dad and all her friends. All in all, her life had been good, she had challenges, but who didn't, we all had a cross to bear at one point or another in their lifetime. Yes, life had been good, and she had learned a lot. She was a good person; a fair one and one her mum and dad would be proud off. She was about to call Tanya to celebrate when her mobile rang.

"Hi Lizzy" The familiar voice rang in her ears, excitement and nerves shot through her, her stomach doing summersaults at 100 miles per second "its Chris." Pause, just breathing "How are you?"

She loved it when she was called Lizzy by him, she felt special even though her closes friends called her that.

"Hi Chris, I am fine, actually, I am great, just got a job." She could not keep it to herself, she was so excited, not only had she managed to bag one of the jobs she had been aiming for a while but the fact that Chris called her at that very moment was the icing on the cake, as if the heavens had decided to grant her all the wishes at once. Were her mum and dad helping from heaven?

"Wonderful, where is it? What is it? More importantly fancy going out to celebrate?"

"Yes, I mean, I would love to do that. I can tell you all about it when I see you! Do you have any ideas where we could go?" She was so excited about everything that she did not realise that she did not answer the first two questions.

"How about if we meet in the Kings Road and we can walk and find somewhere nice?" Silence took over, in Liz's excitement she forgot to answer, she was already planning how to dress. "Hello?" Chris voice strong but gentle. "Are you still there?"

"Sorry, yes, I am here. Why don't we meet somewhere quieter? Near me? Acton Central, I can meet you outside the station and we can go for a drink and walk and see what takes our fancy?"

"OK sure, how about 7:30 p.m.? I will book something just in case, will look at what is available" You could now hear the anticipation in Chris voice, unusual as she never got excited at all about meeting a woman, but he was excited and surprised that he was excited, this was so unusual. He was desperately looking forward to seeing here again. He wanted to savour her lips, listen to her voice, drink her beauty.

## Janine

Chris had finished with Janine as soon as he came down to London, he did not hesitate at all and called her prior to him landing asking her to meet him.

He loved her, like a friend and nothing more, she had been a great friend, company and more so entertainer. She knew the art of entertaining business clients, always planned his dinner parties and never pestered him. She knew she was not the one, it hurt her, but she was old enough to realise the reality of life. Chris was not someone you could persuade and connive.

"I hope you understand" Chris's voice was soft he was watching Janine as he delivered the news. "I think this is it, I think I have met my soul mate and don't want to lose her."

"You understand, right?" Chris asked the question, more as a reassurance to him than anything else that he had been fair to her, that he had not been dragging her along and feeding her false hopes of one day making her Mrs Wandsworth.

"I do Chris, don't worry. I always knew I was not the one and that one day this will happen. She is a very lucky lady." There was no jealousy in her comment, she loved Chris, had always loved him but knew. She did not hate Liz, she envied her but not in a malicious way just more of a resigned way.

"I knew you would one day be brought to your knees, the almighty Chris Wandsworth down on his knees. She must be quite something!"

Janine realised that there was something essential missing from their relationship. They never spent time together for the sake of spending time together, it was either set time to meet for a physical encounter or to talk about something. They never shared time to do nothing, where they would just be with each other in the 'comfort' of doing nothing. It is essential for a relation to be something, to share the comfort of the 'nothing' and if sharing this becomes discomfort, then they have indeed nothing to share and unite them.

Regardless of their wealth, they never just shared a view or even washing the dishes. The little things that bond two individuals to their very soul were missing, they talked to each other liked friends, never sharing their most intimate thoughts or desires, never moving away from the accepted norm or relaxing themselves to the point they were both bearing their soul and their most intimate desires. She knew, now, how unsuitable they were for each other, she understood, finally, sadly!

"She is, Janine, but it is not fair for me to go on about her now. I just wanted to be honest with you, fair. I want you to go out there and find the one. I don't even know if she will have me but now that I know what it feels like, I am willing to fight for it."

"Weirdly enough Chris, we all look for it, you are the only person I know that was not looking for it or caring to find it. I am amazed and envious, but I am more than sure I will find someone. I am only 29, I have time."

The evening was nice, more than nice. They have both made their peace and ensured their friendship was set in stone, they both suddenly clicked that they had to learn to be friends, distanced themselves from the quasi relations they had set up more out of convenience that desire. The drank their wine whilst looking at the view across the Thames. The light breeze gently caressing Janine's shoulders, she pulled her shawl tighter, was it the breeze or just sadness to see it all end.

This was her favourite restaurant, it had a view of the London Bridge and from the balcony where their table was, tucked in privately with some giant plant pots covering, they had their private island. He had so carefully picked this restaurant, you had to have connections to get in here, the list was private, the first floor was for everyone, tourist and Londoners alike but the second floor, dripping in luxury was for a selected elite, those who could afford to pay a pretty penny for a view. 50 tables for only the rich and connected world millionaires. How was it that he always managed to get a table at last minute notice? Was it his charm? She would miss this.

The evening after this was filled with gentle chatting, dreams and aspirations and eventually Janine owned up about her other lovers. None of them inspired her like Chris did but maybe and just maybe someone was waiting out there for her.

On the way out, Chris took her home in his Aston Martin, a beautiful racing green colour, at the door, she was hoping for a kiss, but he had already made up his mind, he squeezed her hand and told her to take care of herself, they would be in touch but only as friends, she knew that.

# The meeting

*'Anyone who can conquer their heart can conquer the world' Anonymous.*

Chris had chosen a lovely local restaurant in Poets Corner in Acton. Actually, it was a pub but had a very nice semi elegant restaurant at the back and the food was good. He had never been there before and thought Liz would probably enjoy being local rather than go somewhere fancy.

He was starting to get to know her, her taste and what made her tick. They had texted each other so much throughout the day, it was hilarious, as they were seeing each other that evening but obviously they could not wait. Her wicked sense of humour kept him going through his meetings, boring ones now, how did he suddenly find his meeting boring, when did that happen?

He wanted somewhere intimate where they could talk and not be bothered by loud music or people shouting. The place was very causal so neither of them had to dress up smart, even though he made sure his pink coloured shirt was nicely ironed to wear with casual jeans and his tobacco-coloured Chelsea boots.

Chris was not a fussy dresser, but he liked looking good. He felt that if you made an effort on yourself, you made a better impression, then again, only once he was proven wrong, when he met a woman called Gladys, he was thirty and they had met at a friend's party, he had not been impressed by the way she was dressed, it looked scruffy and careless but nevertheless they got talking. To his surprise, she was extremely interesting and beautiful, she had just got divorced and it had affected her quite badly which in turn meant her losing her confidence, something she was very conscious of. The fact that she had reached her mid-forties did not help but nevertheless, he felt extremely attracted to her, a mutual attraction that led to a three-month fling, something he never regretted and to his surprise he still kept in touch with her, always having fond memories of their time together. Her mind is what attracted him to her, on a subconscious level he ignored the exterior and went for the essence of her.

"Hi, you look beautiful" Chris whispered near her ear as he kissed her on the cheek. His lips felt warm, he smelled beautifully, and he was better looking that the time before, he had a slight tan and his hair looked slightly ruffled, as if he had run his fingers through it. He had a lovely pink coloured cotton shirt with faded jeans and very nice brown boots. He was so tall and very well-toned; his muscle definition could be seen through his shirt. Liz just could not believe she was here with him and he chose her.

He fully drank her beauty, she was amazing, confident in a shy way, her cheeks rosy and she was a little bit flustered.

"Thanks." Liz was so embarrassed, she felt slightly overdressed, she wore a lovely grey organza top which had beautiful flowers embroidered in white, black and grey thread. She wore a white pair of soft jeans with a buckle belt and had beautiful high heel sandals. The sandals were not too high but high enough for her to be conscious of how she walked. She was so nervous; this was maybe not a good idea to wear such heels.

It has been ages since she had left this way, she was totally self-conscious, so much so that a slight pink blush covered her chicks. She was used to being given compliments, after all, she knew she was an attractive girl, however, she hardly went out on dates, she very seldom found the right person, or it was a disappointment after the first meeting.

Chris had parked his car just outside, it was a Mercedes Maybach, another in his vast collection. He did not need a car to show his power, but he did love driving the beasts, he was like a boy with his favourite toy, cars were his passion, or one of them. It just emanated out of him, exuded energy.

"Do you think it will be safe there?" Liz's voice showed concern.

"Yes, it should be." Chris replied self-assured. Poets Corner is quite a safe area. People just hear the word Acton and think 'rough' but it is not actually. Like any area you need to be careful. People are generally very respectful.

"I know the area, but most people don't park top of the range cars here" Liz's sarcasm started coming out, something she realised she had to put under control. Some people don't react very well to sarcasm, especially with a fresh date who did not appreciate she was joking.

Chris's eyebrow rose slightly at hearing that and laughed "Well, it is about time someone brought some class here." Chris was smiling, a good sign, he was not that against the odd comment or sarcasm, good. She liked nice sarcasm, hated when it got cruel. Chris was more and more proving that he was her type of guy.

She had never been to this gastropub before for a meal, just for drinks, she wondered why she had never been here for anything other than drinks. Strange how our mindset tells us in our subconscious where we want to go and what is best for us but sometimes gets it completely wrong.

They sat by one of the large windows, a nice large curtain floor to ceiling and the table draped in a white elegant cloth, probably Egyptian cotton, very pristine. Very basic but elegant and at the same time relaxing so they did not have to worry about how they were dressed or put up with unnecessary formalities.

The waiter helped Liz with her chair and once seated handed the drinks menu to Chris and food menu to both of them, put some water on the table and left them to decide what they wanted.

"What would you like to drink Liz? Fancy champagne or Kir Royale as a celebration?" His eyes sparkled as he looked at Liz, she not only looked beautiful but really alluring, there was something about her, not only her body language but her voice, her eyes, her smile. She seemed really happy and pleased to see him. It was as if she finally found herself and allowed herself to live. She felt the beating of her heart, faster than usual, as if clapping at her for finally finding her place and her pocket of happiness.

"Kir Royale would be nice, thank you." A shy smile played on her face. Finally, she felt she was fully in control of her life and given an opportunity to not only appreciate her past as a learning experience and let it go but also fully embrace the opportunities being presented to her.

We all have a journey in this life, be it to learn or to teach. A journey that none of us can discard because it is written in the stars, for the university to watch and assess and if we keep failing on the journey, it comes back until such time as we learn our lessons. She was finally understanding that her journey had to be the way it had been to learn and understand. She had somehow chosen a hard path for this life, but she felt she had come out of the other side, scarred but OK. It made her who she is, a better, more understanding human being.

Liz was accepting her parent's life was their life, the tragedy of their illness shaped her but did not destroy her, it made her who she was, with bruises and quirks. But it was her, a fighter, a survivor but most of all a loving individual who was nurtured by her parents regardless of their plights, she had been loved and was loved all the way to their last breath and in their own way which did not dimmish the fact. The challenges her mother had with her father's mistakes was a lesson for her to ensure she chose the right man and look at the whole and not just at one part of the person, regardless how perfect they look. There was more to a partner than the superficial or 'normal' behaviour under perfect circumstances. The 'real' person came out when life sent you its challenges and that is when you want to ensure it was the right person walking side by side with you. She now understood.

As for her, the lessons she had learned from her own personal journey was that even though Tim had loved her and made a mistake, it was not meant to be. If it had meant to be she would have forgiven him. She now needed to bury that past and appreciate it and enjoyed it for what it was, a love of her youth.

The biggest lesson was for her though, to appreciate herself as a valued member of humanity, to be respected and loved for who she was and no matter what anyone said or did, she was worth more than the bad friendships she had been dragging alone for years. She had finally discarded herself of Charlie and moved on with her live, ready to embrace a new better and brighter chapter.

# Epilogue

## A Happy Ending

Life had got better and better for Liz, she had been dating Chris for nearly a year and were now in the process of moving in together, not Chris's choice as he would have wanted to get married straight away but Liz wanted them together as soon as possible. The wedding would be a few months later, a small affair with the people that mattered the most in the life. She also wanted to get to know him slowly and appreciate each stage in their relationship.

Life was good and she was ready for it, with new lessons and challenges for sure but ready and she knew for once in her life that her journey would not be on her own, she would have Chris supporting her all the way.

The key, Liz realised, is that life is all a journey, the ups and the downs and it is better to have someone beside you to share with, the burdens and the joys. Be it a friend or a lover or a family member, she was now fully open to embrace new challenges and ensure she was never alone.

And yes, before anyone asked or wonders, they did share the washing dishes duty, for the simple reason that Liz found it so relaxing to hand wash, Chris in charge of drying. Whilst they chatted, they knew this was a short terms opportunity, as soon as they settled and their family expanded there was going to be more of the rushing and dishwashing machine rather than the handwashing choice. But they were both sure that their connection will continue, deeper and deeper, more profound by each passing year and even though there is the recognition that every relationship has challenges regardless how much in love they started, they both knew they would survive it, they had both had found their other half!

# Family & Friends

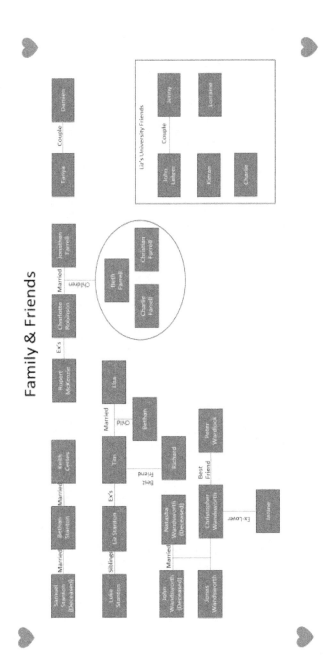

Samuel Stanton (Deceased) — Married — Bethan Stanton — Married — Keith Coates

Luke Stanton — Siblings — Liz Stanton

Liz Stanton — Ex's — Tim — Married — Lisa

Tim — Best Friend — Richard

Tim — Child — Bethan

Rupert Mackenzie — Ex's — Charlotte Robinson — Married — Jonathan Farrell

Charlotte Robinson — Children — Charlie Farrell, Beth Farrell, Christian Farrell

John Wandsworth (Deceased) — Married — Natasha Wandsworth (Deceased)

John Wandsworth — James Wandsworth

Christopher Wandsworth — Best Friend — Hester Wardlock

Christopher Wandsworth — Ex-Lover — Jenine

Tanya — Couple — Damien

## Liz's University Friends

John Lahrel — Couple — Jenny

Keran

Charlie

Lorraine

241

# About the Author:

Yviebeth Bardug is the author's nom de plume. She lives in London with her husband and two kids, two cats and a dog. Her time is spent gardening, writing and ensuring the family is a happy and united, surrounded by love.

Liz, a driven independent woman, facing the challenges of what has shaped her life in her growing years, her journey towards accepting the past, the mistakes and achievements of her family as well as accepting the mistakes people she cared for her made. Moving on and recognising that what she was and made her were effectively those challenges. She was stronger and better because of these events.

By accepting that her journey, by fate or individual design, had created an alluring, successful but at the same time insecure individual who craved the company of her mother, who missed her brother as they were both forced to grow quickly in order to maintain the family unit.

By understanding her past and acknowledging the gift of the future, Liz was able to clearly see the value of real honest friendship and the meaning of rewarding those who cared and moving on from those who did not.

The new Liz opened herself to love and started looking at life through a different lens. Love was giving her another chance, a chance to be happy and appreciate the gift of life and love. Everything that happens to us shapes us and makes us what we are, a better version of ourselves.

Printed in Great Britain
by Amazon

86330182R00139